# The Mercenary's Shadow

# The Mercenary's Shadow

*A Prequel to Wastra*

**Rohan Kailasam**

NU VOICE
PRESS

First published by NU VOICE PRESS 2025
An imprint of Hubhawks Pvt. Ltd
www.nuvoicepress.com



This is a work of fiction. Space and time have been rearranged to suit the convenience of the book. Except for public figures, hotels, and institution names, any resemblance to persons living or dead or the real events are purely coincidental. The opinions expressed in the book are those of the characters, and should not be confused with that of the Author.



ISBN: 978-81-993684-6-0
Typeset by Pooja Sharma
Published by Nu Voice Press

This novel is inspired by true events; however, all names, characters, locations, and timelines have been fictionalised for narrative and entertainment purposes. Any resemblance to real persons, living or dead, or actual events is coincidental.

This book contains depictions of sexual content and graphic violence. Reader discretion is advised.

*This book has been written under extremely hazardous conditions and is dedicated to the unsung heroes who fight other men's wars.*

# Chapter One

*July 2023 0400 Zulu*

The Airbus A350 left the Japanese city of Sapporo behind, encased in lights like an expensive piece of jewellery, as it forged eastbound over the Pacific. The moon was a half-eaten piece of camembert, lighting up the huge carpet of clouds that covered the ocean below in a never-ending white wrap. The radios were silent, and the night was alive with an ethereal enchantment, and it seemed that a mystical and palpable magic was weaving its way through the never-ending darkness that lay ahead at forty-three thousand feet.

They had already been in the skies for six hours, and the next nine would be noise-free, until San Francisco control came alive. Controller Pilot data link or CPDLC contact had been established with Tokyo control, and there was no more radio work to be done. The relief crew would take over in a couple of hours, and he would then climb into the bunks, behind the flight deck, beautifully camouflaged from prying eyes and try to fall asleep. And therein lay the problem, because the ghosts of the past were never far away and always seemed to visit just as he was hitting a REM cycle. He smiled mirthlessly into the dark. The AirPods were jacked into his iPhone, and Steely Dan started to play Aja. The darkness stretched endlessly around him, wrapping the aircraft in a lover's embrace. The song whipped up forgotten memories.

For now, he was perfectly legitimate. The Vozdushnyye Volki had been grounded. They had mounted a resolute defence against a united NATO, and in spite of new generation aircraft, drones, Navy Seals, army rangers, SAS, French foreign legion, to name a few, the imperialists had been unable to make any inroads, and now a deep, harsh winter had begun to set in on the battlefront. This was the type of cold that had broken Napoleon as he marched on Moscow and then the German

6th Army under Von Paulus at Stalingrad. Hopefully, history would repeat itself.

He had been sent back to his job with Vietnam Airlines and, in no time, had blended back into the normal life of a commercial aviator. He had been a master of living a double life since he was a teenager and hadn't questioned his orders, but a month later, when the mutiny made headlines, he understood why. He had understood the need to keep the air wolves out of the family spat. His fighters had been a significant deterrent against the ageing American leader and his sycophantic European counterparts and would no doubt play a decisive role in future crucial battles. But for now, as the ship struggled to right itself, they needed to stay out of action.

As the music reached a crescendo, his thoughts travelled further back in time, and for the first time in a long time, he wondered about the Entourage. After the incident in Bombay where he disposed of Tal Bakre and several of his acolytes, it had become untenable to remain in his beloved Colaba. While most of his enemies now lay dead, there were many hyenas waiting on the sidelines. The identity of Wastra, now no longer controlled information had been due to the betrayal by Vasu and his brother Prabha. They had joined Tal Bakre in the afterlife, but the damage had been done.

The necessity to leave Bombay had coincided with his orders to go south and prepare for battle against the Sinhala oppressors. There had been stupendous successes, and for a while, it had looked like the Tamils would have their own land in the north of Lanka. He felt a pall of grief descend upon him as his mind rushed through the final days. What a catastrophic decision it had been to kill the Indian leader. Had he been aware of the assassination plan, he would have opposed it vociferously, and maybe the defeat could have been avoided. In the same way as Canaris had advised Hitler against invading Britain, because he was secretly working with the Allies, it seemed now, in hindsight, that the possibility of an infiltrator surreptitiously working against the Tamil cause could not be ruled out.

But having done what they did, the LTTE should have been ruthless and removed all the surviving family members from the revenge equation. They didn't, and in the end, the Sicilian widow had had her day under the sun. After the heartbreak in Sri Lanka, the offer to go to Africa had been presented to him by a renegade priest, and he had accepted it without a moment's hesitation. His meeting with the Ragnar group in the Congo changed everything, and suddenly, yet again, he was fighting in another man's war. The forever mercenary.

But now, the prolonged period of peace imposed upon him triggered memories from the past. Where were the Entourage? Where had they disappeared to? They had been an extension of himself and phantom pain of severed limbs that hadn't troubled him in a long while, twinged in the periphery of his consciousness. The music took him further back in time, before the entourage, before the warriors, before Wastra, and he remembered The Plumber. He remembered Lovedale and the Building Boys, memories hidden in the sands of time. He remembered the last attack by the Building Boys.

*

### *May 1983*

Evening came quickly to Colaba, as the last rays of the setting sun struggled weakly to find a way through the trees of Badhwar Park and the ramshackle buildings of the pasta lanes and the Colaba Causeway, before surrendering to the night, in an explosion of orange and pink. They came at him from three sides. They had planned the attack in a rush, in a rage without thinking, and that was their first mistake. If the desire for vengeance and retribution is not tempered with cool logic, the chances are pretty bright that the expected outcome will not be achieved.

On the edge of the twin fisher villages of Sunder Nagari and Geeta, there were five buildings: Lovedale, Atur, Ferena, Sangeetha and Sea King, forming a sort of apartment complex. The Building Boys, the toughest street gang in Colaba, lived in these five buildings. All together, the core membership minus affiliates was about forty strong, led by Mervyn Ramos, aka Catholic Nigger boy or CNB. He lived in Lovedale apartments, which had become the de facto headquarters of the Building Boys. CNB was close to six feet four inches, powerfully muscled and undefeated in combat, single or otherwise.

With his interests focused on sports as opposed to drugs and violence, coupled with the relative affluence of his parents, Arjun was as different from the Building Boys as chalk was from cheese, and being different was enough reason to despise him. Nothing much had changed since the dawn of time. Young Arjun had been the subject of several beatings over the years, but then the incident on the Bangalore-Chennai highway had occurred, followed by several formative episodes. The Building Boys were not aware that the general equation had changed considerably, and definitely not in their favour.

Since they had been fooled effortlessly several times in the past, they didn't expect things to be any different this time around. In this, they had badly miscalculated, and that was their second mistake. They would not have time to make a third. This was not the kid from four years ago. That innocent boy had disappeared in the sands of the Middle East and there had been the rebirth of a violent cold killing machine that had just come back from a mission in the desert where according to multiple reports from both sides of the battlefield, he had tracked General Irfan Al Mansoori, the 'butcher of Khazrat' and his entourage for ten days and had killed all of them while they slept. The official Iraqi count was eleven dead, and rumour had it that it was closer to twenty-five.

But that evening on Minoo Desai Marg in downtown Bombay, the three street fighters who had planned to attack a tennis player called Arjun hadn't heard about the story that was on several Arab and Iranian lips. If they had known the terror of the *rooh*, maybe they would have reconsidered their course of action.

In Tehran, they whispered that many of the dead had had their throats torn out as though they had been killed by a wild animal. No one knew what the rooh looked like, or if he was even of this world, and the deeply religious talked about a djinn striking down the Iraqis for their affront against the prophet. The rumour spread to the equally impressionable Iraqis, and it took personal messages from Saddam himself to restore a semblance of morale.

Everyone in the upper echelons of Saddam's inner circle tried to douse out the rumours of the general and his men being hunted to death in the desert sands. But there were just a handful that knew that the truth was even more disastrous. The truth was that the butcher and his men hadn't been stalked and hunted and then killed. 'The Butcher' had been killed in his sleep in his extremely fortified house on Al Rasheed Street, right in downtown Baghdad. The assassin had slit the throats of the two highly trained *Nephilim* security guards who were in charge of the general's personal safety, but left his wife unharmed, and truth be told, although she wailed and beat her chest at her bereavement, to some it seemed that her heart really wasn't in it. The Butcher was known for his many mistresses and appetites. She was soon seen at the local cafes and upmarket restaurants in the company of a handsome captain whose family had close ties to the Ba'ath party.

It was a complete mystery as to how the assassin had gained entry to such a heavily guarded compound until one of the gardeners was reported missing. His lifeless body was found in one of the large tool sheds, but no one could accurately remember anything about the person who had pretended to be a gardener for the previous fortnight or so. The assassin had evaded all the security measures, bypassed all protocols and had disappeared into the cool Iraqi darkness, leaving a gaggle of corpses in his wake. All those who were not on duty that night thanked Allah for his mercy because one thing was for absolutely certain. As sure as night followed day, the Jihaz El-Mukhabarat, Saddam's dreaded secret service, would be visiting several households, and it wouldn't be to distribute gifts. A lot of people were going to receive 'the meat hook' treatment.

But the three Building Boys who had come to kill Arjun did not know this and other very scary rooh stories. Mervyn Ramos stood an even six inches taller than the rest. He blocked Arjun's path, his dark eyes glittering with menace. He was a fearsome fighter, but in the viciousness department, he was a dwarf compared to Bobby 'Shiv' Kathuria, who was flanking CNB on the left. Short and athletically built, he was born mean and was a good friend of Kevin Rozario, one of the leaders of the Building Boys, who had been attacked and sent to the other side by Arjun a week ago. Even now, they couldn't believe that this young punk had had the audacity, let alone the skill, to take out Kevin.

Technically speaking, it was impossible that this tennis player had left one of their top fighters dead with a broken neck in a pool of his own puke and blood. Kevin was good—very good, but he obviously hadn't been good enough. And the news surrounding his assault and battery and subsequent death was confusing and unbelievable. Eyewitnesses reported Kevin running out of the twin villages in a state of panic, followed by the tennis player in full pursuit.

There were no eyewitnesses to what had actually transpired, but it was safe to assume that there had been a violent encounter at the entrance to the elevators on the ground floor of Lovedale Apartments, where both Kevin and Arjun lived. Kevin's broken body had been found by a maintenance crew member. There was no sign of Arjun. The Building Boys still could not understand why Kevin was running from the village.

The village was Tandel territory, and Shyam Tandel—the head of House Tandel—was a brother from another mother to Kevin. Shyam Tandel ran the twin village of Sunder Nagari and Geeta Nagar with an iron fist, controlling both the Koli and Vaithi tribes, and had the unwavering support of the giant Lhoncha and his Visarjan troops. He was the undisputed king. So it didn't make sense that Kevin was running out of the village and away from Arjun. In retrospect, all this should have raised a red flag. But it didn't. And that was going to prove extremely costly. So the Building Boys actually *did*, in fact, make a third mistake!

Standing to the left was the mildest of the group, relatively speaking. Unlike most of his gang, Sandeep Unni wasn't really cut out for war. He enjoyed the protection and the tough talk of the Building Boys, but rather than fight, his main interest was sticking it to Simi Katkar, the busty beauty from Sangam Bhavan. And of course, there was the weed. Sandeep loved his weed. He had been forced into this conflict by CNB, and something told him this wasn't going to end well. The smile on Arjun's face and the total lack of concern spoke of something else at play. Sandeep was high. The *maal* from Babulal, the dealer from Strand, had been unusually good. But in spite of that, or maybe it was precisely because of that, he knew they weren't seeing the whole picture. And it suddenly became terrifyingly clear. On that lovely evening in downtown Bombay, they weren't the predators. They were the prey. This would be the last attack on the Building Boys.

***

# Chapter Two

He hadn't always been like that. At least that's what he liked to believe, and had tried to convince himself of that over the years. That he wasn't a natural born killer, that he enjoyed the hunt, lived for it. But deep inside his dark soul, he knew the truth. It had nothing to do with that Belgian bitch and her betrayal. The bloodlust had always been there, as far back as he could remember. She had just been a catalyst. He was born wrong. Born bad. Born with a blood moon in his eyes, as his grandmother would say.

He'd felt the urge bubbling to the surface from deep inside like hot molten lava almost immediately after receiving his first mission directives that would take him behind enemy lines. It was a barely controlled primaeval thirst for blood. He was told that he would always remember his first kill. Arjun had definitely never forgotten his. Disguised as an Iraqi corporal, he had infiltrated the 46$^{th}$ cavalry unit. This was a specialized armoured division that was having significant field success against the Iranians. Arjun's job was to eliminate the commanding officer, Khalid al Ansari. Arjun went above and beyond his orders. By the time the death and destruction were over, Colonel Ansari and fourteen of his men lay dead. No culprit was found. The rumour took root that a spirit of the desert, a rooh, had visited the camp. Shortly thereafter, the 46$^{th}$ Cavalry Unit was disbanded.

He found that he truly enjoyed the kill just as much as the hunt, and when he killed, it was like getting high on an extremely addictive drug. And like any addict, he needed to feed his addiction because coming off the high was a terrible experience. Always at the back of his mind, constantly prodding him painfully like a rusty blade, was the beautiful face of Muriel. The only way to fight the anguish and the hatred was to descend into a kill zone. He found that the violence and the blood kept him on an even keel.

Kevin Rozario was a proven enemy, an unrelenting, violent bully. He was more than fair game. On Kevin's part, he had been at the wrong place at the wrong time. In all honesty, no one could really blame him. After all, the twin villages had been his second home. But what he saw had shaken him to his core, and then he realized the danger he was in, and there was nothing to do but make a run for it. Try to get home and warn the others. Try to warn his friends that there had been a seismic change in the power structure in the twin villages. Kevin thought he was safe once he'd entered the building area of Lovedale apartments. There would always be some backup around. But as luck would have it, there was no support visible, and as he waited for the elevator to take him up to CNB's apartment on the twelfth floor, Kevin deliberated on the fact that the wiser mover would be to ditch the elevator and take the stairs. It would be a long run up a hundred flights, but he would be safe, far from the reach of that tennis player who had evidently taken control of the village and the Visarjan troops.

*Never wait or hesitate. Make a decision before it's too late.* Kevin forgot about the old adage as he mentally debated his next course of action. He looked to his left and was startled to see Arjun standing next to him. He hadn't heard or seen the tennis player come up next to him. Yet like magic, suddenly he was there. Kevin stared into the abyss, and the abyss stared back at him. Kevin felt it. The same way the gazelle on the savannah feels it even before it sees the lion—a feeling of overwhelming dread. And there was this look in Arjun's eyes. Kevin remembered a saying from the Bible, 'And I looked and behold a pale horse, and his name that sat on him was death. And hell rode with him.'

There was no escape. No one was coming to save him. Kevin was on his own. Surprisingly, the fighter in him took over, overriding the paralysing fear that gripped his very being. He would not go quietly into the night. He stepped back, dropping into a *niko-dachi*, hands raised to block an attack to the face, balancing on the balls of his feet, ready to throw a front kick. The left punch was a lightning-fast uppercut that broke Kevin's jaw, his teeth biting off a piece of his own tongue as they snapped together violently. Arjun twirled around the falling body, and his left elbow impacted the base of Kevin's skull with terrible force. Kevin was dead before the snapping heel kick that followed, painting an anti-clockwise arc in the air shattered the top of his head, and he collapsed in a pool of his own blood and vomit.

The entire encounter took all of five seconds. Three members of the cleaning staff who were tending to the garbage disposal at the back of the building came rushing to see what had happened. They came upon the impossible scene of Arjun standing over Kevin's fallen body. They came forward to lift the fighter from the ground where he lay, but Arjun stopped them with a motion of his hand and said, 'He stays where he lies. No one is to move the body. I want everyone, and I mean everyone, to know it was me who did this. Spread the word.'

He dropped out of sight after the Kevin incident. There were a couple of reasons for this. Primary on his list was the work that needed to be done in the village following the aftermath of the Tandel incident. He needed to make sure that the transition of the throne went about smoothly, and without incident, before the world was made aware that a new king sat on the throne of the twin villages. The secondary reason was that Arjun knew that his sudden disappearance after killing Kevin would sow anger and confusion amongst the Building Boys. Arjun wanted the rage and the hate to fester to a boiling point. A good general chooses the time and place of his battles, and after a week, Arjun had made sure that CNB and the Building Boys were apprised of the fact through street informants that he had finally been sighted going into Bella Court, an apartment building on Mereweather Road. Everyone would assume he had gone to meet a member of his band who lived there. Arjun knew the Building Boys could not, and would not let it go. Honour dictated that there would have to be some sort of 'eye for an eye' situation occurring soon. And he was right.

'We'll take him as he comes down the Strand Road between Scherezade and Fariyas hotel,' growled CNB.

'Count me in, boss,' said Bobby Kathuria as he sharpened his Bowie knife. 'I have a gift for this fucker. I'm going to get him acquainted with Gina.' He waved his knife in the air.

Sandeep Unni laughed and said, 'What a stupid name to give your knife.'

'Hey Unni, don't laugh and get a weapon. Pramod Builder just called. That fucker has just left Bella Court. We take him in fifteen minutes. You're a part of the strike force,' said CNB. Sandeep stopped laughing.

'Just the three of us?'

CNB swore irritably. 'Yes. Just the three of us. Consider this your initiation ceremony. We don't really need you, but I've noticed that you would rather talk than fight. So I want you to get your hands bloody this evening with some wet work. Don't worry, Bobby and I will soften him up first, and you can finish him off once he's down. I've also sent word to Shyam Tandel that we are going to avenge Kevin. He will definitely want his pound of flesh, but he's going to be too late. But make no mistake, *chutiya*, you are coming, you won't be late, and you will fight.'

*

Arjun looked at Pramod as he hung up the phone. 'I've done as you asked, boss. Please tell Lhoncha *bhai*.'

Arjun felt a rising excitement at the prospect of inflicting crippling damage on several attackers intent on doing him harm. The final battle with the Building Boys was a long time coming. He wondered how many would be there. Would it be with or without weapons? He knew CNB would lead his strike force. Mervyn Ramos was very confident in his strength and fighting prowess. So he definitely would be weapons-free. Then there would be Bobby 'Shiv' Kathuria. He would be bringing along his favourite knife. He wondered if Pradeep Menon would be there. He looked forward to killing him. When he did finally come face-to-face with the attackers, he was surprised and rather disappointed that there were only three of them. What were they thinking? It was quite apparent that they were not expecting much resistance.

Arjun shrugged inwardly. He did not have anything against Sandeep per se, and on the spur of the moment decided not to inflict severe damage on the weed smoker. Maybe just a broken leg. The other two were a different kettle of fish. They were stone-cold killers and would get no mercy. He looked at them coldly. There had been no words exchanged. The entire episode was unfolding in silence. The building boys had expected some sort of plea for mercy, but there was none forthcoming from the tennis player. And as they looked at his stony countenance, CNB and Bobby had no idea that morning when they woke up that they would be receiving a visit from the angel of death that very same evening. While the street fighters were mulling over the reason for the lack of fear in the tennis player, Arjun struck.

He went for Bobby first, striking with blinding speed. Bobby had unsheathed Gina, and it was obvious from the way he was holding the weapon that he was well-versed in the subtle art of knife fighting. But all his hard-earned skills would be of no use to him that evening. Arjun shuffled sideways, fast like a spitting cobra and smooth as silk, his movements blending with the setting sun, making it all extremely surreal and snapped a *hiza-geri* at the short street fighter's knee, just below the kneecap. It was a precision strike, and it broke Bobby's knee in half. He knew that wasn't required, but it's what he wanted to do. He needed to feel it. The drug of violent, bloody combat coursing through his veins. Bobby fell to the ground screaming, but the heel kick, or *kakato geri,* that followed broke his jaw and stopped the screaming like a radio that had been switched off. It also thrust the nose bone violently into his brain, killing Bobby and all his viciousness before anyone could even think *maa ki chooth*.

Sandeep may have been high, but in that instant, his fight or flight response kicked in at full throttle, and as he realized that he was not made of sterner stuff, he ran, fear literally lending him wings, leaving CNB on his own. The same night, Sandeep was sent to live with his aunt in America and would shortly thereafter join the reverend Moon cult, never to be heard from again. Arjun stepped in front of the much taller, brawnier Goan boy. 'Just you and me now. No one is coming. Time to see how tough you are.'

His voice was calm, almost friendly, and Mervyn Ramos felt a stab of hope that maybe this catastrophe could be averted. But all hope disappeared when he made eye contact. CNB felt a cold shiver run down his spine. These were not the eyes of a sixteen-year-old. Those eyes belonged to a predator, a killer. CNB looked around, assessing his escape options and saw two shadows materialize from the darkness. He recognized Namdeo and Kalidas. Once again, he felt a stab of hope. If the two heads of the fisherfolk were there together, then definitely Shyam Tandel, their overlord, would not be too far behind. And then he would not be alone.

The Building Boys had a working relationship with Kalidas, providing him with the necessary manpower and transportation for the smuggled goods that Kalidas' men offloaded from the many cargo liners that stood in queue sometimes for days, waiting for berthing instructions. But Namdeo had rebuffed all efforts by the building boys to establish some sort of rapport. Those fucking Kolis thought they were closer to Gods than to normal mortals. CNB swiftly turned his thoughts to something more positive. At least Kalidas would not turn his back on a business associate. He was sure of that, and CNB felt a boost of adrenaline. There was still a chance he could walk away. He wasn't sure if he could defeat Arjun, even with the help of the two fishermen.

But once he rallied his entire army, they would hunt down and kill this fucking tennis player who had just killed Bobby with no apparent effort. And when the fuck had he learned to fight like that?

As CNB struggled with that disturbing thought, he suddenly realized something was terribly wrong. Another disturbing thought crept into his mind: *Why was Shyam Tandel not with the duo?* He had sent a message to Shyam Tandel, but in his hurry to waylay the tennis player, he hadn't bothered to wait for a reply from the village. Suddenly, he remembered why Kevin had gone into the village. Shyam Tandel had not been seen for a while, and there had been no news about his whereabouts. Kevin had gone into the village to find out about his friend. Then he had turned up dead. Something wasn't adding up.

And as he saw the two sworn enemies bow to Arjun, he understood why there would be no help coming from the fisher village. Namdeo was the Koli Chief, and Kalidas the Vaithi Head. They had been enemies for generations, with the Kolis claiming the original bloodline and Vaithis claiming their birthright from the god of the sea. Shyam had them working together, but it was an uneasy alliance held together through the sheer will of the Tandel name and Lhoncha with his Visarjan fighters. But somehow, impossible though it was, they were obviously quite happily united in their support for this fucking tennis player. Kolis and Vaithis united! With the visarjan and that fucking giant, they would have unbridled control of the streets. He wondered how they had been able to remove House Tandel from power. As far as CNB knew, there was only one way. That seemed almost impossible, yet the absence of Shyam Tandel at the evening's proceedings was proof that assumption was the mother of all fuck ups. He knew he was witnessing something mind-blowing and felt a pang of regret that he would not be a part of it. He wondered how long this union had been in place, and wondered how no one on the streets knew about this.

He realized the trap he had walked into and cursed himself silently that he hadn't brought more of his fighters with him. CNB had sent many an enemy to meet their maker, and he realized that he was going to be joining them shortly in the afterlife. He was under no illusion that he would escape this death trap. It wasn't a pleasant feeling, knowing that his death was imminent. He felt the bluster leave his body like air from a balloon. He wondered about his mentally challenged brother, Myron. Who was going to take care of him? But he realized everything was moot. Nothing mattered anymore. Death was knocking, and it was time to pay the piper. It was at that moment that CNB decided not to be remembered as a coward and turned to meet Arjun with tightened lips. He bent down and picked up Gina, which had fallen from Bobby's dead fingers and straightened up, taking a deep breath, dagger in hand.

Arjun smiled, his white teeth glistening in the fading light. 'I can never understand this thing you guys have for knives.'

*

### *May 23rd, 1983, 2330 Hours, Indian Standard Time*

A passing police patrol stumbled upon the two street fighters lying in an open ditch near the Fariyas hotel. Given the trauma that was immediately visible on the bodies, the initial assumption was that they had been run over by a truck, but upon closer examination, it was quite clear that both the gangsters had been waylaid by a superior force and had been beaten to death, most likely with blunt instruments. The police were conflicted between relief that CNB and his right hand, Bobby Kathuria, had been taken out of the general equation of the streets and irritation, because a coroner needed to be called. This was going to last well into the early hours of the next day. They would have to wait for a doctor from St George's Hospital to arrive. Everyone knew that those damned doctors took their own time in responding. And then of course, there were the orderlies who had to accompany the doctor, who thought they were god's gift to the medical fraternity, and would definitely not be in any rush to answer their call to duty.

Sub Inspector Tambe, following protocol, questioned the taxi drivers who were parked near the Fariyas hotel, hoping to find a witness to the attack. He was not surprised to find that no one had seen anything. Everyone around seemed to be completely shocked at the discovery of two badly beaten bodies, not even two hundred meters away from the taxi stand.

'*Arey*, *saab*, believe us! We didn't see anything. Maa *kasam*!' Bhagya, the de facto spokesman of the local taxi driver union, held the skin of his throat between his thumb and forefinger to emphasize the oath on his mother.

Tambe felt the blood rush to his face, but stifled his anger. There was no point asking anyone there if they thought that the police were fools. They wouldn't say it to his face, but the answer was obvious. He turned around and headed back to the jeep. Maybe someone from one of the buildings would volunteer some information, but he knew it was a forlorn hope. No one would want to get involved. The radio crackled: it was Sub Inspector Baig. Tambe stifled a curse that rose unbidden to his lips when he heard Baig's voice, and his train of thought changed tracks.

'That sanctimonious, holier than thou motherfucker,' he cursed to himself silently. How could he have been so wrong about Baig? They had come up the ranks together right from the police training academy. He knew that Baig came from an impoverished family in the Satara district. He had visited Baig in his village of Vaigaon and had seen the horrendous condition that Baig's father's alcoholism and gambling had left his family in. They were neck deep in debt, and there were two sisters who needed to be married off.

On paper, he was the perfect candidate. He was motivated, had the ability to think out of the box, and had shown that he was not squeamish when it came to unholstering his weapon. But most importantly, he had shown that he was ready to bend the rules if it meant getting the job done. He had more than proven his mettle in the Macha encounter.

Macha was the *Shiana*, or the self-styled boss of Paanch Pairi, an area that bordered the village of Sunder Nagari. He was into some petty smuggling and intimidation of local shopkeepers. Although there had been complaints lodged against him in the Colaba police station, not much had been done because of the lack of cooperating witnesses. The status quo may have persisted, and Mach may have continued with his minor criminal activities had he not decided to diversify into rape.

One sunny summer day in June, Macha happened to see Chetna returning from school. Chetna's father, Shyamlal, was one of many small grocers who plied their trade in the bustling Colaba market. Now, Macha liked his women to have big breasts, and Chetna was certainly developing in that area. She was light-skinned and had long, light brown hair. She ticked all the right columns in Macha's book. There was a slight problem. Not insurmountable in Macha's estimation, though. She was twelve years old.

Macha began to follow her when she went to school and soon began striking up conversations with her. He bought her little gifts of glass beads and necklaces, and very often he got her mango *barfi* from Kailash Parbat, the famous confectioner in Colaba. Chetna loved the walks with her 'uncle' and looked forward to her daily meetings with him. So, one day when he suggested that they go into the Gulmanor building near the radio club for a couple of minutes just to see a a friend, Chetna thought nothing of it. After all, it was her Suresh uncle.

*

Later that evening, a weeping Shyamlal and his wife came to the Colaba police station and lodged a complaint. The complaint was of the rape of their twelve-year-old daughter,

Chetna, by the petty criminal known as Macha. Sub Inspector Baig took down the complaint, sent a van to pick up Macha, and went himself to St George's Hospital to interview young Chetna. He took two female constables with him to record her testimony.

Baig arrived at St George's Hospital just in time to see Macha leaving with three of his cronies. With a sinking feeling in his heart, Baig rushed to the minors' ward where Chetna had been admitted, and when he reached there, he found her sobbing and shaking with fear. It was no surprise that she recanted her testimony, and by the time Baig could get to Shyamlal, he was informed on the walkie-talkie from police headquarters that Shyamlal had visited the Colaba police station and withdrawn the complaint.

Sub Inspectors Tambe and Baig went on a drinking session that night. They started at Leopold Cafe with some beers, then went to Hiroo Kababwala in Colaba and ate some of his delicious kebabs. Fortified with some protein, they proceeded to the Blue Nile dance bar where they got a hefty discount and polished off four large whiskies in under an hour. Baig had been surprisingly calm.

After the fourth round of whiskey, he looked at Tambe and said, 'He's a rabid dog. You know what is done to rabid dogs, right?'

Tambe had nodded completely in sync. There was no doubt what needed to be done. They went back to the Colaba police station, signed out one of the jeeps and went looking for Macha. They found him just outside Sassoon Dock, sitting with the three cronies Baig had seen him leaving the hospital with. Seeing the jeep and the two inspectors, Macha folded his hands in a *namaste*.

'Arey, Tambe Saab and Baig Saab together! What an honour! How can we help you today?'

Baig was most courteous and got to the point immediately. 'Some drugs have been found in back gardens. They have not been logged in as yet. You come across as a gentleman who can be trusted. We thought that maybe you could find a buyer, and we could go fifty-fifty on the sales. What do you think?'

Macha almost fell over his chair in glee. Not only were there some free drugs to be sold, but if it all went right, he would have two inspectors on his payroll. It was too good to be true. He did find it odd that the cops thought he was trustworthy. Macha's own mother definitely didn't share the same opinion of her offspring. But the lure of potential lucre overrode his doubts.

'Of course, sirs!' he said, bobbing his head in deference.

'Okay, let's go now while it's still dark. We don't want some other patrol to find the maal.'

'Of course, of course,' said Macha. 'Can I bring my friends along?'

'Definitely. We will need to cuff you all, though. You understand? Just in case we get stopped on our way by some of our colleagues. We can say we are taking you in for questioning.'

Macha nodded, understanding perfectly. The four petty criminals got into the back of the van and allowed themselves to be handcuffed. They drove in silence to the back gardens behind Campion School. Macha was already thinking of how to cut his three friends out of the deal. Most likely, a good drowning at sea seemed to be in the offering.

The first thing that came to Macha's mind was that it was too dark in the back gardens, and the only ones with torches were the inspectors. The second thing that was quite apparent was that there were no drugs.

'Get the fuck out of the van,' rasped Baig.

As the four hapless criminals clambered out, Macha started to weep. He knew what was coming. How could he have been so stupid! He had lost a few good friends to police encounters. The police always came to you with words of praise and flattery. It was designed to keep you off guard until the very last minute when they put a bullet in your head. But Macha was the proverbial son of the soil. He was sure he could negotiate a deal. He wasn't sure why he had been brought to the back gardens for an obvious 'encounter'. But he was sure that if he could find out the reason, he could negotiate a deal. All these cops were corrupt. He could definitely make them see reason.

'Please, saab! Why have you brought us here?'

Baig slapped the cuffed Macha extremely hard, dropping him to the ground. 'You like little girls, is it? You piece of shit! Tell me everything, and maybe I'll let you go. Tell me about the rape. Tell me everything, and I promise I'll put one of your colleagues in jail for it, not you. But you have to tell me the truth.'

So it *was* the rape! It wasn't like he had killed somebody. There definitely was a deal to be made here. Macha felt a wave of relief wash over him. He smiled inwardly. He could say anything, but there would be no witnesses to his confession. After this, he would visit Chetna one more time, have some fun and dispose of the little bitch in the sea. Then he'd run to Billimoria and throw himself at his mercy. He had done a few favours for the Parsi cop in the past and had given him quite a bit of money. He began to sing like the proverbial canary.

'But, saab, let me tell you something,' he said as he came to the end of his story. 'It may have started out as rape, but in the end, I swear she was really enjoying, saab. I swear, maa kasam, saab.' He winked conspiratorially at the two sub inspectors Baig looked at Tambe. Wordlessly, they unholstered their service revolvers. Macha began to weep again as he realized that hope is always the last to go.

The next day, the newspapers were awash with the news of the killing of the dreaded Macha and his three associates. According to the carefully drafted police report, Tambe and Baig were on routine night patrol when they came upon Macha and three of his criminal colleagues gathered together in the back gardens.

Upon seeing the police, the criminals began discharging their weapons at the police with no provocation. Tambe and Baig were forced to return fire, and in the ensuing violent exchange, the two brave policemen ended up killing all four suspects. It was an act of unparalleled courage and heroism, and there were rumours of gallantry awards being handed out at the next Republic Day.

So, it was totally understandable that Tambe decided to introduce Baig to Sub Inspector Billimoria, who had a pretty sweet and rewarding side operation running. Given the run of events, Tambe was pretty sure the gig was right up Baig's alley. How wrong he had been.

Billimoria had organized a meeting at the New Light of Asia restaurant, opposite VT station. Baig had been most respectful until Billimoria explained that the money was to be made from being hitmen for the rich and famous. Baig's expression turned from shock to disgust.

'You are a disgrace to the uniform you wear. I want you to know that if I catch you, there will be no arrest. I will rid the world of a scum sucker like you.'

He had turned and looked at Tambe and said, 'You may have visited my home and have been my guest. But after today, you are no longer my friend. I will kill you without a second's hesitation if I catch you breaking the law.'

Billimoria had looked out of the restaurant as Baig got on to his motorcycle and said softly, 'I think we will have a big problem with this sanctimonious motherfucker in the future. Something will have to be done about him.'

Tambe listened to what Baig was saying on the radio and forgot about his animosity towards his colleague. A housewife had been murdered, and Baig was asking for backup to secure the crime scene before it got contaminated.

***

# Chapter Three

## *One Day Earlier*

It had taken more than a month before he decided he was ready. He had the timings now down almost to the second. The children left for school at seven thirty. Half an hour later, the husband came down, got into his Premier Padmini and drove off to work. There were two maids, *kaamwalis*. They both came shortly after the kids had left and stayed for about three hours. An hour after they left, Mrs Khemlani received her afternoon visitor. He estimated his window of opportunity was about forty minutes. There would be more than enough time to do what he had to do.

He hadn't picked this particular home at random. She had been chosen. Mrs Khemlani was in her early thirties, attractive with large breasts, and her tight blouse left little to the imagination. In a couple of years at the most, she'd be a typical fat Sindhi lady, but at that moment in time, she was in her prime. And she was a head turner.

She shopped regularly at Swabal Stores, which provided all household utilities and goods under one roof. Although she was chosen, Paresh Nerurkar, the rat-faced son of the owner, still found himself grasping for words in her presence. And then, to his surprise, he got clearance to stalk her in preparation for the ritual. He was rather sad as he began to surreptitiously follow her, trying to find out her schedule. He had developed romantic feelings for Mrs Khemalani. But then, to his shock, as he conducted his covert surveillance of the sexy housewife, he saw that the building watchman, a tall, strapping Afghan named Talib, visited the Khemlani flat almost every afternoon and left just before the children got home. That explained the glow! A vein began to throb on the side of his forehead.

When he was much younger, his own mother was also visited on a regular basis by the building security guard, while his father was at the store. He had surprised them one afternoon, returning home from school early. The watchman, a local from Sudam Jhopadi called Kedar, had got off his mother's naked, sweating body and had then proceeded to beat him brutally while his mother watched. No words were ever spoken, but Paresh had known what to expect if he opened his mouth.

A month later, his mother was drinking her evening *lassi* while listening to her favourite Akashwani radio channel that played old Hindi songs, which she loved. The show came on every Saturday evening for an hour, and for an hour, his mother went into a rapturous, dreamlike state as she listened to love songs of a bygone era. Midway through the show, she started feeling sick, and soon after, she began to throw up. Before she could get to the telephone, she fell to the floor unconscious. By the time her husband came home, she was dead.

The coroner found large amounts of rat poison in her stomach during the autopsy, and her death was ruled a suicide. No one ever suspected the young Paresh.

As his mother's corpse was taken away, he looked at his father's ashen face, and he felt a roar in his ears. It was all-encompassing and captured all his senses. He felt numb and almost fainted. Much later, much after the roar subsided to a murmur, and he despondently wandered the dark streets of Colaba, his life changed dramatically and he had been told that God had spoken to him, and everything was explained to young Paresh in painstaking detail. This was his calling. This is what he was put on earth to do. He was the sword of God that would deliver justice. But it wasn't his time as yet. He wanted to tell the world that it was he who had sent his whore mother back to the creator so that she could be cleansed, but he understood the reason for the instructions to stay in the shadows for a while longer. He was young and had obviously experienced a mental break, and even then, in spite of it all, Paresh displayed an uncanny ability to read the room.

Any confession would result in him being arrested, and he would be sent to one of the many juvenile homes for young criminals. He would get lost in the system and would not be able to fulfil his duty to God. He was told that one day the world would fear him, would know of his kills. But had to wait until he was older and stronger. He wasn't skilled enough yet. To become a weapon of death, he had to become death. Death has no conscience. Death does not suffer from morality. Death knows no mercy, and death knows no remorse.

He was entered into courses that would train his body and his mind. He needed to be able to pick out his prey, stay downwind and out of sight until the last possible moment. He needed to be able to kill with speed and with dexterity. The devil was in the details, and patience was the mother of all virtues. And most important of all, he had to learn to hide in plain sight.

So, as instructed, a few days later, he wept uncontrollably, and when his father comforted his young son and asked him what the matter was, Paresh told him about his mother and the man from Sudam Jhopadi. The police arrested Kedar and beat him with big telephone directories for three nights, after Paresh's father made a fat 'donation' to the Colaba police station. Kedar Vaidya could never really get a proper erection ever again. Rumour had it that he had been gang raped repeatedly while he was in the police lock-up, but it was never verified independently.

Paresh joined his father at the store after school, and a year later, his father remarried happily, and by the time he was fifteen, young Paresh was more or less in charge of weekend operations of the shop, and every day in the evenings after school. He was extremely good in his academics and excelled in science and maths, and the Holy Name High School adjusted his attendance. It was naturally assumed that this was in return for a generous donation that was being shared between the two fat Christian priests in charge of the school. No one thought to question this highly irregular arrangement.

Paresh just went about his business at the store and was very soon a highly proficient manager. Away from prying eyes, he went about preparing his body and his mind. He trained diligently under Oliver, the famous taekwondo black belt, excelling in *kumite* and *sai*, and the years passed as he waited patiently for a sign. He was twenty-two when Mrs Khemlani came to Swabal Stores, and he found himself madly infatuated, but once he found out that she was a cheating whore like his mother, his infatuation with her rapidly disappeared like mist before the rising sun, and he realized that the sign he had been waiting for had revealed itself. Paresh was methodical and patient and proceeded to map out a typical day in Mrs Khemlani's life, then a typical week. Within a month, he had her timetable down to the millisecond.

Almost like clockwork, five minutes after the two maids had left, Talib disappeared to the back of the building into his little room, where Paresh assumed he would eat something and rest a bit before visiting the Khemlani household. That was the time to strike. Paresh crossed the Colaba Causeway and entered the building unnoticed by anyone.

He took the stairs to the third floor, avoiding the elevator that might have given a nosy neighbour something to investigate. He knocked on the door and waited. Mrs Khemlani opened the door, a slightly surprised smile on her face. Surely Talib knew he was early? The Pathan wasn't the brightest star in the galaxy, but he touched her in places she didn't know could be reached. Better early than never was the thought that crossed her mind as she opened the door.

Her smile turned to confusion as she recognized the lean, rat-faced shopkeeper. Paresh struck her precisely and expertly across the jaw with the wrench he was carrying, and she went down like a log. He stepped in and closed the door.

The roar was deafening in his ears, yet he felt a clarity of purpose as he looked down at the prone figure of Mrs Khemlani on the floor. He realized it was the sound of the universe!

*Om*! He closed his eyes and prayed. The noise receded, the telephone rang, and God spoke. 'More is lost in haste than the world understands. Do not rush in your cleansing. Her heart should be pure.' He went into the kitchen and found the right tools. A hammer, a screwdriver under the sink, and he also found a meat cutter that would do perfectly

It would be a while before he would be known by the name, but on the fateful day in May of 1983, the era of 'The Plumber' was just beginning. Later, as the city reeled in terror, The Plumber would cross paths with a young man who, in the future, would be known as 'Wastra.'

***

# Chapter Four

*Later on that same evening*

At the same time as Sub Inspector Baig was requesting backup, a message was being passed on not too far from the Colaba police station.

One of the street vendors on the gateway told Khadpa Naresh that the Afghan known as Sulaiman Dost was looking for Ali Baba.

'Are you messing with me? Do you think I would know someone called Ali Baba?' Khadpa Naresh, with his shock of curly black hair, his dark face ravaged by a chicken pox attack in his youth, looked terrifying to the hapless peanut vendor. 'I'm sorry, bhai,' the vendor stammered. 'But that Afghan just came up to me and told me to pass this on to anyone I knew. And you are the boss of Gateway. I don't know anyone bigger and more powerful than you, bhai!'

'Don't forget handsome, you *madarchod*! Okay, then! You can fuck off. Pass your message to someone else. But don't forget to let me know if that Afghan has any more *chutiya* messages like this. Have to keep a close eye on these guys. Khadpa gave the vendor ten rupees, and the man grovelled for a while with gratitude before scurrying away.

Khadpa carried on drinking his *chai*, totally unconcerned until the vendor was out of sight. Then his expression changed. He knew that 'Ali Baba' meant that he had to pass the message on to Lhoncha in the fisher village. On a normal day, Khadpa lived by the 'ours not to question why' code, and in this case, the Fisher Chief was a friend, so the code really applied there. He had been told to keep a sharp ear out for anything related to Ali Baba. If Lhoncha had some dealings with the Afghans, then it was for a good reason, and that was that.

Khadpa waited another twenty minutes, made sure there were no prying eyes marking him, put the empty glass down on the pavement, which would be picked up later by one of the chai kids, and sauntered off down the Colaba Causeway, chatting with the local shopkeepers along the way. He crossed the Hanuman Mandir that led to Strand cinema, took a left into the Colaba market and to the untrained eye it would seem that he just disappeared into the masses.

Khadpa slipped under the tarpaulin awning of Nandu Tambe's hardware store, cut across the *dhobi ghat*, came up behind Paanch Pairi, the street where Pakistani terrorists would hold hostage and kill a Jewish family many decades into the future, and entered the Sunder Nagari fisher village from the south. He went east, deep into the heart of the village and saw Lhoncha. The Visarjan commander, standing at almost seven feet in height, was a truly impressive sight.

'Wonder what his mother feeds him,' thought Khadpa Naresh as he went forward to meet the young fisher chief with a respectful smile on his face.

'Salaam, bhai! How are you?'

'Never a dull day. What brings you here, Khadpa?'

'That Afghan Sulaiman *dost* is looking for Ali Baba. Just came to tell you that.'

Lhoncha's eyes narrowed. 'Anything else?'

Khadpa shook his head. 'Nothing. I'll be going now. I am always at your service.'

It wasn't that Khadpa was scared, far from that. He had been in a few tight situations already in his young career, but the village was different. He didn't belong, and however friendly Lhoncha and the fisherfolk were, he knew he would always be an outsider, and Khadpa didn't want to overstay his welcome.

Lhoncha smiled at the pockmarked fighter as though reading his mind and said, 'You are always welcome here. You are a trusted friend, and Sunder Nagari values your friendship.'

Khadpa flushed with pleasure at the unexpected praise and bowed slightly. 'Thank you, bhai. Gateway will always fight for you.'

*

### *May 24th, 2330 Hours Indian Standard Time*

The AN-32 cargo plane lifted off from Santa Cruz airport shortly after midnight and headed west over the Arabian Sea. It was a standard run into Sharjah, and they did it three times a week. The usual cargo was beef, which was in great demand in the meat-crazy UAE and vegetables. However, that night, as the powerful turboprop climbed effortlessly to its cruising altitude of twenty-five thousand feet, there was an additional guest on board.

The Russian crew were most curious about their guest. But also because they were Russian, they knew about curiosity and cats. Anyway, they were being paid a princely amount by Russian standards to be blind, and so Stevie Wonder it was.

With two and a half hours to go, Captain Alexei Karatsev, as instructed, opened the large manila folder that had been given to him at Bombay dispatch. His eyes widened slightly, but being the consummate professional that he was, he recovered his poise in double quick time. He leaned over the radio management panel and selected 128.35 megahertz.

'Karachi control, good morning, this is Lease Air 155.'

After a brief pause, the radio came alive. 'Lease Air 155, Karachi Control, good morning. Go ahead.'

'Lease Air 155, changing call sign to Lease Air 175 and activating reclearance flight plan. Confirm reclearance number alpha delta victor 3765.'

There was a brief silence, and the radio came alive again. 'Lease Air 155 reclearance is confirmed. Call sign is changed to 175. Squawk 4200 and from position derbo cleared direct to tango Romeo November.'

'Change transponder, and set course to Tehran vor,' Capt. Alexei ordered his first officer and looked around at his crew, who were acting like it was a completely normal thing to be changing call signs and destinations in mid-flight. He smiled and turned to look at the Iranian coastline lighting up in the distance.

Arjun felt the aircraft bank and sat up in his makeshift seat in the cargo hold. He thought about the reasons for the urgency and couldn't quite figure it out. Based on the Ali Baba code, he went to the pre-arranged dead drop at Shelly's guest house, first making sure that there were no lingering prying eyes around. He knew the Afghans and knew them to be proud warriors, but he trusted no one unless they had proved worthy of his trust, and while Dost was known to be a good enough guy, he hadn't had any direct dealings with him. Hence, the need for enhanced awareness.

'These Afghans are tough guys,' Lhoncha had said. 'Here in Bombay, they are outnumbered, so they pay us to let them sell their coke. Not sure they are too happy about it. The smile just doesn't reach their eyes.'

Lhoncha had taken a deep breath. He knew the young *raees* would be leaving shortly, and it would be a while before he returned. 'I have no idea what your dealings with the Afghans are, Baba, but here in Bombay, the Visarjan have got your back against anyone. But we can't protect you if you're not here. And I am not going to ask where you are going because we both know the answer to that question.' The giant sighed and shook his head in frustration.

Arjun had looked at the young giant and smiled. 'You don't have to worry about me, brother. I can take care of myself. The less you know, the better.'

Taped to the back of the municipality garbage bin outside Shelly's guest house was a piece of paper with a telephone number. He called the number from one of the phone booths outside Telephone Bhavan. A female voice on the line said, 'Ali Baba.' It wasn't a question.

'Yes.'

'Santa Cruz old airport. Lease Air 155. Hangar 12. 0030 hours. Tomorrow.'

He hung without replying. Normally, he had a week to prepare. Normally, he travelled as a passenger to Sharjah. Normally, he got his new papers in the transit lounge. Normally, he then flew to Tehran from Sharjah. Normally, his new papers would show him as hired help to a wealthy Iranian family. Normally, he wouldn't rate a second glance from the lazy Emirati immigration officers. Normally. This was different.

Something had happened, and the entire Iranian High Command was rattled. He didn't get many updates on the war in Bombay apart from the odd mention about it in the *Times of India,* which was dropped off with religious punctuality at his flat. The Afghans and Iranian students in Bombay provided more up-to-date information. As far as he could make out, the Iranians were holding their own against the technologically superior Iraqis, and things were hitting a bit of a stalemate.

So something had happened that had thrown the scales off balance. Something had happened that required the rooh to go behind enemy lines.

***

# Chapter Five

*May 25$^{th}$, 0300 LT*

The AN-24 had been vectored for an approach on runway 29R at Khomeini Airport.

'After landing, roll to the end of the runway, and take the taxiway sierra to the Salam Apron,' had been the curt instructions from the controller.

*Far from prying eyes*, thought Captain Alexei.

A large black Lincoln Navigator had met the aircraft. Two members of the revolutionary guard had come aboard. They were very polite and apologetic as they put a hood over Arjun's head. 'Those *sharmutha* Iraqis have eyes everywhere. We have been instructed to take adequate precautions.' The two soldiers exchanged a quick glance, and Arjun caught it. The Russians would never see Novosibirsk again. Arjun felt slightly bad for them, but he understood the reason why they needed to be eliminated. He was a ghost, and only the chosen few could see his face and live. Still, he felt a twinge of sadness for the hapless crew.

The enormous SUV dropped Arjun off in front of a nondescript office in a quiet by-lane in Nasr Square. Inside the office, in front of a large desk that had the photo of the Ayotollah, sat General Shahzad Gauri, head of the dreaded Republican Guard. He got up and came around the table and engulfed Arjun in a warm bear hug.

'It is so good to see you again, my son. Come, sit down and have some tea and *halwa*. Tell me, how is everything in your country? How are your parents? Do they have any idea where you are?' General Gauri laughed loudly.

Arjun smiled. He knew the welcome was genuine, but the general was tense.

'My country, my parents and all my relatives are just fine. And you know very well that they have no clue that I'm here. Thank you, I will have some tea, but no sweets, please.'

Arjun sipped on the hot tea as General Shahzad Gauri pretended to be deeply interested in some paperwork on his desk. Arjun had been in front of General Gauri before and knew he wasn't one to waste time on unnecessary theatrics. Their relationship was a little more than just professional. So Arjun watched with a bit of curiosity as the brawny General seemed to struggle to begin the conversation. Arjun decided to make it easier on his commanding officer by giving him the opening he seemed to be at a loss to find.

'You went to a lot of trouble to get me here, sir. A lot of planning has gone into this. Before we proceed, I must ask you a favour.'

Gauri looked up at his young assassin and said, 'Anything for my son. You only have to ask.'

'If you haven't already disposed of them, then I want you to spare the lives of the Russian crew. They are innocent and were only following orders, and brought me to Iran safe and sound. They do not deserve to die like dogs in a foreign land. They deserve to go back to their families.'

Gauri nodded and picked up the phone that was in front of him. He spoke rapidly into it. After a while, he sighed in relief and put down the receiver and smiled and said, 'Just in time. They will be airborne within the hour, with instructions to never discuss last night's flight with anyone. They know we can get them anywhere and have promised to take this knowledge to their graves. And may they have long lives.'

Gauri cleared his throat and continued, 'Now, as to the reason you are here. We have a problem. One of our agents may have crossed over to the other side. We need you to go into Baghdad and eliminate this problem.'

It wasn't that Arjun didn't feel fear. The moment he felt it, he just isolated it in a part of his brain that didn't negatively affect his reactions. It was the same thing with pain. He just put it away where it couldn't do him any harm. This ability to compartmentalize had, in turn, developed in him an uncanny sixth sense. He was able to sense danger way ahead of time, and prepare for it, giving himself those few precious extra seconds that gave him the edge, and he was also able to acutely sense when things were not quite right.

For a while now, he'd had a feeling that he wasn't the only assassin the Iranians had operating behind enemy lines. There were a couple of incredible kills that had been notched up to the rooh, including the most recent one, where Al Badawi, a ruthless and trusted general, had collapsed in the middle of a war council briefing, frothing like a cappuccino, a victim of some sort of poisoning, resulting in Saddam being rushed away to safety by his security. A few photographs had hit the world-wide news networks, and suffice it to say, the Iraqi despot wasn't pleased that he looked like an errant child being frogmarched away.

Now, Arjun knew that it definitely wasn't him, because around the time of the assassination, he had been in Bombay, busy practising with the D'rozario brothers and their band 'Les Boys' for the *Live Wire* concert at IIT Powai. He had wondered who it was that had knocked off Badawi and had felt mild professional envy at the meticulousness of the strike.

'You would not have risked so much to get me here so quickly if it were just to take care of a traitor. This is a trusted warrior who has betrayed you or has been captured. And this warrior has classified information that the high command feels could either turn the tide of this war or embarrass someone high up. Perhaps both. You are also not going to tell me what it is that this agent of yours has because I don't need to know. And you are right. I don't need to know. I just need to know the identity of the person I have to kill. I have one question. Is it the one who killed Al Badawi while he was in a war room meeting with Saddam?'

The general got up, which in itself was a rarity because he got up only for Ayotollah Khomeini, who had personally appointed him after the fall of the Royal House. He looked at the teenager with the faintest of smiles that was totally bereft of any humour and nodded. This would be the day that Pandora's box would be opened. He handed him a brown manila folder.

'Before you open the folder, you need to listen to me and understand why we did what we did. We face an existential threat. The Iraqis mean to wipe us from the face of the earth. They are well funded, and the high command and His Excellency were worried that we would have no choice but to capitulate if the war dragged on. We needed to think outside the box. We needed to disrupt their fighting units, supply lines, assassinate their top officials and sow confusion and fear amongst the rank and file. This dire necessity to survive was the basis on which the idea for an elite hit squad was born. Our scientists created the formidable interrogation machine called "The Reaper". We wanted to create a squadron of super soldiers, if you will. Unfortunately, apart from you, only one other was able to withstand the gruelling induction. What made you special was that, unlike her, prior to coming to Iran, you had no military experience. You are truly one of a kind. But then you also had Indrajit.'

Arjun didn't say anything, and his calm demeanour masked the shock he felt when he heard the confession. Without any further words, he opened the folder. He already knew what to expect, but in spite of all his extensive training and heightened sixth sense, when Muriel Steyn's face popped out of the dossier he had been handed, he felt like he'd been slapped in the face really hard, but to the casual observer, he might have been reading the *Times of Tehran*.

So the Afghans had been right. Muriel was here. Well, not anymore, but she had been here all this time. He took a deep breath and controlled his emotions. Now was not the time to give in to anger. His mind moved diagonally away and focused on something else. So she had also gone through 'induction'. She was tougher than she looked, he thought with grudging admiration. You needed to exist in a different zone to be able to survive induction.

'Induction' had been a combat course that had lasted for about six months. He learned how to combine open-hand martial art techniques with small arms and stabbing weapons for close-contact combat against multiple attackers. His anticipation, combined with his ability to blend in with his surroundings, was phenomenal. He was a human chameleon. And of course, there was Indrajit. Arjun was good—very good—but what made him stand apart were the last three weeks.

That module was dubbed 'death camp'. That was where they taught you to withstand interrogation and introduced you to 'The Reaper', named because the general consensus was that it must have been created in hell. The machine itself looked like something out of a science fiction film, with lights blinking and wave patterns flowing across multiple green screens. Electrodes were attached to the temples and to six points on the subject's chest. The technology was groundbreaking and state-of-the-art.

The interrogator could introduce a signal into the subject's brain through the machine neural interface that suggested to the subject under interrogation that a part of his body, for example, the hand or the leg or the penis, was being cut off. It was an introduction to extreme agony with no actual blood being spilt. It was brutal, and no mercy was shown, because everyone knew that the Iraqis loved a good torture session, and there was no question that if you were captured, they would break you eventually, because everyone had a threshold, and once that was breached, it was canary time.

The hope was that the machine would exponentially increase the pain threshold and make a detainee impervious to the Iraqi interrogators' efforts. And if all else failed, if the torture became unbearable and there was no hope of escape, then there was the final option that had been gleaned from their arms supplier and had been incorporated into the arsenal of the rooh.

He hadn't met the Tamils as yet, but he had heard of them. They were providing sophisticated weaponry to the Iranians at a considerable profit that was going to fund their own war back home. Their special forces, called the 'Black Tigers', carried a cyanide capsule attached to one of their molars. If they were ever in a situation that looked untenable, one hard bite down would do the trick. Better to move on to another world than be a guest in a Sinhalese prison, was apparently their adage. Arjun was also fitted with a cyanide pill fixed into his right molar. A must-have for all assassins.

He had heard that the Iranians were extremely impressed with the Tamils, their tenacity, their ability to procure weapons, and their willingness to die for their cause. Arjun didn't care about their politics. He had been wanting to have a one-on-one chat with them regarding a certain Muriel Steyns, but their whereabouts were a closely guarded secret. He didn't know it then, but in the future he would be bound inextricably to the LTTE and their charismatic leader. But then, all he wanted was information on the blonde.

Back at induction camp, Arjun was able to resist pain in such a manner that his instructors were most impressed. He screamed at the point of infliction, but went back to a cool demeanour almost immediately, and he did this every time until his body switched itself off, sending the teenager into unconsciousness before a point of no return was reached. He never broke during 'death camp' in spite of all his appendages being simulated as cut off at one point in time by his frustrated instructors. He should have been a broken husk, but the fact was that he broke the machine. In fact, it was downright scary, and the legend of the rooh took birth much before his first actual kill.

The general blew out a ring of cigar smoke. It immediately polluted the air with a foul smell. The general continued, 'She graduated from the programme a year before you. To be honest, we do not know how she found out, and we were not sure why she volunteered for the assassin program. She was here with the Tamils, brokering arms deals between us and them. She asked to see me and volunteered for the training. There were nineteen trainees at the time and no women, so I thought, why not? I was sure that she would not survive the training, and there was nothing to lose by allowing her to participate. So in she went. But incredibly, she took to the "death camp" almost as easily as you did. She was the only one of that group who came out unscathed. I won't bore you with the details of what happened to her course mates. You've seen what happened to yours. Six of the seven committed suicide, and the last one is in a sanitarium in a vegetative condition. You have to be able to make hard decisions in war, and while I'm not proud of what I did to so many young minds, I can assure you, I would do it all again without hesitation.'

Gauri took a deep breath and continued, 'We knew you had come to Iran in search of her, but she was too valuable to lose. I'm sure you understand that we had to make her invisible to you. At the time, she was the only one of her kind. She had already carried out three assassinations and had shaken the Iraqi power structure to the core. And to be honest, as far as you were concerned, we were sure you wouldn't last a week on the front lines. And then Amdar happened, and we decided to test you. And you went through induction even easier than she did. And we realized that you were also special. And then, we realized something else.'

Arjun completed the sentence, 'Now you had two assassins.'

General Shahzad smiled grimly. 'You can understand that we wanted to avoid any altercation between our two prized weapons. That is why neither of you knew about the other, although I am sure she would be amazed to know that you had reached our borders. We had hoped to put off your eventual meeting for as long as we could. But man proposes and God disposes, and here we are.'

Shahzad had heard the stories surrounding the battle of Amdar, how the 57$^{th}$ Brigade had turned certain annihilation into victory and the role of the young assassin in that blood bath. He didn't say it aloud, but thought that Muriel would have been even more amazed if she knew what had gone down in those killing fields.

Arjun understood very well. He moved on ostensibly unperturbed and addressed the elephant in the room. 'So has she been captured, or has she defected?'

'That is why you are here, my son. That is unclear at this moment. She was to make contact in Mosul with one of our informers and had been tasked with assassinating a high-ranking general. She never showed up. Then we found out that she was a guest of the Mukhabarrat. Now, whether she is a willing guest or an unwilling one makes no difference, you understand? You have to stop the river from overflowing.'

Arjun understood perfectly well. He smiled and shook his head ever so slightly. General Shahzad had a way with words. These Persians! So erudite, so artistic, their women beautiful to a fault, yet both sexes incapable of mercy and forgiveness. His thoughts turned dark. Soon, he would be face-to-face with Muriel Steyns. His journey was reaching its end. His time had come. The endgame would be played out in Baghdad.

***

# Chapter Six

*January 1982*

Bangalore was still, and would always be fresh in his mind. He remembered her, blonde and beautiful, all the tennis players amazed that she had eyes only for him. But their's was an innocent jealousy mixed with a large dose of camaraderie and goodwill. He would face destructive envy later on in life and deal with it destructively.

She had watched him win his match, clapping and shouting words of encouragement. He could never be sure, but the sight of a beautiful blonde screaming for him may have interfered with his opponent Manoj Chandani's concentration. Manoj's mother, who was also watching the match, tried to object to the referee but was told that there were no rules that prevented a spectator from cheering for a particular player. In fact, everyone concerned was glad that there was at least one non-playing spectator watching the Indian nationals.

Manoj Chandani lost after holding a clutch of match points and wept inconsolably on his mother's shoulder. An hour later, as Arjun sat in a coffee shop with the beautiful Muriel Steyns, the heavens opened up. A couple of hours later, the downpour turned to a non-stop deluge, and it was no surprise when the cafe was suddenly full of tennis players. He learned through some of them that the tournament was cancelled due to the forecast of incessant rains for the next 48 hours.

'So now we are stuck together, whatever are we going to do?' She had a warm, dulcet tone to her voice, and he felt completely at ease with her.

'Don't you have any friends here in Bangalore? Where are you from?' he asked.

'I'm from Belgium. My father owns a shoe manufacturing company here. I'm visiting him for a couple of weeks.'

'I guess you like tennis.'

She leaned forward with her green eyes, looking deep into his brown and said, 'I like tennis and I like you. Very much.'

Her intentions were clear, but Arjun had a problem. He had never been with a woman before. The only thing he had done so far was kiss Amili Setalvad from college and hold hands with her as they sat on the rocks at Marine Drive. The kiss had been clumsy and awkward, both of them totally inexperienced.

This was different. This was not some teenage girl who was a slave to her hormones. This was a grown woman. He was breaking new ground. He was in uncharted territory. He had no idea what to say next, and he felt beads of sweat form on his forehead. He felt the eyes of all the tennis players on him. His pulse quickened, and he felt a sudden shortness of breath.

She saw his discomfort and understood immediately. She put her hand on his and said, 'I hear music next door. Let's leave this cafe and all your friends and go and see what's happening there. Do you have a pair of jeans inside your kit bag? Great. Why don't you go and change, and I'll get the bill.'

The music was coming from a small disco on the floor above the cafe. The bouncer at the door saw Muriel and had no problem letting her in with someone who very possibly was a minor. Strictly speaking.

She led him by the hand onto the dance floor. 'Love's Theme' from the movie *Flashdance* began to play. She pulled him close to her, and he found himself lost in the music and lost in her. She was almost his height, and he didn't have to bend down to kiss her. They say everyone remembers their first kiss, but for Arjun, it was his second kiss that he would never forget. Years later, when things went from very good to very bad, he found that he could always close his eyes and suddenly he was with Muriel on a dance floor in a small disco on MG road, dancing and kissing to *Flashdance's* 'Love Theme.'

She tasted of caramel and honey. 'I've never been with a woman, you know?' He stumbled over his words.

She put her arms around his neck and kissed him on his left ear, sending a jolt of electricity down his spine and said, 'I know. All that will change after tonight.'

It was all extremely surreal. He felt dizzy and overwhelmed. She sensed his insecurity and pulled him to her and melted her lips into his. She tasted of honey and caramel, and he was lost in her. Even though he was a virgin and completely inexperienced, her next words had a sense of familiar inevitability.

'Where are you staying? Let's go there right now.'

It wasn't long before they were in Arjun's rather Spartan hotel, given that most of the tennis players were on a tight budget. There were no phones in the rooms. There was only one phone at the reception, and one had to make an appointment if they wanted to use it.

The rain came down in sheets, and the wind rustled the leaves outside the window. They sat together on the floor, their backs against the bed, the dim light from a nearby lamp casting a warm glow around them. The air was thick with unspoken words, a tension that had been building since the evening on the dance floor..

He glanced at her, the way the light danced in her eyes, and felt a rush of warmth. He tried to speak, tried to say something cool, but he was unable to raise his voice above a whisper.

She turned to him, a smile playing on her lips. 'It feels like I have been waiting for you my whole life,' she said, her voice soft and inviting.

With a sudden burst of courage, he reached out, tucking a loose strand of hair behind her ear. The simple touch sent a shiver down her spine, and he could see the way her breath caught in her throat.

'Can I kiss you?' he asked, his heart racing as he searched her eyes for permission, her gaze locked onto his.

'Yes,' she breathed, her voice filled with anticipation.

He leaned in, closing the distance gentle, tentative kiss. It was soft at first, a delicate exploration that quickly deepened as they lost themselves in the moment. He felt her warmth enveloping him, a sweet surrender that made his heart race. As the kiss intensified, he pulled her closer, feeling the softness of her body against his. Her hands found their way to his face, fingers tracing the contours of his jaw as she kissed him back with equal fervour. Every touch ignited a fire within him, a longing that he had never experienced before.

'Wow,' he murmured against her lips, pulling back slightly to catch his breath. 'This is . . . incredible.'

She laughed softly, her eyes sparkling with joy. 'I know,' she said, her voice breathless. 'I've wanted something like this for so long.'

With a newfound confidence, he leaned in again, capturing her lips with his, pouring all his feelings into the kiss. It was a dance of passion and tenderness, a connection that felt both exhilarating and safe.

As they kissed, he felt a sense of freedom as if all his fears and worries had melted away. It was just them, two souls connecting in a way that felt both thrilling and profound. He knew this moment would change everything, but for now, all that mattered was the heat of her body against his and the taste of her lips.

'The bed looks rather comfortable,' she said.

Naked, he was unsure and shy at first. But she was patient and was the perfect guide. He exploded way too soon, unable to control the ecstasy.

'Don't worry. You'll last longer the next time,' was all she said.

And she was right. They devoured each other, stopping only to leave the room to get food and water. The air was filled with the gasps and sighs of their lovemaking. In the afterglow as they lapsed into a languorous stupor, she murmured words of love to him that would forever remain branded into his memory. Arjun was sure this was love and it would last forever. He was wrong.

*

On the third evening, around eight, as they lay intertwined in each other's arms, someone knocked on the door. Arjun answered the door in a haze of happiness. It was the bellboy. He looked past Arjun and spoke to Muriel.

'Good evening, madam. There is a phone call for you.'

The first thing that popped into Arjun's mind was that no one knew Muriel was in his room except for Ranjit Shinde, who was another tennis player and a close friend. He looked back at Muriel, confused, and the second thing that popped into his mind was that somehow, Muriel had changed. It was her eyes, he realized. In the brief seconds between the knock on the door and the bellboy's announcement, her eyes had gotten cold. She went from almost naked to fully clothed in what seemed like under thirty seconds. Then she spoke, and a strange feeling kicked him in the gut.

'It was really nice to have met you. I have to go now. Good luck with your tennis.' She was distant and remote.

*Good luck with your tennis?* Before he could even think *what the fuck?*, she was gone, leaving behind a faint scent of expensive perfume in her wake. But even then, long before he became the rooh, the qualities that would make him feared on both sides of the battle lines kicked in instinctively. He shook off the numbness brought about by the shock of the abruptness of her departure.

Arjun shifted gears. There was no time to feel sorry for himself. It could not be over just like that. He needed to talk to her. Get her to understand that he felt something in his heart for her. He slipped into a black vest and blue jeans. Slid into his sneakers and ran downstairs to the lobby just in time to see Muriel leave in a green Padmini. Obviously, there had been no phone call. The bellboy had been paid to get her out of the room. And with a sadness he had not felt before, he realized that it had all been a setup. He'd been played.

He isolated the pain and the hurt far away in the farthest recesses of his brain where it could not paralyse his thinking. He sprinted behind the car just long enough to memorize the number plate, made a mental note of the direction in which the car disappeared and jogged back to the hotel. He knocked on Ranjit's door. The handsome tennis player opened the door with a look of irritation on his face, which cleared when he saw Arjun.

'Arey, sex machine! How's it going? Where's my blonde *bhabi*?'

He saw the look on Arjun's face, saw the uncharacteristic bleakness.

'What happened, buddy?'

'She's gone. The bellboy came up and told her she had a phone call. Next thing, she wished me luck with my tennis, and she left in a green Padmini. I think she was just using me to stay out of sight or something. I'm not sure. There's something else going on here, Ranjith. I want to know where she has gone and with whom. Will you help me?'

Ranjit shrugged. 'Fuck her! Let her go. You had a good time. There are other fish in the sea.'

But Arjun was adamant. 'I need to know. What was all this about? Why did she choose me? You don't think that I am owed an explanation? She used me, Ranjit. She has to look me in the eyes and tell me why she did it.'

Ranjit saw the anger in his friend's eyes. He understood that the situation needed to be resolved. Ranjit was more wise in the ways in the ways of women. Maybe she just needed a break, or maybe two days was her limit. But either way, she should have been upfront about everything. He nodded. 'Absolutely. Let's do this. I've got Dinesh Reddy's car with me. But how do we find her?'

'I have the number plate. They were heading in the direction of the Bangalore-Chennai highway.'

Ranjit nodded, but was not really sure. It was all getting a little bizarre. But he couldn't back down now. 'Sounds like a plan. Let's go. I've also got a few things I want to say to her.'

Dinesh Reddy, a Bangalore-based tennis player, was the son of a successful businessman and had several cars at his disposal. He had loaned a white ambassador to Ranjit for the duration of the tournament.

Traffic was still a little heavy as they headed towards the highway. Arjun looked for a green Padmini, but no joy. Then they were on the highway. The traffic eased considerably, but there was still no sign of their target vehicle. An hour on the highway and with still no sign, Ranjit started getting restless.

'Maybe we are on the wrong track. Maybe the bitch is headed for Mysore.'

Arjun had already started to second-guess himself. But then suddenly there it was, parked on the side of the road. Ranjit eased up behind the car and engaged the parking brake.

'Doesn't look like anyone's inside.'

Arjun nodded at a wooded pathway sloping downwards on the right. 'They must have gone down there.'

'Buddy, there are no lights. We are going to be walking in darkness, and I don't have a torch. Do you? Arey, this is all getting a little intense, *yaar*. Fuck it, let's go back. I'm getting some bad vibes.'

'Okay, you stay here. I'll be back in a bit.' Without waiting for a reply, Arjun set off down the road.

Ranjit looked at Arjun fading away into the darkness, decided that safety in numbers should be the norm for the night and set off behind his friend. 'Wait! I'm coming with you.'

Half a kilometre down the wooded path, they saw a glow lighting up the brush ahead. They followed the glow, and it led to a large shack. It was not visible from the highway, and no one would have known it was there.

Again, Ranjit voiced his concern. 'Arjun, buddy, this is some weird shit. Let's go back to the car. If the blonde is in there, she's up to no good,' he whispered. 'What the fuck is going on? I got a bad feeling about this.'

'Another five minutes, okay?' Arjun whispered back. 'Then we'll leave. I just want to see what's going on.'

Ranjit sighed in frustration. 'You are so stubborn. You just don't know when to stop. Okay, but just five minutes.'

There comes a time in everyone's life when they hit a fork in the road. Most will take the well-trodden path. Most will go on to live unremarkable lives. And there are the chosen few who decide to take the path less travelled. They will either crash and burn or go on to become legends. In the ten minutes that followed the decision by Arjun and Ranjit to take a look at what was going on inside the shack, both of the above happened.

The duo crept up to the shack. There was a makeshift window at about shoulder height. They looked in. What they saw made their blood run cold.

There were four men on their knees. Their hands were clasped behind their heads. They were surrounded by eight or nine gun-toting, dark skinned men. And Muriel Steyns, standing in the centre of the group in front of the kneeling men, was looking very comfortable with the gun she had in her right hand. She was talking to the kneeling men in a harsh tone in a language they didn't recognize. She raised her voice at the kneeling men. Again, the questioning tone. One of the men being questioned shook his head and spat at her.

Muriel took a deep breath, wiped the spit from her face, and very calmly shot the kneeling, defenceless man in the head. He keeled over without a sound. The remaining three men began to scream in terror, and Muriel screamed something at them. Then she shot one more man. Again through the head. It was absolutely terrifying chaos. But the men with the weapons didn't seem to be fazed at all by the terrible violence. They just stood there, weapons in hand, and watched Muriel do her thing.

Both Arjun and Ranjit were transfixed in shock. Realizing that it was time to get the hell out of Dodge, they turned to quietly slink out of ground zero before they were discovered, and came face-to-face with four well-armed dark-skinned men. Instinctively, they raised their hands. The men silently motioned them to go inside the shack. Muriel had circled around the survivors, so she was with her back to the entrance when Arjun, Ranjit stumbled in, followed by the armed retinue.

She twirled, her green eyes flashing with rage at the intrusion. She saw Arjun, and the fire died out in her eyes as though doused with cold water.

'What are you doing here? I said goodbye, you idiot. Why didn't you just go home? You stupid, stupid boy.'

Arjun couldn't answer. The sight of the dead bodies and the smell of blood, coupled with the piteous weeping of the remaining two kneeling men, had overwhelmed his senses.

Ranjit was also frozen in complete horror. Muriel looked at the boys and looked away for a bit. When she looked back at them, there was a sadness there.

'I can't let you go, you've seen too much. I am sorry.' She looked behind Ranjit, and one of the guards stepped forward and shot Ranjit in the back of the head. As the young tennis star flopped forward, the guard swivelled to Arjun, gun pointed at his head and as Muriel screamed, 'NO!' he fired. Arjun felt a searing pain and fell forward.

*

When he regained consciousness, dawn was breaking, a warm and vibrant glow in the east. He tried to get up, but almost passed out with a shooting agonizing pain in the back of his neck, and lay back down again. His body was weak, but his mind was still willing. He quickly took stock of the situation. Number one—and it was no surprise—Muriel and her band of merry men had disappeared. Number two, the place was teeming with police. And number three, there were four bodies on the ground that he could see. They looked pretty dead. No one paid any attention to Arjun until someone saw him move, and then that someone yelled hysterically, 'This one's alive! There's a survivor!'

And then, he became the centre of everyone's attention. Some gentlemen with stethoscopes rolled him about, and they informed him that he had a gunshot wound to the neck. He was further informed that he was lucky to be alive. Miraculously, the bullet had missed the carotid artery. Later on in life, he would learn to assess such a wound and call it a deep graze. But on that fateful day on the Bangalore-Chennai highway, it was labelled a gunshot wound.

Then he saw Ranjit. There was a gaping bloody hole where his right eye had been. His remaining eye was open and lifeless. He didn't need the doctors to tell him that his friend was dead. He began to cry. Tears rolled down his cheeks. What was he going to tell Ranjit's father? Ranjit's father was a tennis coach. He had dedicated his life to moulding his pride and joy into championship material. The hope had been that Ranjit would be able to use his tennis to get a scholarship to a good American university, make something of himself in the land of opportunity. Who was going to tell the old man that his son was dead, killed like a dog, far away from his loved ones? Who was going to tell Coach Shinde that all his dreams had died with his son?

Strapped to a gurney inside an ambulance, as he sped towards Bangalore's Chinmaya Hospital, Arjun thought about the events that would follow. He was the sole survivor of a massacre. There were going to be questions. Hard questions. He decided to tell the truth—there was no way out.

When the interrogations did happen, it was in Chennai, under the protection of his grandfather. The officials were CBI, independent and answerable to no one. But then again, no one wanted to cross the 'Iron Man'. The officials were polite, and he provided answers to all their queries. He told them the whole, unadulterated truth. What they told him in return was even more unbelievable. The executed men were Sinhalese. It looked like some sort of war between the Tamils from Sri Lanka. Did he know about the LTTE, they asked?

Arjun didn't lie when he said he had no idea, but saw a subtle change in his grandfather's face—he knew something. The CBI officials went on further. There was no proof of any blonde girl's involvement. In fact, there were no witnesses to prove that she even existed. Was Arjun sure about the events as they had taken place? After a while, Arjun's grandfather put an end to the incessant questioning. Everyone involved wasn't given a choice. They were just informed that the 'interview' was over, and that was that.

Privately also, the old man didn't press the issue with Arjun. It wasn't just about the gunshot wound. He knew the damage was much deeper. He looked into his grandson's eyes, and what he saw worried the old man. For some unknown reason, he remembered Mark Antony standing over the dead body of Julius Caesar saying, 'Cry havoc and let slip the dogs of war.'

*

Many months later, on the front lines of the Iran-Iraq war, Arjun had asked about any possible sightings or information about a blonde girl working for his new employers. No information was forthcoming. He knew the intel from the Afghans was solid. They had told him she was in Iran, and that meant she definitely was there. But his pay grade didn't allow him access to anything but the most basic of information. And then, as the rooh, his inquiries still hadn't made much progress apart from one solitary report describing an arms deal brokered by a blonde woman. The paper trail ended abruptly, making him wonder about her security clearance.

She had destroyed his innocence on the Bangalore-Chennai highway. But in doing so, she had created an unflinching, unwavering, remorseless predator with only one goal in mind. Now, as he read her file, the dust cleared and he understood everything. His pulse rate slowed as he prepared for the next steps. He had no doubt he would kill Muriel Steyns. His concerns were simple. Would he be able to interrogate the Belgian before he dispatched her to her God? Would there be time to find out why she had fucked him over on the Bangalore-Chennai highway?

***

# Chapter Seven

*May 31$^{st}$, 1983, 0900 Beirut Time*

When Adnan Bazzi received the order to infiltrate Baghdad and launch a rocket strike at the Mukhabarrat headquarters, he had been overjoyed. Finally, here was an opportunity to prove to his Iranian masters that Hezbollah were not just a ragtag group of dissidents.

The instructions had been clear. In three days, which fell on a Friday, at precisely 2330 hours, his team was to attack the Mukhabarrat headquarters. They were to engage the enemy in a firefight for about twenty minutes to half an hour, and then disappear. But Adnan had his own plans.

The weapons were Russian and had been smuggled across with a Bedouin caravan. Posing as carpet dealers from Syria, they booked themselves into the Imperial hotel, which was down the road from the Mukhabarrat headquarters, and gave them a direct line of sight of their target.

*

When they did finally come in, the reports were conflicting. Some said the attack was coming from the north east, and some said it was from the south. Actually, both reports were pretty accurate, but then there was also talk about the devil walking on earth, spreading death and destruction in his wake, and that he had the face of a child, so to be honest, the high command was not sure what to make of the panic-filled radio chatter.

Adnan not only carried out his orders, but he also went above and beyond the call of duty. The general belief was that Arabic fighters were not the brightest of the stars in the galaxy. Successive inexplicable, humiliating defeats at the hands of the Israelis had cemented that opinion. But Adnan was a part of an organization that would, in the future, halt the IDF in their tracks in Lebanon and actually push them back, resulting in an impasse, and would be hailed worldwide as a moral victory for Hezbollah.

It would be besides the point to mention that the Hezb would bring beautiful Lebanon to its knees economically and reduce Beirut to a bombed-out husk. That was not the point. The point was that they were able to hold their own against a tactically superior force, and all that began with fighters like Adnan, who displayed independent military acumen.

Splitting up his forces, they attacked the garrison from two directions. As the first rockets lit up the neighbourhood, the initial Iraqi response was one of complete confusion. Overconfidence is a cruel teacher, and as the entrance to the headquarters became a bloody mix of sandbags and bodies, the Iraqis would bitterly remember the lesson. There is no fortress that cannot be breached. Most of the elite Nephilim were asleep, or on vacation for a couple of days after enduring the standard two-month hell on the war front.

The new conscripts, most of them green and not tested in battle, had been put in charge of guarding the perimeter; such was the confidence in the invulnerability of the garrison. Their reaction to the rocket attack resembled that of a headless chicken. It never entered the Iraqi minds that the attack was a diversion.

Dressed in a Nephilim sergeant's uniform, Arjun was one with the shadows in Al Ramza street, two hundred meters south of the Mukhabarrat garrison, when the attack began.

As the Iraqi guards rallied to defend themselves against the unknown attackers and multiple explosions rocked the headquarters, they suddenly found themselves face-to-face with a Nephilim sergeant who seemed to have appeared from the wrong side of the action. They began to cheer because the Nephilim were the deadliest of the Iraqis, and where there was a sergeant, logic dictated more Nephilim would follow. Then, when it was much too late, they got a look at his face.

*

In his debrief back at the Hezbollah compound outside Beirut, Adnan would recount the massacre in reverential tones. '*Wallahi azim*! I have never seen anything like that,' he said. 'It was the devil. It cannot be anything else. We were sent as a distraction so that the devil could kill Iraqis. I understand that now.'

The first three cheering Iraqi guards were slashed open by a black sword that seemed to glow, which had magically appeared in the hands of the Nephilim sergeant. They were dead before they hit the ground, but the sergeant was already moving. His speed was blinding. 'It seemed that he was gliding on air, he was moving so fast,' said Adnan. 'There is no way a human being could move like that. Wallah, it was the devil.'

Arjun threw himself into a roll and landed in the middle of five confused Iraqi defenders. 'He killed five of them in the blink of an eye,' whispered Adnan. 'He had some kind of sword. I could not see clearly because I was too far away, coordinating the rocket attack. There was some sort of glimmer, maybe from the blade, and I looked through the binoculars and saw the chaos. The remaining eight, who were guarding the main entrance, were slashed and were dead before they could even understand what was going on. In the end, there were no more guards alive at the gates. If I had not seen it with my own eyes, I would not have believed it. Wallah, I know that they are the enemy, but…' Adnan did not complete the sentence, and the debriefing officers were confused at the fear and awe in the voice of the Hezbollah commander.

And then he said, 'Do you want to know the strangest thing? He was killing his way into the Mukhabarrat headquarters. Can you believe that? Who would want to go into that accursed place? I don't understand why.

'And there is one more thing.' Adnan was no stranger to blood and had no fear of death, but a tremor racked his body. 'I got a good look at its face. The "*Shaitan*" had the face of a child. So young!' Adnan clicked his fingers four times around his face, a sign to ward off evil, as had been taught to him by his grandfather. The debriefing officers just shook their heads. Obviously, Adnan was in great need of some rest and recuperation.

*

The second line of defence in the Mukhabarrat headquarters was a pair of large iron gates with grills, patrolled by armed guards behind the gates. As per the report given by a surviving guard, he saw a Nephilim sergeant rushing towards the gates, firing behind him and screaming in a very common *bedou* accent, to open the gates for Allah's sake. They had instinctively responded to the entreaty cum command.

'Where is the girl?' asked the sergeant, once he was on the other side of the barrier. 'Quickly, quickly, I have orders to secure her.'

'Second floor in the main interrogation room,' said one of the soldiers, responding to the panic in the sergeant's voice. And then another soldier, smarter than the rest, signed everyone's death warrant.

'Which brigade are you with, sergeant? Show us your face, please?'

Time seemed to slow down dramatically as the sergeant removed his headscarf. Everyone involved realized that the sergeant was firstly not Iraqi, and secondly, he was impossibly young, and everyone went for their weapons.

He twirled as though he were in a dance, metal flashing as he slashed around him, the blade leaving a psychedelic trail in its wake, and eight Iraqis lay dead in pools of blood, intestines and excrement.

He tossed his headscarf aside, sheathed the black sword and joined the general chaos, making his way deeper into the headquarters, screaming that the Iranians were at the gates and men either ran away or into each other as officers yelled and tried to restore a semblance of order among the terrified rank and file.

He went up the beautiful, broad stone stairs to the second floor. Interrogation room two stared back at him directly ahead at the end of the walkway.

*

Interrogation can either be a fine art or a blunt instrument. When used as a fine art, interrogators are extremely successful in obtaining actionable intelligence because the subject more often than not willingly gives up the information being sought after. As a blunt instrument, it is used to try and break the will of the detainee by using torture to inflict indignity and pain, and pressing home the futility of hope, as a means to achieve said goal.

So when Arjun entered interrogation room two, the first thing that met his eyes was a bloodied naked blonde girl strapped to a chair surrounded by three sweating Iraqis, one who was about to stub out his cigarette on one of the extremely well-shaped breasts of Muriel Steyns. He understood that the Iraqis were taking the 'blunt instrument' route.

The interrogators, confident that their troops would repulse the external threat, had continued with their artistic enterprise, and they didn't think much of the Nephilim sergeant dropping in unannounced. Everyone wanted a look at the blonde *Gehba* who had been captured. It was only after two of the interrogators lay dead, as a result of two well-placed bullets in their faces, did the remaining soldier, Colonel Sayed Al Hamrawi, realize that things had suddenly gone south and dropped his cigarette with startling alacrity.

Muriel raised a bloody face to check out the cause of the rude interruption. One of her eyes was swollen shut, and her left cheek had caved in, suggesting a broken cheekbone, and she was obviously in great pain. But in spite of all that, she stiffened in the chair as she recognized the young tennis player.

For some strange reason, he realized that it was a Saturday in Bombay. Fort Convent, the all-girls school on Wodehouse Road was having its annual Disco night. It was the only time of the year when males were allowed inside the hallowed all-girls school for a social gathering from six to eleven in the evening.

Tickets for this event would have sold out within a couple of hours. The Casanovas from Strand, Mandy and Puri would be headlining the male platoon as they descended in droves for the event of the year, dressed in their Sunday finest. There would be a lot of loin stirring as both sexes prepared for some hip grinding under the watchful eyes of the pious catholic nuns. He should have been there, somewhere in the background, hoping someone would dance with him. But he wasn't. He was very far away from Colaba. Far away from peace and quiet. The truth was that he didn't much care for the evening at Fort Convent. He was exactly where he wanted to be.

He was cold as ice as he spoke, although his insides were a thunderstorm of emotions. 'So I guess you didn't defect.'

She was flippant in her reply. You would have thought they were in a restaurant having coffee, but for the bright red blood that frothed out of her mouth, indicating severe internal damage. 'We do meet in the strangest of places. Are you here to kill me or rescue me? You're going to have to do either one pretty fast. Our friends are going to figure out this "attack" is a diversion.'

Through a red flecked smile, she said, 'There's no one stupid enough to launch an attack on the Mukhabarrat headquarters. I just didn't realize I was the target. But then again, I do know where the skeletons are buried, so I guess I understand you being here. Wasn't required, though. I wouldn't have talked. Of course, that's assuming you're here to kill me.'

He had often wondered what he would say when he caught up to her, but suddenly he was bereft of the appropriate words.

And somehow, it didn't feel important anymore. Which was weird, because he had gone through some pretty far-out stuff to get to where he was, and it had all been because of fucking Muriel Steyns.

'Can you walk?'

'I'll try to put my best foot forward.'

He went behind her and cut the bindings. She stood up and buckled with agony. He caught her before she fell and rested against him for a bit. Her hair smelled of honey, but maybe he was imagining it. She straightened herself up, wiped the blood away from her mouth, and smiled a tiny smile.

'You wouldn't happen to know where my clothes are, would you?' She turned her head and they both looked at Colonel Hamrawi, who wordlessly pointed to a bunch of tattered clothes in the far corner.

She limped painfully, picked up her clothes, and as she put them on, she continued speaking. It was all really quite bizarre.

'Well, look what these Neanderthals did with my clothes. We will have to find something else for me to wear if you are going to take me out for a drink. Oh! And what do we do with the good Colonel? We've got a little close in the last couple of days. Nothing like a good interrogation if you really want to bond. He has a wife and three children. Did you know that? He told me so just before he closed my eye for me.'

She turned and faced the Colonel squarely. 'Why did you share your family history with me, ya *hamar*?' She stuck her hand out behind her, and Arjun placed his stabbing knife in her right palm.

Colonel Hamrawi went weak in his knees as his life hung on the razor's edge.

***

# Chapter Eight

The Hezbollah faded away into the darkness without losing a single fighter. In terms of operational success, it was beyond fantastic. They hadn't lost even one fighter. The Iraqis had had no clue what was happening. All that could be heard on the Iraqi radios was that they were under attack and that they had lost many men. Then there was some crazy talk on the radio about the devil killing everyone. It was a good thirty minutes before the Iraqis realized that there was no return fire.

Then, someone from the army headquarters monitoring the chatter ten miles away asked the all-important question.

'Has anyone checked on the Sharmutha prisoner?'

*

'Looks like you're in a bad place, Colonel.' The 'place' had been two guns, a stabbing knife and Colonel Hamrawi's very weak knees. In Hamrawi's wintered opinion, that statement was not very accurate. 'Bad place' didn't quite describe his predicament. He was completely and totally fucked.

Either this bleeding blonde and that scary kid in a Nephilim sergeant's uniform were going to cut out his gonads, or if he miraculously survived this catastrophe, Saddam would take his time. First, he would have Hamrawi's pretty wife raped and then garroted while the good Colonel watched, and then he would strangle his two sons and daughter before finally making Hamrawi die in extreme agony.

Muriel Steyns was a consummate professional. While every fibre of her being wanted to end Hamrawi, the logical side of her saw the necessity of keeping him alive.

'You are a dead man when they find out I've escaped. You are going to be the sacrificial lamb. I see a meat hook in your immediate future.'

Hamrawi saw the same future, and it was very bleak. Muriel spoke again. 'But there is another option.' Colonel Hamrawi brightened up considerably. 'I could get you and your family to Europe. Does any particular place come to mind?'

*

General Rizwan Ahmed, head of the Mukhabarrat headquarters, had been with his mistress and had switched off his radios, and only his trusted aide-de-camp knew where he was. By the time anyone was able to get hold of the good General, the better part of an hour had passed.

Rizwan almost passed out from shock. The Mukhabarrat headquarters was under attack! And he had been with Fatima at that exact time! 'Allah save me,' he repeated silently as he rushed back, his heart pounding as he thought about what was going to happen to him once Saddam heard about the disaster. He heard the enquiry about the blonde prisoner over his now switched-on radios. His initial rage over the lack of help from the army headquarters dissipated, giving way to paralyzing fear as everything became shockingly clear.

It hadn't been a breakout. It had been a fucking break-in! He had heard about the rooh at several intelligence briefings. Could it be him? It had to be. 'Allah help me,' he prayed. As it turned out, Allah wasn't in a helpful mood that night. The interrogation room was empty. Not quite, though—there were the two interrogators lying on the ground, very dead.

Eyewitnesses reported seeing Colonel Hamrawi exiting the interrogation room with the prisoner. He had screamed in a very loud voice that he had orders to take the Gehba to the army headquarters in Nablus for safekeeping from the attack, and demanded unfettered access to the southern exit, where the motor pool was. No one thought to question the commandant. He had taken a Land Cruiser and had left the headquarters in a hurry.

Oh, and yes, no one had thought anything was wrong, since he was accompanied by a Nephilim sergeant. The strangest thing was that no one was able to quite remember what he looked like, except that he was very young. Hamrawi was not seen again for a very long time. Time enough for all concerned to believe he had been executed by the rooh, and his body dumped somewhere in the cold, unforgiving sands.

*

## *June 4th, 1983, 0500 Iraq Time*

'You need to see a doctor. We will be splitting up after this. Hamrawi is bringing a Taureg to take you guys across Syria to Lebanon. The Mukhabarrat will be expecting us to make a run for the Iranian border. They will concentrate their resources at likely entry points. They will never expect you to go west. I'll find my way back.' Arjun's tone was neutral.

They were at the safe house in Al Mansour Street, a stone's throw from the Mukhabarrat headquarters. Hamrawi had circled back and dropped them off. It was so audacious, and the Iraqis never suspected the fugitives were so close. He had then proceeded with extreme haste to pick up and bring his family back to the safe house. His instructions were clear: he had one hour to get back, and if he wasn't on time, then he was on his own.

'Don't forget to dump the Land Cruiser,' Arjun had said. 'They'll be looking for it.'

'I'll find alternate means of transportation,' assured a much-relieved Hamrawi.

Muriel lay down on the surprisingly comfortable bed and rested her weary bones. Her injuries were severe, but not life-threatening. She understood the rigours of the journey that lay ahead of them. She needed to be much fitter. She also knew Arjun was worried about her. She felt a pang of guilt as she looked at him. He was looking out at the street through the drawn curtains, and she looked at his back framed in the shadows.

If she hadn't decided to seduce him, he would be living a peaceful life playing tennis and going to college. Looking back, she thought about that spur-of-the-moment decision in Bangalore at a tennis tournament she was never supposed to be at. After everything she had been witness to in her young life, she had given up on the belief in God. But the world had definitely turned since she decided to shack up for a few nights with a young tennis player, leading up to the present situation. She had to wonder whether there was actually a higher power at work.

What was done could not be changed. Arjun had been dealt a bad hand of cards. But he had made the best use of them. He would never be mediocre, never be a part of a pack, never be mundane. She wasn't sure what was going to happen with the young tennis player, but a woman's intuition assured her that it would be something people would talk about years into the future, years after all the madness had passed—she was sure of that.

She smiled. 'Still my knight in shining armour.'

He looked at her, and she realized it was time.

'I guess I need to clear the air about Bangalore.'

Arjun was impassive as he waited for Muriel to continue. 'I need to start at the beginning. The LTTE was formed to protect the ethnic Tamils in Sri Lanka against the Sinhalese-dominated discriminatory practices.'

Arjun cut her short. 'I am not interested in a history lesson. Give me the abbreviated version.'

Muriel nodded. 'Understood. There was a colonel called Nandana Dasanayake in the Sri Lankan secret service who created a task force with the sole aim of eliminating the upper echelon of the LTTE. He was a ruthless man, and his cruelty knew no depths. The top officers of the LTTE had disappeared into the jungles and could not be found. So, he started with the families left behind. He had the women raped and children killed when no information was forthcoming about the location of their men.'

Arjun nodded. 'Terrible things are done in war. It is to be expected.'

Muriel continued. 'I agree. So the LTTE decided to deal with the violence appropriately. They leaked information about a secret arms deal that was to take place in Bangalore. All the top leaders of the LTTE would be there. Since it was outside of Sri Lanka, security would be minimal. One strike and the entire upper echelon of the LTTE would be eliminated before they could do any more damage in Sri Lanka. The news leaked that the elusive Prabhakaran would be there.'

Arjun took a deep breath. His theory had been right. He'd got in the middle of a military operation. 'What was your role?'

'The leaked communiques detailed the presence of foreign brokers sympathetic to the LTTE cause.'

Arjun sat down and leaned forward, his thumbs under his chin. 'In one stroke, this colonel could deal a death blow to the entire organisation. Destroy the top command and eliminate the brokers. Too good an opportunity to pass up.'

Muriel laughed. It was a very pleasant sound. 'The colonel took the bait. Bangalore became ground zero for his six-man hit squad. We kept the line of information flowing about the location of the secret meeting through sources that the colonel perceived as unimpeachable. Our informants in the local police kept us up to date about the arrival of the colonel and his hunting party in Bangalore.'

Muriel laughed again. 'The double agents did not even know that they were feeding false information to the good colonel. They had been identified as compromised quite a while back. Instead of eliminating them, we kept them in play, waiting for the one big moment.'

Arjun nodded, and Muriel continued, 'All that was required was to separate the colonel and his party from the local police back-up. Information about the location of the safe house where the LTTE leaders would be meeting with the arms dealers was leaked through the usual rock-solid sources. Further information reinforced the original assessment that security would be minimal.'

Against his will, Arjun found himself caught up in the story. 'Go on,' he said.

Muriel turned on her side and grimaced with the pain. 'Colonel Dasanayake told the police to follow me while he and his team scouted the location of the safe house. The police wanted to arrest the ring leaders, but the colonel had other ideas. He could not afford to let the leaders live. He was going to fake an encounter while the police followed me. Kill everyone at the meeting and then claim self-defence. Better to ask for forgiveness than for permission.'

'So the police followed you, and you landed at Cubbon Park, where I was playing my match.'

'Don't sell yourself short. I like tennis, and I definitely liked you. I could see you were a fighter. I enjoyed the match. I would have liked to see how far you would have progressed if the rains hadn't washed out the tournament.'

'So I was a diversion.' It wasn't a question.

'Yes. I'm sorry. The colonel and his team got a nasty surprise. We had a full team waiting for him and his men. Unfortunately, the colonel escaped. The rest were taken to the shack on the highway, and everyone waited for me.'

'Meanwhile, the police, following you, saw you with me. You kept them occupied outside my hotel, while your team turned the tables on the colonel and his men. Then you waited for the police to get bored. They must have got information that contact was lost with the colonel at the safe house. They left the hotel in a rush. Members of your team were lying in wait. They sent a message with the bellboy to my room about a phone call. That was your signal to move. So the four gentlemen you executed were the colonel's team. You were in the middle of an interrogation to find out where the colonel could have run to. Ranjith and I interrupted you.' Arjun was toneless in his summarization of the terrible night.

'You were not supposed to be there. That was a tragic mistake.'

'Bulshit. Don't sugarcoat anything. I get it. No witnesses. Standard protocol.'

Muriel was silent. Arjun continued, 'You're blown in Tehran. They will execute you if I take you back. They will never be sure you didn't defect, and how much information you shared. And you know about the Iranians and second chances.'

She nodded, understanding perfectly. 'So we go west, and you go east.'

Arjun nodded and got up. He looked out the window. 'Here comes Colonel Hamrawi.' He spoke into his walkie-talkie, 'Party of five. Lunch and dinner.'

Arjun looked at Muriel. 'What made you such a high-value target? You must have some extremely compromising information.'

Muriel smiled. 'Let's make that our next conversation piece.'

Arjun saw Colonel Hamrawi looking anxiously out of one of the windows, but knew that he also had one ear tuned to the conversation.

'Hopefully our paths will never cross again.'

'It would be so boring without me. And I know you don't mean that. You're just trying to be tough.

Colonel Hamrawi smiled slightly.

*

His journey back to Iran had been relatively incident-free, apart from an encounter with an over-enthusiastic group of Iraqi border guards. They were found sliced to pieces by what seemed to be a very sharp blade. Back in Tehran, he made a verbal report to the General Shahzad. It was short and to the point.

'Hezbollah played their part to perfection. I was able to infiltrate the Mukhabarat headquarters and neutralize the agent.'

Shahzad lit an expensive Cuban cigar and laughed heartily. 'We received a rather long and detailed report from Hezbollah. I think it's safe to say you neutralized the hell out of the Iraqis. Their commander witnessed what he called a massacre. And that is only what he saw from the outside. Can you fill me in on the details of what happened once you got in?'

Arjun shrugged his shoulders, keeping his tone flat as he replied. 'I had some great instructors. They taught me well. Not much else to say. I had to neutralize some opposition once I entered the Mukhabarrat headquarters. To be fair, I don't think they were expecting anyone to break in. I would assume it's normally the other way around. I utilized the element of surprise and—'

'Yes, yes, you neutralized them. I think we all got that memo on both sides of the border. Can you be more descriptive?' Shahzad cut in on the rather vanilla report.

Arjun was silent for a moment. He knew the general wasn't angry or irritated. He just liked listening to a good story, and if it came from the horse's mouth, even better. But he wasn't there to be the dancing bear of the moment.

He continued, 'Then I found the agent. They were interrogating her, and she was not in very good shape. I killed two of her interrogators and used the remaining one, I think he was a colonel, to commandeer transportation out of the headquarters. I took the target along with me. Once I was clear of the city, I eliminated both prisoners out in the sands. Their bodies have probably been picked clean by the vultures and the ants.'

'Probably better this way. They would not have suffered. Imagine if they were still under interrogation? Those Mukhabarrat dogs are an abomination.'

'I still don't know why this agent had made her such a high-value target.' Arjun was curious.

'Even I don't have access to that information. It's above my pay grade. Don't worry about that. All that matters is that you did what you were sent to do.' Shahzad laughed a trifle bitterly. 'Yours is not to question why.'

Arjun smiled, but it didn't quite reach his eyes. 'Well, I did and I didn't die. So I guess no harm, no foul.'

'You acquitted yourself with honour. Those animals, the Mukhabarrat, would have had no mercy. It was an act of kindness that you ended the agent's suffering before it actually began.' Shahzad sighed dramatically as he realized there would be no out-of-the-box entertainment and rested his cigar on a gold ashtray that could have probably fed a couple of villages in Africa. He also needed to end the dialogue before he was pressed into answering questions that were rather compromising.

Arjun smiled to himself. Calling the Iraqis brutal was like the pot calling the kettle black. Arjun was well aware of the brutality of the Iranians, but kept his opinions to himself. Two sides of the same coin! He was aware that General Shazam's pay grade was probably the second-highest in the country. There was nothing that he was not privy to. So his obfuscating meant that Muriel had been more than just an embarrassment to her handlers. Pity he wouldn't be able to find out what all the fuss had been about. That would require a conversation with Muriel, who, by his estimate, should have boarded a freighter to Marseilles at that precise moment. He would not see her again, and that left him with mixed feelings of relief and regret. Either way, he had found his prey, and in doing so, he had found out a lot about himself. But as far as his loyalty was concerned, it would always be for his alma mater. He bowed ever so slightly.

'I am always in your debt, General. Without you, I would have never been able to complete my journey. I want you to know I am always at your service. If you or your loved ones ever need me, please do not hesitate to call for me. I will be there. We will always be family.'

Shahzad came from a line of warriors that went back ten centuries, and he was not given to emotion. But he was suddenly and unexpectedly inundated with a wave of sadness. He knew this was goodbye. He probably would not see this mysterious young man from the east again. He sighed deeply and nodded.

'It was an honour to be your supervising officer. Your journey is not at an end. It has only just begun. You have the heart of a warrior. But even the best warrior tyres. And if some day your spirit is in need of rest and you long for home, remember: Iran and you will always be especially welcome in the house of General Shahzad Gauri.'

***

# Chapter Nine

*Bombay, 1985*

The newspapers called him 'The Plumber'. That irritated him mildly. He had been hoping for something more dramatic, like 'Shiva', or 'The Destroyer', because that's what he felt he was. But he remained The Plumber. And it was all because he had used that damned wrench with Mrs Khemlani, and some stupid cop had spoken to some unimaginative reporter about that. Then, it had been plastered all over the newspapers, and he had been forced to use a wrench in all the subsequent eleven killings. He didn't want someone else to take credit for his kills. Peer pressure is a killer! What really upset him was that in spite of the way he treated his victims, the effort he put into serving them up to the creator had gone seemingly unnoticed. All everyone was talking about was the damn wrench.

For his thirteenth victim, he had chosen Mrs Contractor. She was a mild-mannered Parsi lady whose husband was an ill-tempered ex-sailor. He had left the high seas and now ran a liquor shop in Fort. It was an inheritance. It was a money spinner. The license, along with the shop, was worth a fortune and had been handed down to him by his father, who had acquired it from the departing British. He refused to water down the alcohol, and there was always a steady stream of high-value customers in and out of his shop.

It wasn't that Mrs Contractor was sleeping with the building watchman. In fact, the chances were bright that sex didn't figure in her spectrum. It was well known that she lived in fear of her husband, who could be quite nasty after a few drinks. It was rumoured but never confirmed that he preferred the company of the local ladies of the night who hung around the periphery of the shop, enticing potential customers. Long story short, sex wasn't a recurring event in the Contractor household. At least not for Mrs Contractor.

Her only mistake was that she had come into the store, had smiled very sweetly, and asked if the store provided a delivery service.

Maybe it was the smile, or maybe it was the dress that she was wearing that showed a hint of her knee. He could not tell. But suddenly, he felt the familiar roar building up to a crescendo in his ears. He could barely make out what she was saying. He knew that God was speaking. God had made the selection. He was no one to question the will of the Almighty. He made a show of looking for a pen to write down her address as he waited for the roar to subside.

He looked up and smiled. 'Of course, madam. We provide door delivery service up to 8 pm, every day, except Sunday. But for you, madam, I will come myself if you need. You are VIP customer.'

Mrs Contractor looked a bit confused about the 'VIP' bit. Then she did a mental shrug. After all, she was a Parsi, and the shopkeeper obviously knew her husband. She smiled back and said, '18 Scherezade Apartments.'

Paresh nodded and wrote the address down. Mrs Contractor handed him a list of things she needed. 'Can you deliver this today?'

Paresh nodded emphatically. 'Of course, madam! It will reach your residence within one hour. I will set up an account for you, and you can pay at the end of the month.'

Mrs Contractor beamed. 'This is really VIP service. Thank you, *Dikra*.'

*

Paresh spent the next two months making regular deliveries to the Contractor residence. He knew that the husband, a rude, arrogant man, left the house every day at about 11 am.

The son left the house shortly thereafter. He had found out that the boy was an only child and was studying to be an architect. That was great. There was no need to factor in the timings of several siblings, as he had had to do with some of his previous killings. He would return much after seven in the evening. The kaamwali came shortly after that and stayed for two hours. The entrance to the building was shrouded by beautiful old trees that had seen the British enjoy a privileged colonial life in a land far away from their gloomy, dark, cold, rainy island in the Atlantic. There was one old security guard who was almost never there.

By his estimate, Paresh figured he could have Mrs Contractor all to himself, undisturbed, for most of the afternoon. It was almost perfect. Almost. There was a slight potential hiccup—his normal route to Scherezade Apartments would have been from the south, through Colaba market. This meant he would have to pass the taxi drivers who waited in the queue for customers from the Fariyas Hotel. Most of the customers were foreigners, and paid very well for a sightseeing tour. Many paid a lot more to get high and get laid. The taxi drivers were the one-stop shop of iniquity. They were also extremely territorial. One of their lookouts might remember him.

He decided to take the long way on the appointed day. His amended route would take him down the Strand Road, keeping the cinema theatre on his left. He would pass the Sangam Bhavan complex on his right, and then turn right and make his approach from the north. The trees would cover his arrival. Chances were bright that no one would see him.

He had heard the saying that 'assumption is the mother of all fuck ups'. It was from some movie, he wasn't sure which one, but it stuck in his head. To make sure no one recognized him, he decided to use a disguise. On the Colaba Causeway, he had come across a make-up set for kids in Paragon, the toy shop. The set came with a grey stick-on moustache, some easily washed off white paint for the hair, and a pair of zero-power reading glasses. It was the perfect gift set for a ten-year-old.

It was even more perfect for him. He decided to go as an old man—it was a cruel and callous world, and no one gave the elderly a second glance. He would be virtually invisible to the average onlooker from any of the buildings or a passerby.

He was stressed. The timing needed to be right. A sacrifice to God made at the wrong time was no sacrifice at all. He knew it would be in the next three weeks, but he still didn't know the exact date. He knew the devil was in the details. Then, as he read the *Times of India* two days later, the answer appeared to him. He had a date. God had spoken. Soon it would be time to do his bidding.

*

It was around one in the afternoon on the 27th of June, when the doorbell of Mrs Contractor's house rang. She was sitting down to some delicious *đhansak* as she listened to the news on the radio. She was looking forward to an afternoon nap. Mr Contractor had been particularly nasty that morning—his coffee hadn't been hot enough, and the orange juice hadn't been cold enough.

Mrs Contractor wished she had the courage to kick him in the balls really hard, pack her bags and leave. But she had nowhere to go, and she didn't relish the prospect of living in Cusrow Baug. Too many inquisitive Parsis around. Everyone would know about her situation, and she didn't want to be the topic of gossip. Unsurprisingly, she was a little distracted when the bell rang and opened the door without thinking. She was surprised to see an old man.

Paresh buckled her with a straight punch to her solar plexus. Mrs Contractor collapsed on the floor. She wanted to scream, but found herself gasping for air. She was unable to breathe—a hard punch accurately delivered to the solar plexus will do that to you. Paresh stepped inside and closed the door. The whole operation took three seconds.

Once inside, he took his time with Mrs Contractor. He knew she had to experience extreme agony. Pain was the ultimate cleanser of the soul. He bound and gagged her and laid her on the ornate antique dinner table that was rarely used by the Contractors.

'I'm sure you never thought you would be the main course at your own table.' He laughed lightly at his own joke. His smile was almost kind. Mrs Contractor whimpered into the gag as she saw him open his bag. She screamed in terror when she saw the unassuming old man take out the wrench. She knew she was face-to-face with The Plumber.

But what tipped her over the edge was the foldable hacksaw and other assorted cutting and slicing instruments that appeared from The Plumber's bag. She swallowed her tongue; such was the terror of being in the clutches of The Plumber.

Paresh was momentarily distracted by the fact that he was trying to come to a decision on which of his tools he needed the most. Out of the periphery of his right eye, he saw Mrs Contractor begin to convulse and realized she was choking, and cursed.

'Stupid woman!' he said as he turned her on her side, removing her gag. Vomit dribbled all over his hands, and he cursed again. He stuck his right index finger inside her throat and felt around. The tongue was stuck inside. He moved his finger around and felt the muscle respond to his touch. He slipped his finger under the tongue and pulled gently. He heaved a silent sigh of relief as the tongue popped out along with lumps of half-digested *dhansak*.

He was back to his gentle self. 'Let's start again, shall we? First, I need to wash myself, and I'll be right back.'

He put a fresh gag in, making sure the tongue could not curl back into the throat again. Then he removed his moustache and glasses, and Mrs Contractor's eyes widened in horror as she recognized the owner of Swabal Stores.

'Sorry about the white hair. It's all part of the disguise. Just for you, Mrs Contractor. Let's begin, shall we? I wish I could say that this is not going to hurt. Truth be told, it's going to hurt a lot.'

*

### *June 27th, 1985, 1700 Hours, Indian Standard Time*

It was the son who found the body. Or what was left of it. Mrs Contractor had been sliced open from throat to pelvis. Her sternum had been cut, and her rib cage had been pulled apart by a sternal retractor, which was still in place. Her heart was missing. It was a bit of a mess, as is often the case when the heart is cut out of the body.

'He cut her heart out while she was still alive,' said the medical examiner matter-of-factly.

Sub Inspector Baig shook his head. 'I don't understand what goes on in this animal's head. What drives him to do these things? It's that damned Plumber of course.' He pointed to the wrench at the end of the table.

The medical examiner was bent over the mutilated body. He looked like a teenager, far too young for such a job. He shook his head. 'No, Sub Inspector Baig. An animal would never do something like this. This is pure evil. This man takes pleasure in inflicting terrible pain on his victims, and then cuts their hearts out while they are still alive.'

He straightened himself and continued. 'I have seen him improve with every kill. He is learning. He is driven by perfection.'

'What do you mean?' asked Baig.

'I have been called in for every victim since the first one at Cuffe Parade, four years ago. Housewife. It was extremely messy. He obviously didn't have the right tools for the job at that time. He'd used a hammer to break open the chest. He didn't know how to pry open the ribs. He used pliers, I think.

There were bone fragments and shards all over the place. It was an extremely sloppy job. He must have been drenched in blood. In my opinion, he was lucky to get away.'

Baig was curious. 'How did you know he would kill again? I mean, after the first one?'

The medical examiner smiled wryly. 'I'm in a specialized line of work. I get to see a lot of corpses.' They both laughed grimly.

The ME continued, 'You develop an instinct after being around dead bodies for a while. Especially with homicides. And with this guy, I don't know. After I saw the first kill, I just knew he wasn't done. I felt he was just beginning. Unfortunately, it turned out that I was right.'

Baig looked grudgingly impressed. 'You're quite young to be an ME.'

'I'm still a medical student. I'm in my second year. We all have to do morgue duty at least once a month. I found I liked forensics. It's amazing what you can learn from a corpse.'

Baig nodded his head wisely, but not understanding at all. The ME continued. 'I asked to be informed if there were any more similar cases to the Cuffe Parade killing. I got the call a couple of months later. This time, it was a housewife in Brady's Flats in Colaba. The kill site was still messy, but there was an element of finesse to the slaying. The rib cage had been opened up more professionally. I'm not sure, but maybe he used forceps. Of course, there was The Plumber's wrench. It was the same guy. After that, the legend of the plumber was born, and I've only seen marked improvements in his technique with each subsequent kill.'

Baig hid a sneer. 'You sound as though you admire this maniac.'

'Incorrect, Inspector. He's not a maniac. He's a cool, calm predator. I don't admire him, but he has piqued my interest.

This is not your ordinary run-of-the-mill killer. This man has an agenda. He is not driven only by bloodlust. I mean, yes, he likes the killing, but that's not what drives him. I'm not sure, but it's something else. I also don't understand the wrench.'

Baig was a family man. He has two small children, and he wondered how he would cope if he came back home and found his wife slaughtered. Not very well.

He turned and yelled at a passing constable. 'Hey, Bhave, you fucking idiot! What are you doing here? Where's the son? What about the husband?'

Surinder Bhave had been surreptitiously wending his way out of Ground Zero, hoping he wouldn't be noticed. He ground to a halt, snapped a weak salute and said, 'Saab, the boy is downstairs at a neighbour's flat. We called the husband. We didn't tell him anything except that there was a family emergency and that he needed to come home.'

Baig grunted. 'So you're not completely useless. Now don't keep staring at me. Fuck off downstairs and bring me the son. I need to talk to him.' He turned back to the medical examiner. 'Do you have a time of death?'

'Somewhere between one and three in the afternoon. He took his time with her.' The medical examiner's voice was grim. 'She vomited most of the contents of her stomach. Either it was fear, or the gag. Maybe it was a combination of both. What a terrible way to go.'

The young ME looked at Baig. 'You have your work cut out for you, Inspector. It won't be easy to catch this guy. You're going to need help. And please don't tell me that you have your colleagues. Most of them aren't very gifted in police work.'

Baig laughed. 'You may be right. But what do you suggest?'

'Let me ask around. You'll need help from the streets, and your *khabaris*, or informers, won't be of any help. You need someone who sees things differently. Someone like you. And I mean that as a compliment."

He removed his gloves, closed his medical bag and headed for the door. "I'll be in touch."

'Hey! Hang on a sec. What's your name?' asked Baig.

The ME smiled, and Baig thought he suddenly didn't look so young anymore. 'My name is Eknath Wadekar, but my friends call me Shinde.'

***

# Chapter Ten

In the summer of 1985, a decision was taken to kill Shabaz Khan. It was not a decision taken lightly, or in haste, because Shabaz was feared both by his friends and his enemies. He lived by the code that it was better to be feared than respected, because if you were feared, then you stayed alive, and respect, like beauty, was only skin deep. The decision to take out Shabaz Khan had been arrived at after a great deal of thought, since apart from being a fearsome warrior who had been able to cheat death successfully in the past, and then wreak bloody vengeance on his would-be assassins and their families, he was also the nephew of Kasim Lala.

Kasim Lala had come to India from Baluchistan in the fifties, just after the bloody partition had claimed millions of Indian lives in the name of their gods.. He had set up his criminal empire from humble beginnings in the dockyards of Masjid Bunder. Lala was born in the heat of battle, his mother giving birth to him while his village was under attack by a rival clan. It was said that it was a miracle that the mother and child had escaped the slaughter, and an even greater miracle that the young widow and her suckling infant had survived the treacherous terrain and the even more treacherous denizen that dwelt in the lands through which she had to travel to get to India.

The newly made border between India and Pakistan was still very porous, and eventually Jamila and her young son had finally reached the safety of Bombay and had taken refuge in the house of relatives in Bhendi Bazaar. Young Kasim grew up in the tough neighbourhoods of Dongri, Nagpada, and Agripada. While he didn't receive a formal education, he was well-versed in the language of the streets by the time he was sixteen. Being naturally tall and brawny, he quickly found work in the dockyards of the eastern lines and, just as fast, realized that there was a fortune to be made in smuggling.

The Indian government's policy of 'Be Indian Buy Indian' had given birth to a fanatical craze for all things foreign, and even the most modest of Indians was ready to pay a premium price for anything made abroad. This included anything from tobacco to toothpaste, and from garments to booze, but the biggest craze was for electronics. Television sets, cassette players, and radios went for double and triple their actual price, such was their scarcity. Kasim and his gang ran a smuggling ring using dinghies and speed boats that rendezvoused with cargo liners lying off the coast of Bombay, and unloaded tons of foreign cargo bound for the customs yards. Through various Malayali shops that dotted the streets of South Bombay, they peddled their smuggled goods at astronomical prices. Even after the hefty overheads, which involved paying huge bribes to the police, Kasim was able to buy a six-bedroom apartment in Bhendi Bazaar and moved his mother and his bride into the luxurious quarters, which were within walking distance of the local mosque.

He made sure his lieutenants were well paid, because happy lieutenants were loyal lieutenants, and his power grew until he was one of two dons who ruled Bombay. He spread his wings into prostitution and *havala*, which involved money transactions between the Middle East and India, and then went into providing manpower to the burgeoning economies of the UAE and Saudi Arabia. It might have all had a happy ending had he not decided to expand his business and get into the drug trade.

*

If you decide to invest in the narcotics business, you will very suddenly be thrust into the world of extremely ruthless people, where God is money, and money is God. They don't think of themselves as the rotten apples in the world's basket. They consider themselves to be businessmen who supply a very global demand, and just like successful and profitable international corporations, they are high-performance oriented and just as unforgiving of mistakes and failures.

Kasim Lala was pragmatic about himself and realized that he lacked the ruthlessness of the drug lords. He wasn't a coward and had proved himself time and time again to be a dangerous adversary in a fight. But these drug lords took ruthlessness to a level that was reminiscent of Genghis Khan, had no compassion, and did not hesitate to wreak devastation on women and children if their business was threatened. Kasim needed a face, an equally ruthless axe for the operations, while he remained the brains, and thus entered Shahbaz Khan.

Shahbaz proved to be more than equal to the task, and his ruthlessness sent shivers down the backs of friends and foes alike. He wasn't really Kasim Lala's nephew, but as in all stories, it was not the story itself but the telling of it, and after a while, it became the truth. He was handsome, well over six feet, and hid his evil behind a winsome smile. You underestimated Shabaz at your peril, as more than one gangster found out.

Take, for example, Spanjo Shekar. He was a drug dealer who had been given the franchise of Mulund by Kasim Laila. He was dangerous, loyal, and made his payments regularly. But after six months, it became clear that the accounts weren't tallying, and the finger of suspicion pointed towards Mulund. Now Spanjo was a good earner, and that should have earned him some brownie points with Kasim Lala, and to be honest, it did. But not with Shabaz. The brawny Pathan paid Spanjo a visit one night. He had a hit squad with him, along with the famous, 'Mulund James' of the Mohawk haircut.

Spanjo was a seasoned veteran himself, having escaped a number of assassination attempts. He had been in a million street battles and had survived relatively unscathed. He knew that the angel of death danced on his shoulders and knew that unless he was incredibly lucky, he would not live to a ripe old age. 'Anyway,' reasoned Spanjo, 'who wanted to live to an age where his body would be racked with disease, unable to take care of himself? The greatest gift was to die when one was at peak health.'

Still, he was entirely unprepared for the violence that was unleashed on him. There was no hint of Shabaz's true intentions as they all sat down for a few drinks, chatting about the latest goings-on in the city. After his fourth peg, Spanjo was pleasantly high as the conversation ranged from the latest dance bar girls in the circuit to drug shipments inbound from the north. He saw Mulund James get up and go out, and thought he was going out to relieve himself.

'Arey, bhai! No need to go out. I have a Western-style toilet at the back.'

There was no reply from Mulund James for a bit, and suddenly the night was pierced by a shriek of fear, and before Spanjo realized what was happening, his wife and ten-year-old son were dragged in front of Shabaz and his bodyguards. Spanjo sobered up double time and also realized that he was a dead man, as he found himself face to face with a number of handguns of different makes. Quite illogically, he found himself admiring the Skorpion machine pistol in Shabaz's hand and wondered if it was a gift or if Shabaz had paid for it. He knew he would never find the answer to that question. It was stupid to have skimmed from the earnings, and he cursed himself for not having some loyal warriors around. At least they could have made a fight of it.

'This is how it's going to go,' said Shabaz, conversationally, 'First, we are going to kill your son.'

One cue, Mulund James cut the throat of the young boy who gurgled and slowly crumpled in a heap as a halo of red gathered around his head. Spanjo was numb, stunned beyond grief as he looked at the lifeless body of his pride and joy.

'I know you don't want to hear the moans of your wife as I take her, so I'll send you to Allah first.' Saying this, Shabaz put a bullet into Spanjo's face, which exploded, spraying fragments of bone and flesh everywhere. Spanjo's wife began to wail as Shabaz got up and gently led her into the bedroom and shut the door.

The story of Spanjo's final journey made its rounds all over Bombay. Not too many people were willing to go head-to-head with Shabaz after that. So, when the decision to kill Shabaz Khan was taken, it must be stressed that it was not taken lightly. But after repeatedly raping Kasim Lala's favourite whore, Laila, the choice was removed from the old don's hands. Inaction would have been perceived as weakness, and in the jungle, there were many jackals just waiting for the right moment to strike down an ageing lion.

***

# Chapter Eleven

The task of killing Shabaz was given to Hamid and Majid Pathan. The brothers were fearless fighters and were the first to use kicks effectively in street fights. It spoke of military training, although where they had received such training was not clear. There was a saying in the Muslim heartland of Bombay that if you saw a crowd running down the road in Nagpada, chances were pretty bright that Hamid and Majid would be seen not too long after, striding down behind them.

The brothers were not fazed by the legend of Shabaz Khan and the blood thirsty tales surrounding his rise to power. They had a few tales of their own. Every run-in with Shabaz and his entourage had always ended in a stalemate. But the brothers had always felt that if push came to shove, they could take Shabaz. As Majid Pathan once said, 'Victory is not about weapons or manpower. It is the willingness to do what the enemy wouldn't.'

When the *supari* was handed to them, they approached it with caution. It could have been a trap. Majid, the more assertive of the two brothers and their unofficial spokesman, insisted that he hear the orders from the great Don himself. At a secret meeting held at 'Candy Castle' in Cuffe Parade, the brothers met with Kasim Lala. The Don arrived with only one bodyguard as proof of his commitment. The brothers came with no one.

The Don had aged significantly. The brothers had heard of his heroin addiction. His physical frailty, decaying teeth and glassy eyes were evidence that the great man from Baluchistan was on a downward spiral. But when he spoke, the legendary strength was still there. 'Shabaz is my son. I love him, but his actions will cost me my empire. You boys have been chosen because you can be his successor and mine. I will not give you any lectures about Shabaz and how dangerous he is. You already know that. Let me know when the job is done.'

The don sighed deeply and got to his feet. He may have looked frail, but he walked out the door with no help. Hamid nodded with admiration. 'That's a tough old dog.'

The brothers were cautiously elated. They knew that success meant that they would have Bombay at their feet. They did not think about the consequences of failure, because failure was not an option. But they knew that they had to come up with an extraordinary plan. The devil was in the details.

They started a covert surveillance of their quarry. Knowledge of his movements and his schedules would give them an idea of his security, favourite hangouts, favourite hookers, etc. Information was key. With the right information, they could plan for the right moment to strike, and they knew that moment had to be perfect. They wouldn't get a second chance. 'When you aim for the king, you best make sure you don't miss.' And tough as they were, the brothers didn't want to tangle with the likes of Mulund James and a vengeful Shabaz Khan if they failed.

The Pathan brothers underestimated Shabaz Khan's popularity. Members of the surveillance teams that were tailing him broke the news to Shabaz that he was a marked man and that he was no longer his uncle's favourite nephew. But then, much to the consternation of his allies, Shabaz Khan did the unthinkable. Rather than go to war with his uncle and the consortium that had decided his fate, Shabaz decided to run. That was his fatal mistake. He had always been feared, and that inspired fanatical loyalty.

Truth be told, one could never really have been able to predict a sure winner, had Shabaz decided to go to war. In the jungle, to be feared is the key to the throne. To be an apex predator, all other predators must fear you. It should also be emphasized that all predators look to the throne with envy, lust, and desire. It is fear that keeps their aspirations at bay. And all predators, big or small, can smell fear. And they all smelled it the moment Shabaz decided to run. Unknown to him, there was an immediate defection in the upper echelon of his ranks.

Shabaz planned for the late-night Air India flight to Dubai. His departure was at 3.40 am, and he planned to be there at the very last moment possible, to exclude any possible assassination attempts. Hanif Kuttha was sent earlier on with the bags and was tasked with checking the luggage in and getting the boarding cards. Shabaz and his wife Anissa would arrive at the airport at 2.40 am. They would meet Kuttha at the departure entrance of Santa Cruz airport. There would be no time for fond farewells. A quick handover, and once they were inside the airport, they were safe.

Shabaz knew that punctuality was the key to success, and arrived at Santa Cruz airport at precisely 2.40 am in a nondescript taxi. He got out, followed by Anissa, his eyes everywhere, scanning for death, heart racing. He was completely exposed without any weapons. But the coast seemed clear, and his gaze fell upon Hanif Kuttha, who came through the airport entrance doors, boarding cards in hand, and he relaxed. Then, with a shock, he saw the look in Hanif Kuttha's eyes, swimming with treachery and turned to hug his wife. From behind two pillars on either side, Hamid and Majid stepped out, Makarov machine pistols in hand.

*

In faraway Strand, in the heart of Colaba, a phone rang in a flat in the Mohini Mansion. Richard D'Souza, warlord of Strand under the Subash Raut umbrella, picked up the receiver and listened silently. He hung up, looked around at his fighters sitting around and said, 'Wicket *gir gaya*. A wicket has fallen!' It was self-explanatory, and there was a hum of conversation in the room as everyone gathered and began to pour out their experiences, both real and imaginary, with the late Shabaz Khan.

It had been a bit of an edgy relationship between Shabaz and Richard. There had been mutual respect between them, but they hadn't necessarily liked each other. That was because of Richard's close relationship with Majid Pathan. The news was that it was Majid and his equally crazy brother Hamid, who had killed Shabaz. Richard ran the computation through his mind and shook his head irritably. He really hoped he wasn't going to be dragged into a turf war that didn't really concern him. Why had they killed the wife? That was quite awful. She was innocent.

He knew what Majid would say. 'There are no innocents in war.' And he knew that he would not be able to say no to Majid. Not out of fear, but out of friendship.

Richard's gaze was drawn to the end of the room, where Vasu was sitting with the young tennis player, Arjun. The kid was not a part of his organization. Also, as far as Richard could remember, he hadn't been around for quite a while. He'd sort of popped up that afternoon with Vasu. Now Richard didn't mind the young tennis player called Arjun. What he couldn't put his finger on was the relationship between the two. From what Richard could see, he felt that Vasu was talking to Arjun with a lot of respect, deference even. As though the tennis player was his superior.

The subservience didn't make any sense. Vasu was a cold-blooded killer and feared no one. But from what Richard could make of the body language, Vasu clearly considered himself not equal to the tennis player. Richard could make out bits of the conversation. Vasu was detailing Shabaz's relationship with Strand in general and with Richard in particular.

What further surprised him was the slight hint of amusement in the young tennis player's face. A great warrior had been assassinated, and everyone and his uncle were preparing for war. Shabaz was notorious and feared by all.

The Pathan brothers were equally so. But the young tennis player seemed unimpressed. It seemed that he was suppressing a smile. Richard felt his hackles rise, but controlled himself. There was no need to go off all crazy on the kid.

Of course, the kid wasn't smiling. It was some sort of persecution complex. Richard looked away, berating himself mentally for his immaturity. There were more important things at hand to worry about, now that Shabaz had departed this world. War was coming to Strand, and he couldn't believe he was thinking of whipping a poor kid who was obviously completely innocent.

Then the phone rang again. Richard answered the call with his usual '*Bol*.' He listened in silence, and his expression changed. 'When?'

He listened carefully, and silence descended on the room. These were experienced fighters, and they knew something important had happened. They waited for their boss to share the news. Richard put down the phone. His face revealed a shock that was alien to everyone around. He turned his gaze to Arjun.

'Arey, Vijay Amritraj, I need to tell you something. Sit sit.'

But Arjun and Vasu were already on their feet. Richard sighed, his shoulders slumped a bit, and continued. 'You know your *bawa* friend?'

'Homi? What happened to him?' There was a bit of underlying panic in Arjun's voice.

'Nothing has happened to your friend.' Richard swallowed a bit as he tried to continue and try to convey the shocking news. 'But his mother has been killed. It looks like the work of that *madarchod* Plumber. Arey, wait! The police are there. Be careful.'

But Richard was speaking to an empty space where the two youngsters had been.

***

# Chapter Twelve

***Bombay 1984, One year after Baghdad***

He hadn't ever expected to see Muriel again.

Twenty minutes after Colonel Hamrawi had arrived with his beautiful wife and two adorable daughters in tow, a battered Land Cruiser pulled up outside the safe house, and a lone Arab in a dusty white dish-dash stepped out.

'It's okay,' said Hamrawi hastily as Arjun and Muriel moved into offensive positions, weapons drawn. 'He's with me. He is Mohammed. He will take us across Syria into Lebanon.'

Mohammed was tall and lean, with the classic Tuareg nose that gave him an aristocratic profile. He had sharp eyes and an easy smile. He looked at Arjun with deep respect.

'Salaam, brother. It is my honour to meet you. You are a mythical creature like the phoenix. Up and down the Magrebi trail, your exploits are discussed over the campfires. They say that Saddam lives in fear that he might be next on your list.' He laughed and continued, 'Now I understand when they say that rooh has the face of a child. One day, if I live to be old enough to have children and grandchildren, I can tell them that I met the most feared warrior of my lifetime.'

Against his will, Arjun smiled. 'I am not worthy of such praise, but I am in your debt. Thank you for taking my friends across the sands.'

Mohammed nodded and took out a packet. 'I am being paid for my courier services. Also, some time back, the good Colonel allowed my son to be released from his accursed prison. A minor petroleum trafficking charge. Why, I will never know, but he did. So, I am in his debt. This is black henna. It is a dye for the hair.' He looked at Muriel. 'Your golden hair is as beautiful as you are. But it will stand out, and there will be eyes watching our every move. We have to assume that there will be a reward for your head. And of course, you too, Colonel.' He smiled as Hamrawi blanched.

'Do not worry, *habibi*. I will take you and your family safely to Beirut.'

He looked at Muriel. 'You need to blend in. They will be looking for a golden-haired *phiranghi*. With your black hair, you could pass as Lebanese from the Hatta mountains. I deeply apologize if I have offended you, but I need to deliver you unharmed to your port of departure, and preparation is the key to success.'

Muriel winced with pain as she smiled. 'Aren't the Lebanese the most beautiful of all Arabs? I'm okay with that.'

Mohammed scowled with amusement. 'Be careful of Lebanese women. It is said that even King David from the Bible of the Christians was brought down by a Lebanese woman. They are beautiful, but extremely unreliable, and money is their God.'

Muriel took the packet and went into the toilet. The two men and the boy looked at each other. Mohammed spoke. 'I don't understand. The rooh came to kill the phirangi lady, but changed his mind? The rooh never misses his target.'

Arjun said, 'Well, technically, the rooh did not miss, did he?'

Everyone laughed, Hamrawi a little louder than the rest. When Muriel returned half an hour later, she was freshly showered, looking slightly less battered, and she was now dark-haired. And she was still breathtaking. Mohammed, being a creature of the desert, made his feelings clear.

'Allah took his time when he was making you. You are indeed special. But this young man here has risked his life and reputation to help you escape. Love, hate, and envy are the driving forces of the universe. A person who can arouse any one of these emotions in another is special. I am not sure which emotion drives the rooh. But it is also none of my business. I am to take you to Beirut, and this is what I will do.'

A night owl hooted in the distance. Mohammed stood up. 'My people are here. Colonel, please take your family and wait outside. We will be joining a caravan. Safety in numbers.'

He bowed to Arjun. 'You have ten minutes to say your farewells. I know we will not meet again in this life. It is my honour to have met you. Rest assured, I will take your people to safety. I will wait outside.'

The moment the door closed, Muriel came into Arjun's arms and kissed him. She tasted sweet and pure, and for a few brief seconds in time, he allowed himself to be lost in her. Her lip opened up, and he tasted her blood. With great reluctance, Arjun broke the kiss.

'We are against the clock. You must go.'

'What will you tell the general?'

'The truth. That his threat has been neutralized.'

'They have their spies in Saddam's inner circle. There will be talk.'

'Don't worry about me. I can take care of myself. You need to stay healthy and reach Europe. You'll be safe there just as long as you never return to this part of the world.'

Muriel was not one for sentimental chitchat, but she said, 'I am yours, always. We will see each other again.'

Arjun laughed, his turn to be flippant. 'Try not to kill me the next time you see me, if that's alright with you.'

As the Land Cruiser departed, she turned, and their eyes met. She smiled. He was emotionless in his response as he waved goodbye, although the deep emptiness that invaded his heart was wet and cold. He didn't expect to see Muriel again. He couldn't have been more wrong.

*

Six months had passed since the Mukhabarrat affair. Arjun was focusing on his piano skills as his band Helmsdeep prepared for the intercollegiate festival, *Malhar,* which was being hosted by Xavier's College. Interestingly, there were a lot of pretty young things who had made it their sole purpose in life to show up for band rehearsal at the auditorium in their college. Homai Shroff, the authoritarian headmistress, had grudgingly allowed the band to practice, since they were representing Elphinstone College.

There was a new player on the streets. His name was Paul Dandekar, and Vasu was enamoured by Paul's charisma, guts, and fighting skills. Now, since Vasu was Arjun's best friend, Arjun had decided to give Paul a chance. He found Paul a bit of a loudmouth, but then it was the most qualifying trait for aspiring street kings. All things said and done, though, on the whole, Paul was quite likeable. He wouldn't have lasted an hour in the Arabian desert sands, but then neither Vasu nor Paul needed to know that minor detail.

It was a Friday afternoon, and rehearsal was coming to an end. Arjun was packing up his keyboards and was chatting with Brian when he saw the face of his handsome lead guitarist stiffen imperceptibly. He turned around and saw Vasu and Paul approaching the stage. Brian was a really decent kid who would go on to do great things in the world of banking in a couple of decades. He wasn't one for living on the wild side, and absolutely disapproved of Arjun's street friends.

Vasu smiled at Brian, but Paul totally ignored him and focused only on Arjun. 'Arey *chotey*! Your singing is fantastic, yaar! That *Gulbina* song is way ahead of its time. I think one day, this song will be very famous. Your band is shit without you.'

Arjun felt a polar draft from his right and struggled to avoid eye contact with Brian. The eternal problem with every band was that every member had a huge musician's ego and always felt that the lead singer got all the credit and adulation. And in many ways, that was true. It was a team effort, each member showcasing individual expertise with his or her chosen instrument, and syncing in time and harmony with the other members. But the crowd only remembered the lead singer, or the frontman. It was the reason why so many talented bands, all the way back to The Beatles, had split up way before reaching their full potential, denying the world the gift of their music. Arjun hoped that Helmsdeep could get in a few good shows before the egos kicked in. Paul wasn't doing much to help the situation.

Paul carried on, unruffled by the general frosty atmosphere. 'Arey, *chotey*! Let's go. I want to take you and Vasu to see my *guruji*. He's expecting us in half an hour.'

Arjun controlled his temper. Chotey was an underworld term used by the bosses when talking or referring to a subordinate. Paul was trying to build his reputation as a leader, and essentially, what leaders needed were followers. While Vasu had most definitely become an acolyte, Arjun knew he was born to lead, not follow. But he needed to stay under the radar, so Chotey it was. He also knew who Guruji was. Paul liked to smoke *chillums*. These were handcrafted pipes filled with *hashish*. It could be an individual effort, but mostly it was a bunch of guys gathered around, taking deep drags of the chillum and getting high. A 'puff puff pass' scenario, which did not appeal to Arjun at all. His interest in tennis and his lesser-known combat skills were at odds with the concept of destroying your body in order to experience a feeling of well-being. Arjun had no idea why Paul always liked to have him around when they smoked their chillums. But he did, and no one said no to Paul.

Guruji was a supplier of high-quality hash that Paul swore by. His real name was Ghani Khan. He had taken up residence in the gardens that were inside the Opera house *Dargah*, or mosque. It was actually a graveyard for the Muslims, but apart from the occasional burial, one could spend the whole day there undisturbed by any over-enthusiastic keepers of the law. Guruji had obviously made some sort of deal with the keepers of the gardens.

Vasu and Paul had motorbikes, which was the fastest way to get through the crazy Bombay traffic, and also the most versatile way to throw off any potential tails.

'Come on. You're riding with me,' said Paul

'Let me pack up my keyboards.'

'Leave it here, buddy. No one will take it.'

'Paul. My keyboards go with me.' There was steel in Arjun's voice that surprised Paul.

'Boss! He won't go anywhere without his keyboards strapped to his back,' Vasu said with a small laugh. 'Just let him bring it along.'

***

# Chapter Thirteen

Bhandiya and Chor Salim were waiting for them in the gardens, chillum in hand. Like Vasu and Paul, they were also addicted to the pipe. The logic was that it was all right to smoke hash because, unlike cocaine and the synthetic drugs, hashish was actually good for you and kept you young. Arjun was always amazed at how the human brain was able to justify addiction.

Three chillums down, the conversation slowed down to a languid pace as all participants ascended into a thoughtful state. Paul had stopped talking about his exploits on the battlefield and about how respect for him extended way beyond the borders of Bombay. Instead, he was lying down on the grass, eyes shut as the paralysis of the high took control of his body and his mind. Vasu and the rest of the band of merry men were all in similar states of repose.

With the exception of Arjun, who, after refusing the first chillum, had been left to his own devices after Paul had realized that there was no way the musician was going to partake. Arjun actually liked the gardens. There was a certain peace to be found walking amongst the resting places of the dead that appealed to him. The departed were beyond love, hate, jealousy or greed. They rested, waiting for the time when they would stand before their creator and be judged. At least, that's what their holy book and their holy men propounded. But until that day, there was nothing to do but wait.

Arjun was in the middle of wondering whether the dead sometimes longed for a television programme or a book to pass the time while they awaited judgement day, when he felt the air suddenly change. Charged with menace, it assailed all his senses. There was danger close! Shadows flitted in his peripheral vision. They were not alone! He looked at Guruji, who had also been partaking, and saw treachery in his eyes.

His heartbeat slowed down as he took two deep breaths, oxygenating his system. He prepared for battle.

There were ten of them. Standard Bombay street fighters, they were of medium height, a couple of them well built. But, although there was a general skinny look amongst the attackers, Arjun was not fooled by their appearance. He knew that they were hard as nails and equally ruthless. The lack of the telltale bulges indicated that there would be no firearms involved. So, it would be sharp objects.

They were in a semicircle, flanking the prone group on the ground. No one paid any attention to the kid in the background behind one of the tombstones. Paul opened his eyes, saw the group standing around him and his chillum buddies. To be fair, he snapped out of his reverie pretty fast and came to his feet. Vasu was the next to wake up. He shook Bhandiya, who didn't react with the alacrity that the situation warranted. Neither did Chor Salim, who remained passed out. And still, no one paid any attention to Arjun.

If Paul was fazed by the appearance of the intruders who obviously were intent on doing him harm, he didn't show it. 'Arey Rafiq! What brings you so far from your rabbit hole? Did your mother give you permission to leave her pussy?'

At about one hundred and seventy-eight centimetres tall, with oiled locks that fell to his shoulders and a feral look about him, Rafiq stood at the centre of the semicircle. He flushed at the insult. He spoke with barely contained hate. 'You are going to die here today for what you did.'

Paul laughed derisively. 'Is that what this is about? Chutiya, you are not able to get it up when it's required. You should be thanking me for satisfying your wife, not trying to kill me.'

So that's what this was all about. Paul had slept with Rafiq's wife. No big deal. This happened all the time. It would probably end with everyone having a chillum and then a few shots of cheap whiskey. Arjun relaxed. And that's when things got bad. Real fast.

Bhandiya laughed and said, 'She must have been really grateful. Paul is hung like a horse.'

Something changed in Rafiq's eyes. Arjun saw it and shouted a warning, but it was too late. There was a flash in Rafiq's right hand. He leapt forward and plunged a blade into Bhandiya's stomach.

Bhandiya screamed and collapsed on the ground, clutching the handle of the blade that was protruding from his stomach. He tried to pull out the knife, but the agony was overwhelming, and he screamed again. Chor Salim dropped down next to him and tried to staunch the wound, but only ended up aggravating it, and Bhandiya screamed again. 'Leave me alone, madarchod. Don't pull out the knife, I will bleed out.'

But Rafiq wasn't finished. He hadn't come for a simple stabbing. He had become the laughing stock of the underworld. His wife sleeping with Paul had raised all sorts of painful insinuations about his manhood, or lack thereof. His boss, Chandrakant Shendge, was the head of the deadly Golden Gang and had been extremely unambiguous. Either Paul died, or Rafiq's wife would need a new husband.

'Maybe she'll marry Paul after you are dead. Anyway, he's been doing a great job, I've heard,' he had said. It hadn't been a one-on-one type, closed-door type of meeting, so everyone within earshot had been privy to the dressing down, and there had been a great deal of mirth all around.

What the attackers lacked in firearms, they more than made up for it with swords, machetes and obviously, several hidden stabbing knives. Rafiq had killed before and was no stranger to blood. He swung the machete, which he had grabbed from one of his men, downward. It caught Chor Salim on the nape of his neck. All things considered, it was a pretty well struck, and it took Chor Salim's head clean off his shoulders. There was a spurt of arterial blood, like a fountain from the neck of the headless torso, as Chor Salim collapsed on Bhandiya, driving the blade further into his stomach, further in, making him scream in horror and in agony. Guruji emptied the contents of his own stomach on a gravestone next to him.

Paul, also no stranger to blood, lived every day like it was his last. His famous saying was, 'Only the good die young, and I'm the best of them. Fuck it! Who wants to live till they are old and grey? I want to die in my prime.'

It looked like his wish was going to come true. Armed with a nasty-looking Bowie knife, which he had acquired on his travels to Nepal, he drew it, dropped into a crouch and prepared to kill. Vasu, on the other hand, was completely unarmed. But he took his shirt off and wrapped it around his left forearm. He would use the covered forearm to block knife attacks. He would use his right arm and both his legs to attack and defend to the best of his limited ability. Maybe he would get lucky and be able to grab a knife or sword from one of the attackers. All in all, it looked very much like they were all going to meet a bloody end, and it was all because Paul couldn't keep it in his pants. Vasu smiled grimly. Such was life!

There was a short swishing sound. A blade struck Guruji in the throat. He died with a surprised look on his face, choking on his own blood. There was a pause as everyone looked at Guruji with a certain amount of confusion. Something flew past Paul, and a metal star embedded itself in the throat of one of Rafiq's men. It was very precise. Another swishing sound, and another of Rafiq's men went down with another similar metal star in his throat. Everyone turned to look at the source of the mysterious metal stars. Arjun had opened his keyboard case and dropped it to the ground. Apart from a Juno-7 keyboard, there was an assortment of metal objects that looked remarkably like the two stars embedded in the throats of Rafiq's associates. And some short, extremely sharp-looking blades with short wooden handles.

To be fair, it wasn't only Rafiq and his men who were taken aback. Vasu and Paul were looking at Arjun, completely dumbstruck. It wasn't computing for either of them at any level. They would later be told that the metal stars were called *shurikens* and were used by ninjas in Japan. But that would be much later. At that moment, to their surprise, the boy they both thought to be a good-natured musician drew a medium-sized, straight-bladed sword from the keyboard case. This, they would later on find out, was called a katana.

He was blindingly fast. Before either Paul or Vasu could blink, Arjun took two steps, executed a somersault in the air, and landed in the middle of Rafiq and his men. As he landed, he twirled, the katana moving so fast that no one was sure what was happening. The head of two of the attackers went flying in the air, smashing against the branches of an overhanging tree. Arjun turned again and thrust backwards at waist height, his blade going through Rafiq. He didn't even look at the falling body as he pulled the blade free and twirled again.

The katana flashed, and two more of Rafiq's men said goodbye to their heads. The remaining five ruthless, hardcore sons of the streets felt a fear that they had never experienced before, and they ran. The katana flew in the air and caught one of them between the shoulder blades. He was dead before he hit the ground. Arjun moved forward. To Paul and Vasu, he seemed to be gliding, but it was actually very fast footwork, learnt at the feet of a great samurai. He bent down, pulled the blade out of the fallen fighter's back, straightened up, and turned around and looked at his friends.

He shook his head ever so slightly and said, 'If I didn't interfere, they would have killed you both.'

Paul had never been short of words. His mother used to say that he had come out of her womb talking. But on that pleasant monsoon afternoon, Paul found himself grasping for words unsuccessfully as he tried to make sense of what had transpired in front of his eyes. Vasu resembled a guppy fish. It would have been hysterical, if it wasn't for the dead bodies, the smell of drying blood and the swarms of flies that had gathered for a feast.

Arjun spoke. His voice was calm and measured. 'Before you ask, it's obvious that your stupid Gruji had led you into a trap. So he was the first to go. We need to move. The police will be here soon. No one has seen us as yet. But that's going to change if we hang around here.' He looked at Bhandiya, who had passed out, most likely from a combination of pain and blood loss, and said, 'Paul, put Bhandiya on the bike behind you. I will ride with Vasu.'

Paul and Vasu didn't question the order. They didn't ask where they were going. They just obeyed. In that moment, the dynamics of power shifted. In the future, many men would go to war and die for a man called Wastra. Looking back, one could pinpoint that moment in the graveyard as the birthplace of the legend.

*

They collected all the shurikens, but left the blade in Guruji's throat as a reminder of what happens to snitches. Arjun put all his tools back inside the keyboard case. Then they left the graveyard, never to return. It was another hour before they reached the borders of the fisher village Sunder Nagari. No one, including the police, was allowed inside. It was well known that Lhoncha was the head of the fisher village, and that he was a giant, and that he was extremely territorial.

In the past, there had been some courageous keepers of the law who had entered the fisher village unannounced. They had been found dead a few months later. No connection could be made to the village, or to Lhoncha. But everyone knew. Now no one approached the borders uninvited. So one could understand the discomfort felt by Paul and Vasu as they approached Sunder Nagari.

*Fuck! From the frying pan into the fire!*, thought Paul. *As if it wasn't enough that we almost got slaughtered an hour back. Now this? That Lhoncha is no Rafiq. He's going to kill us for sure. Fuck! But then again, this Arjun is some crazy ninja-type of guy. Maybe it will all work out.*

Paul had accepted Arjun as his leader, and Paul, if nothing, was a damn fine soldier. He looked at Vasu on the other bike, who had gone a lighter shade of pale. Then he looked at Arjun, who was riding pillion with Vasu. The musician looked completely relaxed. It was unbelievable that he had just killed so many men. He looked at the keyboard case strapped to Arjun's back. Then he looked back at Vasu. They both shrugged and continued towards the border, silently thanking their stars that they had been good to this damn musician who had turned out to be some sort of killing machine.

There were several able-bodied men at the entrance to the village. Some were openly carrying handguns. There were two big trucks that could be moved into position as barricades. There were drivers at the wheel. It all spoke of a well-oiled operation. Paul understood why the police or anyone never entered Sunder Nagari without being invited. So, he was not able to understand why they would tempt fate after having just escaped the jaws of death. Then he saw why.

Initially, the security of Sunder Nagari had moved into intercepting positions until they saw Arjun. The change in the general atmosphere was instant. There was deference. There was respect. There were smiles. Again, nothing was computing for Paul and Vasu. But they rode on into the fisher village. They reached the village square and although Paul had heard of him but had never seen him, he still drew in a breath as the huge frame of Lhoncha came into view. Good God! He really was a damn giant! Definitely at least seven feet, according to Paul's estimate.

They got off their bikes and went up to meet Lhoncha, who was walking towards them. The sun was setting behind him, and it seemed to set his giant frame on fire—it was all extremely surreal. It was only after Lhoncha had stopped before them that they witnessed the unthinkable. Lhoncha actually bowed to Arjun! The most feared man in Bombay, north, south, or east, bowed to the tennis player! The giant ignored everyone present and spoke only to Arjun. His tone was deferential. Paul and Vasu were sure that they had got tickets to the wrong movie, but they both decided to stay for the rest of the show. It would last a lifetime for both of them, although at the time, they had no idea about the momentous shift in their lives.

'Baba, I have some news.'

'What is it?'

'There's a blonde girl looking for you. She's very beautiful, but she's also very violent. She was asking for you. Anand Badwa and Chotu Sharbat tried to get a little handsy.'

'What happened?' A smile played around Arjun's lips.

'She kicked the shit out of them, but stopped short of breaking any bones. She knew what she was doing. She then told everyone around to send a message to you. She's in Strand Coffee House, having a chai. Shall I send a squad to deal with her?'

'No need, brother. You'll lose a lot of men unnecessarily. And she's a friend.' Arjun got up to go. He pointed to his travel mates. 'You know Vasu from Strand. The other one is Paul. Bring them up to speed. They'll be joining us.'

As Arjun left for the Strand, he found that he was slightly breathless. He remembered her last words, her face framed in the window of the Land Cruiser as it prepared to head west into Syria.

*We will see each other again.*

***

# Chapter Fourteen

Puran Doshi, self-acclaimed sex symbol of the Strand and the Rakish Mahendra, or Mandy, as he liked to be called, was already at Strand Coffee House, chatting up Muriel, when Arjun arrived. Puran was in the middle of a soliloquy about his jewellery business, and Mandy was trying to cut in with his own nuggets about how he was in the final stages of being cast for a movie. They both fancied their chances with the extremely hot blonde and her sparkling blue eyes that reminded them of a summer day on the Arabian Sea. So, one could well understand their consternation when Muriel, who had seemed so interested in their affairs, suddenly looked at them like they were complete strangers, got up, and without a by your leave, pushed past them, walked out at a rather fast pace onto the street, and enveloped the young tennis player who was approaching the restaurant from Colaba market, in a warm embrace, and kissed him long and tenderly on the lips.

It was about five in the evening, and the area was quite crowded. Richard D'Souza, gang boss of Strand, watched the scene unfold from his balcony in Mohini Mansion through hooded eyes. Although not a ladies' man per se, he still had access to several hookers and dancers because of his position. It made no sense to him that this beautiful blonde would have some sort of connection to the tennis player. Rasul, his tough second in command, sitting next to him, also took in the events below. He took a deep drag of his cigarette.

'Boss,' he said to Richard very philosophically. 'You can never tell what drives a woman to man.'

Richard nodded and made a mental note to quiz Arjun at the first opportunity he got. He looked down at his little kingdom. Apart from a few fisherfolk who seemed to be out and about, nothing else seemed out of place. Still, one had to be careful with the fisherfolk. One wrong move and you'd have an army coming out of the village laying everything in its path to waste. It just didn't make for great optics, since everyone on the streets of Strand thought Richard to be the boss. Then, of course, there was the extremely unusual scene of the blonde who was walking out of Strand towards the Colaba Causeway with Arjun. She just couldn't seem to keep her hands off him. It was all very strange. Out of the corner of his eye, he thought he saw Kalidas, the Vaithi lord, but when he turned, there was no one. Most likely a mistake. He shook his head, got up and went inside to make himself a drink.

In a by-lane off Mereweather Road stands the Garden Hotel. A beautiful stone building, it had been constructed in the early 1900s while the British still held India in a vice-like grip. While thousands of Indians were sacrificed in different theatres of war, waged by the British based on a hollow promise by their white masters of freedom from enslavenment, the Parsis took on a different, more pragmatic approach. Plying the British with women and sharing the profits of the lucrative opium trade, the original political refugees received vast swathes of land from the British, enriching themselves, while the masses of Indians languished in poverty.

The Garden hotel stood on land that had been bequeathed to a wealthy Parsi family by a grateful British master. However, the next generation of that Parsi family was not functioning on all cylinders, mentally speaking. This was probably due to the high incidence of inbreeding amongst the Parsis in a desperate attempt to preserve their dwindling bloodlines. They were committed to a sanitarium and the building went into an opaque Parsi trust that turned the building into a hotel.

It wasn't the Taj or the Oberoi, but the rooms were way more beautiful and luxurious. Muriel had booked a suite on the first floor, and it was absolutely majestic. A set of extremely comfortable sofas in the living room and a beautiful four-poster bed adorned the bedroom, which had a high ceiling and an antique fan that was surprisingly quiet. The bedroom opened out into a generously large balcony. It was on this bed that Muriel threw Arjun and proceeded to undress him.

Their lovemaking was passionate, intense, with barely a word spoken as they tried to make up for lost time. She opened herself completely to him, and he entered her warmth, feeling her soft lips on his. He was relentless, thrusting ever deeper, lost in the ecstasy of possessing her. She tasted of wild honey. Her beautiful breasts heaved as her lungs tried to keep pace. She wrapped her legs around him, welcoming him with every essence of her being. Sweat and breath mingling, murmuring words of love, their minds and bodies moved as one.

Much later, as they lay in each other's arms, soaking in the afterglow, young Arjun understood the meaning of love. He did not know what the future held for him, but he knew she would always be by his side. He knew for sure that the fisherfolk had established an invisible protective perimeter around the hotel. He smiled as he thought of Kalidas, who would surely be close by smoking one of his awful beedis. Arjun himself was perfectly capable of neutralizing any threat. He knew that his killing skills were incomparable. And so did the fisherfolk. But it felt good that they had his back. And for some strange reason, having Muriel by his side made him feel safe. It was the weirdest feeling, but he felt happy. It was all totally confusing and wonderful at the same time.

*

They spent the next days walking around Colaba, as he showed her his hidden kingdom. She met Lhoncha, Namdeo, Ghaniya and Kalidas. They were cautious at first, not knowing what to expect. But her winsome personality and her ability to drink them under the table melted the hearts of the fisher lords. At college, Brian and the rest of the band were initially dumbfounded by the appearance of the beautiful blonde with Arjun, but they were warm and welcoming. As Arjun saw Brian chatting with Muriel, he saw how effortlessly she was able to put people at ease. It was the skill of a killer, he knew, but Arjun also knew this was different. There was a bond between Muriel and him that went beyond the physical. They were soul mates. And as he looked at Brian, he realized what an incredibly decent boy his lead guitarist was. He felt guilty that he could never tell Brian about his real life. But of course, Brian could never know the truth. No one associated with him could. He was a ghost, and the fact was that everyone close to him was so much safer by not being aware of the grim reality.

Elphinstone College, being what it was, had its fair share of tough guys, and it was inevitable that some of them would try some macho stuff. It was bad enough that this tennis player and his stupid band were all that the college girls were talking about. Now he had landed up in college with one of the most exotic-looking blonde girls they had ever seen. He needed to be taught a fucking lesson.

It was Ashfaq Siddiqi who decided to make his move. Well above six feet and brawny, he hailed from Dongri, which was legendary for its streetfighters. He walked up to Brian and Muriel and started a conversation.

'Hey, blondie! What's your name?' Without waiting for an answer, he continued, 'What are you doing with that chutiya?' He pointed at Arjun. 'Arey, that *Kalia* won't be able to satisfy you. You need a real man.'

There was some raucous laughter from his sidekicks, and Brian stepped forward, fists clenched.

'Why don't you fuck off and leave us alone?'

Ashfaq moved within striking range of Brian and said, 'Chutiya, I'll show you who's going to fuck off now.'

Arjun casually moved into striking range himself. He wanted to avoid a fight, but these Dongri guys were ultra-aggressive, and it looked like things were going to go south very quickly. Muriel stepped in between Brian and Ashfaq. She spoke loudly and clearly so that everyone could hear her.

'If I were lacking a real man, which I am not, why would I come to a guy like you?'

Ashfaq resembled a guppy fish as he struggled to find a repartee and then made the fatal error of trying to slap Muriel. She easily avoided his strike, kicked him in the stomach, and as he doubled up with pain, she placed a nicely timed uppercut that broke his front teeth and shattered his nose. The brawny street fighter collapsed in a heap, mewling like a newborn baby. None of his friends tried to take up cudgels on behalf of their fallen comrade. But it didn't matter. Later that evening, they were found beaten within an inch of their lives. They did not recognize their attackers, but said they smelled strongly of fish. The macho stuff ceased abruptly. Apart from that unfortunate hiccup, everything else, for the most part, was idyllic.

*

'How long can you stay?' They were sitting in Samovar, the quaint restaurant in the Jehangis Art Gallery opposite his college. Arjun dreaded the answer, but was practical enough to know that he needed one. Muriel went seemingly off topic.

She smiled a trifle sadly. 'I'm so sorry for everything. I'm sorry your tennis friend died.'

He held her hand. 'It was another time. It was your job. We are what we are. Nothing can change that.'

'You are right. And nothing can change what happened. But going forward, what we do now is in our control. I need you to know that I belong to you.' She said, and he gripped her hand even tighter and continued.

'You know about the LTTE and me?'

'I know you have been with them a long time. But I don't know how you joined them. Or why.'

Muriel took a sip of her *nimbu paani* and said, 'Let me tell you. You need to know everything. Did you know I grew up in Colombo?'

'I did not know that,' said Arjun.

Muriel nodded and said, 'My father was the ambassador to Sri Lanka. We moved to Colombo when I was six years old. It was such a fantastic time. The country, the people, the food, the language—it was all fascinating and beautiful.'

An old, grumpy waiter who had been with Samovar for at least twenty years bought two glasses of nimbu paani and two chicken sandwiches, and dumped them on their table. He ignored Arjun, but Arjun noticed he had a smile for Muriel, though. *Fucking racist*, thought Arjun with a smile.

Muriel continued. 'I went to a primary school in Dharmarama Road called the Royal Preparatory School. It was favoured by the diplomatic corps of most of the nations stationed in Colombo. One day, when I came back, my parents had a surprise for me. They had decided that I needed to have a grounding in reality that my posh diplomatic school could not give me. They arranged for me to have a friend of my age who was not from the usual snob circles that my parents socialized in.'

Muriel took a sip of her lime juice. 'These chicken sandwiches are fantastic,' she said, taking a mammoth bite.

Arjun laughed and said, 'The rumour is that they actually serve rat meat well done.'

Muriel laughed and shook her head. 'Oh no, this is not rat meat. I've tasted rat before. This is definitely not rat meat.'

Arjun smiled. He himself had eaten a variety of meats, including rat, during his sojourn in the desert. Actually, he hadn't minded the desert mouse too much.

Muriel continued, 'My parents had a chauffeur who was a local. His name was Ramanathan. He had a daughter. Her name was Shanti. She was dark with beautiful, big, brown eyes and long black hair down to her waist. She was gorgeous. She spoke a little English. We bonded immediately. I was an only child, and it was fantastic to have a companion. Very soon, she became the sister I never had, but always wanted. We did everything together. I can speak Sinhalese because of her. We even took her back to Belgium with us one summer, and it was simply wonderful.'

Muriel's eyes clouded as she took a sip of her lime juice and bit off a piece of her sandwich. 'One day, Shanti didn't come to the bungalow like she always did after school. Her father also didn't show up. My father was a little worried, but he was sure it was nothing. The next day, they didn't show up again. This time, we went to the local police, but they had no idea about where Ramnathan and his family had gone. My father lodged an official consular complaint.'

Arjun felt a tightening in his chest. He had an idea what was going to follow. Muriel continued. 'The next day, we had a visit from the Sri Lankan secret service. They were extremely respectful, since my father was the ambassador. They said that Ramanthan and his family had been detained for questioning. You see, Shanti and her family were of Tamil origin. Tamils were being persecuted by the Sinhalese, and of late, there had been talk of an underground movement to fight for the rights of the Tamils.'

Arjun knew all about the LTTE and their struggle, but it was not his fight. Muriel continued. 'We never saw Shanti or her father alive again. Their bodies were returned a week later. The official cause of death was a road accident. But my father flew in a medical examiner from India. His autopsy report detailed severe torture, broken limbs and . . .' Muriel's voice broke. 'Shanti had been raped several times. She had died from the repeated assaults. She was only twelve. My father lodged a protest, but it was shut down by the Belgian government, which did not want to interfere in the internal matters of the host country.'

Muriel sipped the lime juice and continued, 'My father resigned from his job and relocated to Amsterdam with my mother. They linked up with LTTE sympathizers. They began to supply the fledgling movement in Sri Lanka with money and weapons.'

Arjun looked around. The restaurant was full of college students. In the far corner, he saw Chhaya and her friend Taruna. He liked Chhaya, but Taruna not so much. He wondered what they would say if they heard his conversation with Muriel. 'So you grew into the family business?'

Muriel was silent. 'Are you sure you want to know?'

'I absolutely want to know.'

Muriel stood up. 'I'm going to the washroom. You pay the bill, and I'll meet you outside. Those two girls in the far corner are way too interested in us. Since I don't know them, I guess one or both of them has a crush on you. Anyway, it's been too long here. Let's go somewhere else.'

Arjun smothered a smile. He wondered what Chhaya would think if she found out that she was trying to eavesdrop on a conversation between two assassins.

***

# Chapter Fifteen

The rooftop of the Garden Hotel overlooked the Colaba Causeway. The sun had set, but the western sky still burned a cacophony of red diffusing with blue, bathing the causeway in a pink haze. They sat on comfortable garden chairs, eating the delicious chicken sandwich prepared by Pratap, the in-house Nepali chef. Their lovemaking after their return from Samovar had been intense as it always was, the passion and desire unending. Now they needed sustenance. As they waited for the *dal makhani* and *rotis*, Muriel continued.

'The war for our homeland was fought in the jungles of the north and the east, but the Sri Lankan secret service knew that in order to win, they had to cut off the supply of arms and money. And with that endgame in mind, the State Intelligence services created a shadow organisation called the AXE OF GAMINI, named after the famous Sinhalese king, to hunt and eliminate LTTE sleeper cells and financiers in Europe. The man in charge was none other than Colonel Nandana Dasanayake.'

'So this enmity was a long time in the making,' said Arjun.

Muriel nodded and continued. 'It was a covert war fought on the streets of Brussels, Amsterdam, Antwerp, and Rome. It was fierce, with no quarter asked or given, and lasted a few years, but in the end, we had all but shattered their network. And that's when my parents made a critical mistake. They attended a donor meeting held by some influential Tamil families at Liege in Belgium. It was at a beautiful villa on the Rue de Steppes Boulevard. They were never seen in public, and their movements were known only to a few chosen confidantes. But they were told that their presence would be a morale booster to the Tamil community in Belgium, all of whom were contributing to the Tamil cause.'

Arjun was curious. 'You mean your parents were in charge of the clandestine war against the Sri Lankans in Europe? They would have been high-value targets. Always living in the shadows. Constantly watching their backs. And then they also had to look after little Muriel. How hard was it for you?'

'Well, I could dismantle and reassemble a Kalashnikov in 90 seconds by the time I was fourteen. How's that for learning on the job?'

Arjun whistled silently, impressed, and Muriel continued.

'The meeting was compromised. I will never know who it was that leaked the location. The AXE of GAMINI launched an all-out attack on the villa at Rue de Steppes, and in the ensuing battle, both my parents were killed.'

'Where were you?' asked Arjun.

'They left me in Brussels with Ramalingam. They went to the meeting without me.' Muriel's tone was bitter. 'I never even saw the bodies of my parents. The news of the battle reached us a few hours later, and I was spirited away to the safety of Paris. Six months later, I was in Vavuniya in northern Lanka, training with the Tigers. The Bangalore plan was my brainchild. Dasanayake has been my obsession. It was imperative that he be removed from the equation.' She smiled. 'No one was ready for you, though. Especially me. You were the variable in my plan that I was totally unprepared for. Can you understand that? I have no idea why I was drawn to you. There was something about you. You stood out in that crowd of tennis players. The moment I saw you, I knew we would be together.'

They both laughed, and Arjun said teasingly, trying to make light of her seriousness, 'So I was just a piece of meat to you?'

Muriel leaned across the table and kissed him. 'A very tasty—but what I did not realize at the time—a very dangerous piece of meat.'

'Well, you did try to kill me. I am also your creation.'

Muriel's eyes clouded. 'I'm so sorry for what happened in Bangalore. You understand my obsession with Dasanayake? He had escaped again, and I was not able to see past my hatred. It was wrong, and I would do anything to go back in time and change the events of that night.'

'Don't be too sorry. If you hadn't done what you did, I would be living an unremarkable life today.' Arjun laughed as he continued, 'I got to see the world because of you. Met a few interesting people. And learned a few skills along the way.'

'I doubt you would have ever been unremarkable, regardless of whether we met or not.'

Muriel's tone softened. 'I have to leave tomorrow.'

Arjun knew that the LTTE was Muriel's calling, but had not known why until that evening.

'Will you be going to Lanka?'

'Do you want plausible deniability?'

Arjun shook his head. 'I need to know. This Dasanayake guy is out there. He must definitely know about you, and must be doing everything to find out your movements. You are a threat to him. You killed his team, and it was providence that he escaped. He knows that, and he knows that he needs you removed from the equation. You are safe in Bombay, but out there, I cannot protect you.'

Muriel laughed. As always, it was music to his ears. 'You mean out there in the big bad world? Little Muriel on her own? I'm a big girl. I can take care of myself. You just worry about your tennis. This is a war, and it demands sacrifice. Now, I don't intend to go off into the next world just yet. But if it happens, then it's a price I'm willing to pay.'

'Are you in this war for the Tamils, or are you trying to avenge your parents' murder? They must have also known that a premature death was a likely outcome? They chose to fight for an ideology. I am not sure what you are fighting for.'

Muriel bristled at Arjun's words. 'You have no idea about fighting for a cause.'

'That's not entirely true, is it? You were my cause for a few years. And I did travel quite a distance just to get in touch, don't you agree? But I get what you are saying. Maybe I don't know what it is to experience loss like you have had to endure. That is indoctrination enough. The truth is that I don't want you to go for selfish reasons. I like having you around. Life will be rather dull without you. And I need protection from the bad boys in college.'

Muriel smiled, disarmed by his honesty. 'You don't need any protection. You just want me around for the sex. I promise I will be back as soon as I can.' She sighed dramatically. 'Whoever thought that I would get seduced by the rooh? The name that inspired terror amongst friends and foes alike! Oh, what a life!'

He started to frame a witty comeback about how it was he who had been seduced, and not the other way around, but she was already out of her chair, heading for the door. She looked back.

'It's our last night for a while. I don't want to waste it talking.'

As usual, he was lost for words when she became direct. But he wasn't naïve enough not to understand what she meant, and hurried along behind her retreating back.

The soft glow of the bedside lamp cast a warm glow across the room, throwing shadows and illuminating the sheets that were draped over the bed. Arjun smelled lavender and jasmine in the air, and it wrapped around Muriel and him in a comforting embrace. Lying side-by-side, they faced each other, their bodies barely touching, but their eyes drinking in each other. Her hair spilt across the pillow, a cascade of gold and her eyes sparkled with mischief.

She stroked his cheek and traced the strong, masculine line of his jaw. 'I still remember you on that tennis court in Bangalore,' she said, her voice a low murmur that had the ability to get his pulse racing every time.

He smiled and said, 'How can I ever forget? The famous Indian Nationals that got washed out by unseasonal rain. You and I in a disco on MG Road. Later on in that ridiculous hotel.'

'I had no idea you were a virgin.'

'You are the only woman I have ever been with.'

She laughed and said, 'Let's try and keep it that way for as long as we can.'

He chuckled, his voice, she realized was unusually deep for his age, and she was lost in the memory of their first time together. It seemed like another life and memory hung between them, like a shared secret. Her gaze softened, and she reached out, her fingers intertwining with his. The world outside faded away as they leaned closer, the distance between them evaporating.

He could feel the warmth radiating from her body, the rhythm of her breath syncing with his and the rhythm of the night. Their foreheads touched, and in that moment, everything else ceased to exist.

'I want to tell you something,' she said.

'Of course,' he said, his eyes searching hers intently.

'I belong to you, now and forever.'

'And I am yours, in this life and the next.'

Her heart swelled at his admission. She knew he meant every word he said, and she squeezed his hand tighter.

'You make me feel alive,' she said, her voice trembling with emotion. With a gentle tug, he pulled her closer, their bodies finally meeting, the warmth of skin against skin igniting a fire within them. He brushed his lips against hers, a tentative exploration that quickly deepened, a dance of passion and tenderness.

Time slipped away as they lost themselves in each other, the world outside forgotten. The kiss was sweet and lingering, filled with promises and dreams yet to be spoken. As they pulled away, breathless, he rested his forehead against hers, their hearts racing in unison. She rolled him on his back and got on top of him. His breath quickened again in anticipation of the heat he knew that was about to envelop him in a blaze of rapturous desire.

*

It had been three months since Muriel returned to Lanka. Arjun didn't have any first-hand knowledge about the Tigers' battle for independence, except for what was in the newspapers. But from what was being written, it was evident that the Tigers were winning the war. Their guerrilla tactics were paying off big time as they trapped the Sri Lankan army again and again in the jungles and slaughtered them. Stories of bedraggled Sinhalese soldiers staggering out of the jungle, blinded by hunger, thirst and terror dominated the newspapers.

Morale amongst the Sri Lankans was at an all-time low. Velupillai Prabhakaran had become a household name. The LTTE had their official headquarters in London and their own radio station. They were recognized as a legitimate rebel army struggling against a dictatorial regime. Money was rolling in, arms were rolling out. Everything was perfect.

Muriel had talked about a logistical problem the Tigers were facing. Transporting shipments from Rameshwaram to Jaffna and other points on the Sri Lankan mainland under Tamil control was done by a fleet of fishing boats, the Sea Tigers, who used fast-moving rubber dinghies with three-man crews to ward off attacks from the Sri Lankan navy. Although large amounts of weapons and food were getting through, the Sea Tigers were suffering heavy losses at the hands of the heavily armed Sri Lankan naval frigates and coast guard cutters.

Arjun had an idea about how he could significantly cut down those losses. He didn't want to get involved in another war, but knew someone else who would be chomping at the bit and would not hesitate to jump in with both feet. He smothered a smile as he thought about Lieutenant Commander John Moses of the Indian Navy, in command of the southern coast guard fleet. He'd broach the topic when Muriel returned. He was sure the LTTE could benefit from a collaboration with 'Crazy' John Moses.

As he entered Strand, he saw Vasu standing with a group of tough guys armed to the teeth. They were in earnest conversation. Vasu saw Arjun, detached himself from the group and took Arjun into a corner near Janata stores.

'Something big is happening. I think someone in the underworld is getting hit. The news is that Hamid and Majid have been contracted to do the hit. I'm sure it's Shabaz Khan. We are all going to Richard's house. Why don't you come along with me?'

Now, Arjun wasn't too keen on getting involved in gangland politics, but it was either that or go back home to drunken daddy and some domestic violence. It wasn't really a hard choice.

'Okay, let's go.'

The time was two in the afternoon. Although he did not know at the time, life for Arjun would begin to change irreversibly at six in the evening.

***

# Chapter Sixteen

*June 27th, 1985, 0800 Hours, Indian Standard Time*

Following the explosive disclosure by Richard about The Plumber killing Homi's mother, Arjun and Vasu raced to the Ferena Building. There were police everywhere, and the air crackled with radio chatter. They found Homi sitting down near the entrance. He looked forlorn and broken. He looked up, saw Arjun, and his face crumpled, and he slumped his head over his knees. Arjun put his arms under his friend's armpits and lifted him up.

'Not here, buddy. Come with me. Let's go over the walls before the police realize you're gone. We need to talk where there are no curious cats around.'

When Constable Bhave came looking for Homi, he found that no one was able to tell him where the Parsi kid had disappeared to. One minute he was there, and the next minute he wasn't. Bhave cursed his luck as he pressed the button for the elevator, which would take him back upstairs to a waiting Inspector Baig. He didn't look forward to explaining to a highly irritable Baig that the son of the latest victim of the Plumber had disappeared from right in front of a posse of Colaba's police station's finest.

*

They sat deep inside the fisher village, overlooking the Arabian Sea, surrounded by Lhoncha and his fighters.

Arjun put his arm around his friend and said, 'I'm going to get him, I promise you. I will find this Plumber and bring him before you.'

Bolstered by a big glass of chai, spiked with a mild dose of *arrack*, Homi had recovered considerably. He spoke calmly.

'How exactly are you planning to do that, Arjun? How are you going to do something that the entire police force of

Bombay is unable to do? And in any case, it won't bring my mother back, will it?'

Arjun nodded. 'It won't. She's gone, and she's not coming back. But there are some things you need to know about me. But I need to be honest with you. What I am about to reveal to you is so classified that, apart from the people you see sitting here, only one other person knows about it. And even the people here are not entirely sure what exactly it is that I do.'

Homi, in the future, would go on to be a prolific architect. He possessed way above average intellect. He looked at Arjun for what seemed to be a very long time, and then said, 'Does this have to do with your long periods of absence from Bombay?'

Arjun smiled and nodded. 'Once I tell you, it is binding, Homi. You cannot change your mind once you know everything. If you are in, tell me now; otherwise, you still have the option not to know, and I will never hold that against you. You are, and will always be, my dearest friend. Regardless of your decision, I will hunt for The Plumber and I will find him. Hunting is what I do very well. If you choose to know my secret, then I will bring him in front of you, and I will give you the opportunity to send him to hell with your own hands. If you choose not to know, and frankly speaking, that's a much safer choice, I'll find this fucker and deal with him myself. The killing will stop, but you will never have the opportunity to look him in the eyes and end the motherfucker. It's nothing, but you will know your mother would have been avenged.'

Homi began to reply and was interrupted by Kalidas.

'Bhai, there is someone I want you to meet. He is the medical examiner on The Plumber case. He has been tracking the kills of this madarchod Plumber since the beginning. There is no one with better knowledge about this killer than my friend.'

'Do you trust him? Enough to bring him into the village?'

'Yes, bhai. He is not conventional, and he doesn't play by the rules. He's quite unpopular with his colleagues, but unlike them, he thinks outside the box. He's the one who first made the connection that all the killings were at the hands of one unsub?'

Lhoncha stirred in the background and asked, 'What does unsub mean?'

Arjun answered, 'Unknown subject. It's a term used to describe a person of interest who is the perpetrator of a crime, whom the authorities have not been able to put a face or a name to.'

Lhoncha raised his eyebrows at the sudden infusion of knowledge.

'Okay then. Bring this medical examiner to the village tomorrow afternoon,' said Arjun.

Kalidas bowed and got up. 'I will go and call him and invite him here tomorrow. I'll use the phone in the Tandel house to call him. He has a phone at home because he needs to be available all the time.'

'What is his name?'

'Eknath Wadekar. But he's known to most people as Shinde.'

Arjun turned to Homi and smiled. 'What say you, my old friend? Are you in, or do you prefer not to know?'

Until that moment, Homi had only heard of the fisherfolk in stories. Of course, the whole of Colaba talked about Lhoncha, and there had been multiple unconfirmed sightings of him. But suddenly, Homi had been transported to a world he had only heard of as folklore. And what was wildly exciting was that this mysterious world existed right on the borders of his home. And Homi could now independently confirm the existence of a giant in the fisher village who, for some strange reason, seemed to be overawed by his friend Arjun. In fact, it seemed that these mysterious fisher people regarded Arjun as their leader. It was simply quite amazing.

'I'm in,' was the simple answer from Homi.

Arjun nodded and said, 'Let us begin.'

And while the police searched unsuccessfully for Homi, deep inside the fisher village of Sunder Nagar, the target of their search was receiving an indoctrination that would hold fast for a lifetime.

*

***The next day, 1800 Hours, Indian Standard Time***

They sat around an ornate table in Tandel House. Sitting proudly on the border of Sudam Jhopadi and Sunder Nagari, the old structure, a beacon of history and culture, was the shining jewel of the fisher community.

This small yet magnificent building has been the home of the rulers of the fisher people for three hundred years, and its walls were steeped in the stories of the past. As he approached Tandel House, the first thing that struck Eknath Wadekar was its unique architecture. To his untrained yet appreciative eye, it bespoke a blend of traditional and colonial influences that reflected the diverse history of the region.

The house had been constructed from locally sourced stone, which gave it a sturdy and timeless appearance. The stones, weathered by centuries of sun and rain, had taken on a warm, earthy hue that complemented the lush greenery surrounding the property. The roof was made of terracotta tiles, a nod to the traditional building styles of the area, and it sloped gently to allow rainwater to run off easily during the monsoon season.

The entrance to Tandel House was marked by an intricately carved wooden door, a masterpiece of craftsmanship that had been lovingly maintained over the years. The door was adorned with motifs of fish and waves, symbolizing the close relationship between the rulers of the house and the sea. Above the door, a small balcony jutted out, offering a perfect vantage point to survey the surrounding landscape.

Stepping inside, Eknath was greeted by a grand foyer that immediately transported him back in time. The high ceilings were supported by wooden beams, each one carved with delicate patterns that told the striped stories of the house's past inhabitants. The floor was made of polished stone, cool underfoot, and scattered with vibrant rugs that added warmth and colour to the space.

The walls of the foyer were lined with portraits of the rulers who had called Tandel House home. Each portrait was a window into a different era, capturing the unique personalities and styles of the house's former residents. The eyes of these figures seem to follow Eknath as he moved through the room, a reminder of the legacy and responsibility that came with living in such a storied place.

To the left of the foyer was the grand hall, a space that had hosted countless gatherings and celebrations over the centuries. The hall was dominated by a large wooden table, its surface polished to a mirror-like sheen.

Around the table were chairs of varying designs, each one a testament to the changing tastes and influences that had shaped the house over the years. Above the table hung a magnificent chandelier, its crystals catching the light and casting rainbows across the room.

The walls of the grand hall were adorned with tapestries depicting scenes from the history of the fisher people. One tapestry showed a fleet of fishing boats setting out at dawn, their sails billowing in the wind. Another depicted a bustling market, with vendors selling their catch of the day to eager customers. These tapestries not only added beauty to the room but also served as a reminder of the deep connection between the house and the community it served.

'Please let Ghaniya show you a bit of our headquarters. To the world, it is still known as Tandel House, but in light of recent developments, let me be the first one to tell you that the name has changed. I will tell you all about it said Arjun. But first, I need to make some phone calls. I will be with you shortly.'

The bedrooms of Tandel House were located on the upper floors, each one a cosy retreat with its own unique character. The master bedroom, with its four-poster bed and rich, velvet drapes, exuded an air of opulence and comfort. The smaller bedrooms, though more modest in size, were no less inviting, with their soft linens and carefully chosen furnishings. It was really quite magnificent.

One of the most enchanting features of Tandel House was its garden. It was a small, lush oasis. The garden was filled with fragrant flowers and plants. A small pond, home to a family of ducks, added to the tranquillity of the space, its surface reflecting the changing sky above.

The garden also contained a small shrine, a place of reflection and prayer for the rulers of Tandel House. The shrine was simple, yet elegant, with a stone altar and a carved wooden statue of a deity revered by the fisher people. Offerings of flowers and incense were placed here daily, a testament to the enduring spiritual connection between the house and its inhabitants.

Arjun returned and saw the awe that Tandel House had inspired in Eknath Wadekar. He grinned and said, 'When you look at the ducks, you almost forget that the foundations of Tandel House are soaked with blood and violence. Tandel House has been called by different names over the decades. It all depended on which clan had control over the fisher villages at the time. Fifty years ago, when the last Shirke chief died without an heir, a young Pandurang Tandel challenged the nephew of the deceased Shirke chief to a combat to decide who would rule over the villages. The fight would be to the end. There would be no quarter asked or received. Come, let us sit around the table. You can carry on smoking and drinking at your leisure.'

As they all settled around the table that had seen many a blood brother come and go, Shinde lit up a Gold Flake and poured himself a glass of beer.

'The history of the Visarjan troops is not so clear. All that is known is that they date back to the time of the great Shivaji, who battled the Moghul tyrants and inflicted many a defeat on the superior Muslim forces. They are known as the bodyguards to the kings. They are always neutral and exist to serve the ruling house of the time. Succession to the head of the troops is always decided by battle.'

'But of course,' said Shinde, chugging down his glass. He looked at Lhoncha and almost asked him how he had acquired the title. But there was a look in the giant's eyes that definitely seemed to discourage any questions. Another time.

*

'Why are you called Shinde if your name is Eknath?' The question came out of the blue and caught Eknath off guard.

Eknath had been blindfolded the moment he met up with Kalidas at the pre-arranged location of Strand Coffee House.

'It's for your own safety, my friend,' said an apologetic Kalidas, 'this way, if things don't work out, you can go your own way and stay alive.'

Eknath was suffering from mixed emotions of trepidation and expectation. All he had been told by Kalidas was that he would be meeting a very important person, and it concerned The Plumber. As far as Eknath was concerned, that was enough, and he had agreed to all the terms, including the blindfold.

He was surprised to find himself in front of Tandel House. You didn't have to be a genius to figure out that you were deep inside the Fisher Village. And then, there was the structure he was being led to. Journalists talked about it, and he had heard some cops talk about it at the morgue. He wasn't sure all of them had actually seen it, but there was a reporter called Shantanu who was quite incorruptible, unlike the rest of his colleagues, who insisted he had seen the building from urban folklore. He had described it in detail to Eknath one evening after a few drinks. At the time Eknath had been sceptical, but now, as he sat inside the building, he realized that Shantanu had been here and he wondered about the circumstances that had brought the reporter to the hallowed halls.

Then there were the cops, and you know what they said about cops? You knew how a cop was lying? His lips were moving. He was almost sure none of them had ever been allowed inside the village. Eknath was also surprised to find himself seated in front of a giant, who obviously was Lhoncha, and a young man who could not be more than twenty two, according to Eknath's estimation. The question came from the giant, but as he started to answer, Arjun raised his hand. There was an immediate silence that followed. So the kid was in charge. How weird was that!

Arjun spoke: 'I have only one question. Do you have something to hide? Something that might come back and bite us in the ass in the future? If there is, tell me now.'

'There is nothing. My life is an open book. When I was little, my grandmother used to tell us kids stories about Shinde the Fox. Now, Shinde wasn't as big as his contemporaries, but he was fierce, and once he got his teeth into a mystery, he would not let go until he had solved it. I'd like to think I'm a bit like that.'

There was a round of raucous laughter around the table. Everyone knew about the tales of Shinde the fox. Arjun had joined in the general mirth. He said, smiling, 'Shinde it is then. Right now, I need you to tell me what you know about The

Plumber. Spare no details. Tell me everything, even if you think it is inconsequential.'

Shinde began a soliloquy about his findings. He began with the first killing, the clumsiness of it. He spoke about how the police had viewed it as a mindless, brutal murder, but he had seen it differently. He had seen it as a sign of things to come. He spoke of the development of finesse in the subsequent killings, The Plumber's wrench being left at every crime scene and the fact that the killer always made time to make himself a cup of tea before he left. Everyone in the room listened wordlessly. After he had finished, Arjun took a deep breath and looked around the room.

'Any thoughts?'

Shinde replied, 'A couple come to mind right off the top of my head. How does he decide who is going to die? What's the deal with the wrench? He's not really using it in the actual killing.'

Arjun spoke, 'The wrench is his calling card. And he's killing housewives. He knows they are alone at home with the husbands at work and children at school. I'm sure the police have figured out that. But how does he choose which housewife? Now, if we can unravel that mystery, we will be so much closer to understanding The Plumber's mind. And if we can think like him, then we can anticipate his next kill, and I can be there to welcome him.'

Lhoncha said, 'He's killing at seemingly random intervals. Maybe there's a system he's following. Something religious, maybe?'

Shinde interrupted them. 'Before we go further, I would like to bring in another person. He will be of great assistance in our hunt.'

Lhoncha laughed sarcastically and said, 'For years, no one has ever entered the village. Yet in the last month, we have had a wave of guests. That's just great. We should just have a monthly party and invite everyone to have a look at our village. Maybe organize a guided tour. Let everyone in on secrets that have been kept hidden for a thousand years.'

'Who are you thinking of inviting?' asked Arjun, raising his hand for silence as a burst of laughter took hold of the room.

'His name is Sub Inspector Baig.'

'A policeman? That's just great,' said an exasperated Lhoncha.

Shinde was adamant. 'He's a good man. He has honour, and he operates by a code that I admire. He's incorruptible and he's courageous.'

Lhoncha laughed. 'You're quite the fanboy, aren't you? I have yet to meet an incorruptible cop. He doesn't exist.'

Shinde wouldn't give up. 'I believe he will make an excellent addition to the team. It's his day off tomorrow. I am requesting permission to bring him here. Talk to him.'

Shinde looked at Arjun, ignoring everyone else in the room, and said, 'I see all around me, legends and characters from urban legends. Take, for example, the giant.' He looked at Lhoncha and continued, 'That, I am guessing, is Lhoncha. He's a story mothers tell their children at night. "Go to sleep, or Lhoncha will come for you." I know Kalidas because I've helped him a couple of times with some injury issues to his fighters. I know he is inaccessible to the general public and is feared by the police. I am suspecting that the rest of this company is equally dangerous and has some sort of mythical quality associated with their names.'

Shinde looked back at Arjun and said, 'These guys gathered together under one roof, I can understand. Yes, I can understand. But you? I definitely don't understand how you fit in with these venerable gentlemen. You are an anomaly. You shouldn't be here. You don't dress like a fisherman, don't sound like one, and definitely don't smell like one.' There was another round of laughter, but Shinde continued, unabated. 'And you're a kid. Unbelievable as it seems, you are the one in charge. I don't understand it, but I accept it. Just as you have to accept my judgement that this policeman will be invaluable in our hunt for The Plumber. And so, I'm asking you for permission to bring Inspector Baig to our next meeting. You have to trust me.'

Arjun was silent as he assessed the medical examiner. Kalidas had been correct—this was no ordinary medico. He was extremely intuitive, as evinced by the fact that he had figured out who the real head of the organization was. He was obviously fearless. He had not been scared to air his opinions in a room full of violent men who could have sent him to the wild beyond without batting an eyelid. But the ten crore rupee question was whether he could be trusted? An air of tension descended on the room like an invisible cloak. Shinde felt his sphincter muscles contract. There was a good chance, he realized, that he would not see sunlight or any light for that matter ever again.

And then, Arjun relaxed and made a decision that would reverberate down the decades. He smiled, suddenly looking more his age and asked the visibly relieved Shinde, 'Would you like a drink? For the second time in two days, I am going to tell you a story that not too many people know about. But before I begin, I'm going to give you the same choice I gave another person yesterday. You can decide now. Do you want to hear the whole story or not? If you do, then there's no going back. You are in till the end. If you don't want to know, and again, I think that's the smarter option, it will not be held against you. You will be taken back to Strand with my best wishes for a long and productive career.'

Shinde took out a packet of Gold Flake cigarettes. 'Do you mind if I smoke? And yes, I would absolutely kill for a beer if you have one. And in response to your question, I'm in for a penny and the damn pound.' Shinde didn't know it yet, but much into the future, he would give a gritty reporter the same choice, and she would respond with the same idiomatic expression.

'I think we can arrange that for you, doctor,' said Arjun as the mood in the room lifted considerably and a smattering of conversation wove its way around the room, and orders were given to procure a large jug of beer and a bottle of black label whiskey.

Shinde got up, lit a Gold Flake, stretched his back and then came and sat down next to Arjun. 'How old are you?'

'I am eighteen. I guess you are not much older than me.'

Shinde nodded and said, 'Not much older. And I suspect the story you are about to tell me is going to be rather unusual. Of that I have no doubt."

Arjun laughed and replied, 'I just might have to agree with you. Where should I begin?'

The beer had arrived, and Shinde poured himself a generous glass. He took a big swig of his beer, took a drag of the Gold Flake and said, 'Where you should, sir. At the beginning.'

***

# Chapter Seventeen

There were five people in the room. Lhoncha, Kalidas and Namdeo drank whiskey, Shinde destroyed half a jug of beer in record time, and Arjun did not drink at all. It was half past six in the evening, but the sun still wasn't ready to call it quits. The muggy heat had dissipated, and the temperature inside had dropped a few degrees. Heavily armed security patrolled the perimeter. No one was allowed within thirty feet of the building.

They sat around a carved wooden table that spoke of a generation gone by. Arjun looked at Shinde, capturing his mood and said, 'We are all invaders in our own way. From the moment we enter this world, our very existence in this world is an invasion. Tandel Lodge was not mine. It existed long before me. I acquired it in battle.'

'And the leadership rights that came with it. And of course, as you have mentioned, the name has changed.'

Arjun nodded and said, 'Yes.'

Shinde lit a Gold Flake, took a long swig of his beer and waited. Arjun began.

*

'My parents moved to Bombay from Chennai when I was five years old. My father was chasing his dream job. But he is now a broken man. They say you should be careful what you wish for. Unfortunately, that applies to my father in spades. The job he yearned for and for which he sacrificed everything to get has turned out to be his Waterloo. He was out of the city for extended periods of time, and when he came back, he lost himself in the bottle. He was periodically violent towards my mother, and while I demonized him at the time, I now realize that he knew the secret that I thought only my mother and I were party to.'

Shinde took a nonchalant sip of his beer and asked, 'What was the secret? Is it supposed to shock me? You are aware that I work with corpses?'

Lhoncha shifted in his seat and threw an ambiguous look at Shinde. Arjun caught his eye, and Lhoncha leaned back and continued drinking. Arjun smiled and said, 'Not at all. I just need you to know me. The real me. I need you to know the circumstances that created me. If we are to work together, then we need to understand each other. And for you to understand me, you need to know where I come from. One day, I may ask you to tell me something about yourself that you don't want anyone to know. If that day comes, I need to know that you will tell me the truth. I am merely leading by example.'

Shinde drained his glass, refilled it to the top, and took a long swig of his beer. He looked at Arjun and said, 'I will never lie to you. I may be the bearer of the harsh truth sometimes, but I will never lie to you. Please tell me the secret that you shared with your mother. But you also have to explain to me in detail how a kid with no connection to the fisherfolk took control over the fisher village? And I'm sure you can appreciate my curiosity about the turn of events that led to that. And then there is the village. One could misunderstand my words when I say "village". There are actually two villages, am I right? And this is a kingdom, and you are its ruler. How has that happened?'

Arjun nodded. The medico was ticking all the right boxes.

'My mother was very beautiful. Men were attracted to her like bees to honey. I think it all must have begun as a temporary tryst with excitement when she had her first affair. But it soon graduated to a permanent way of life when my father was away. There were several admirers, and while I am sure some visited her during the day when I was in school, some would pay my mother a visit in the evening. On those days, I would be given some money and would be told to come back later.'

'When did all this begin?' Shinde sounded genuinely shocked.

'I must have been eight years old.'

'So your mother was kicking you out into the streets when you were eight years old? That's terrible. And I guess that although you didn't tell your father, he knew about it. That would explain the alcoholism and the violence.'

Against his will, Shinde couldn't help but feel sorry for the kid sitting in front of him. Life had a way of dealing you some terrible cards, but all things considered, this kid had made the best of a bad situation. He was curious to hear how this story played out. He wanted to know what this kid had done to get him the throne of Tandel house and the loyalty of the fiercely territorial fisherfolk.

Arjun saw the questions written all over the medical examiner's face and said, 'Don't worry, doctor, you will leave here tonight with all your questions answered. Let me continue.'

Shinde drained his glass and looked at Lhoncha. Lhoncha stared back and met the unwavering gaze, nodded appreciatively and yelled for some more beer. It arrived with amazing alacrity because if there was one thing everyone in the village knew, it was that Lhoncha hated to repeat himself. Shinde poured himself a glass and lit up a Gold Flake.

'You know you smoke quite a bit?'

'Yes, I know that. I also like my beer. We are both going to die. That is the only certainty in life. The difference is that you will die healthy, and I will die an unhealthy death."

There was a ripple of laughter, and Arjun smiled again. He was beginning to like the medico. He continued. 'One evening about seven years ago, I came back home from tennis, and my mother would not open the door. I wandered around Colaba for a couple of hours as the twilight gave way to darkness, and when I came back home, my mother still would not let me in. Apparently, the "uncle" sitting inside was really upset and needed to talk. So, I was kicked out into the streets again.'

A dog howled in the distance, and Shinde heard the crackle of radios. *These fisherfolk were communicating with each other using shortwave radios*. This was a bigger organization than he had imagined.

Arjun continued, 'I was tired and hungry, and just as I had given up all hope, this beautiful lady came up to me. She introduced herself as Lesley and asked me where my mother was. She must have seen that I was close to tears, so she took my tennis bag from me and invited me to her apartment in the Esperanza building.'

Shinde raised his eyebrow. 'Sexual predator?' he asked.

'Quite the contrary. She was a godsend. She and her boyfriend, Greg, took amazing care of me. They refused to send me back to my mother, whom they described as abusive. They got my grandfather's number from me and called him. They told him what had happened, and my grandfather flew to Bombay and took me back to Madras. I stayed there for a few weeks, and I'm not sure what happened, but I was back in the loving arms of my mother not too long after that. The uncle visits stopped, and I received regular meals, but for love and attention, I went to Lesley.'

Shinde drained his beer, took a long drag of his Gold Flake, and waited for the story to continue. He knew they were getting to the juicy part.

*

'You may use the restrooms at the back if you need to. One of the bodyguards will escort you.'

'I'm fine, thanks.'

Arjun continued. 'Now I will not bore you with a description of Lesley. Suffice it to say, she was extraordinarily beautiful. It was rumoured that movie directors and producers were lining up to sign her to their label, but the reality was that Lesley was a simple girl with simple dreams, and being on the silver screen was not one of them.'

Arjun's face turned grim, and Shinde caught a glimpse of the predator hiding behind the face of the kid.

'Shyam Tandel inherited the throne of Tandel House and the power that went with it from his father, a great warrior, but more importantly, a great unifier. His father had bought the warring Kolis and Vaithis under his leadership using the carrot and whip technique, offering immense wealth and power if the tribes followed him. As always, there were individuals and groups that differed in their thinking. There would always be rebels and detractors. These he bought under his control, using the power of his Visarjan troops, who were blood loyal to him. You either kissed the ring or you died. Lhoncha is now the head of the Visarjan troops and had been so before me. He has attained that position through trial by combat. That is the only way the Visarjan decide their leader.'

Shinde took a drag of his Gold Flake, drained his glass, and as he poured himself yet another beer, he nodded, understanding the power structure as it had been, and understanding the fear the giant and his troops inspired. He wondered what it was about the kid that had inspired such loyalty among these fierce warriors. And he wondered where this Shyam Tandel that Arjun was talking about was.

Arjun continued. 'Shyam Tandel had all the qualities of his father. A great fighter, he had a forceful personality and inspired loyalty in his troops. He was of average height and had a fighter's lean physique, did not drink or smoke, enjoyed the ladies in moderation, and truth be told, his future as a leader looked very bright. But Shyam Tandel knew that although he was unquestioned King of the fisher village and that big businessmen and politicians were queuing up to meet him, they were happy to do so in the shadows. No one wanted to be associated with the Fisher people in public. The optics were just not good.'

Arjun paused and took a sip of water. Shinde took a large sip of his beer and took a drag of his Gold Flake, while the rest of the gathering looked on with grudging admiration.

Arjun continued. 'Shyam Tandel was a man of many faces. He was a ruthless warlord, a generous benefactor, and a charming entrepreneur. But to be accepted by the superficial upper class of Bombay's fickle society was his secret and unquenchable desire. For that to happen, Shyam felt that he would need to have a partner on his arm that would stoke envy and desire amongst the social elite. And again, he found himself in an unenviable quandary.'

'Where to find a trophy wife who would deign to be seen with him in public. And looked like she was enjoying herself,' Shinde completed the sentence, and Arjun nodded.

Arjun continued as Shinde drained his glass, took a drag of his Gold Flake and pointed to the empty jug.

***

# Chapter Eighteen

*May 1983*

'Olympia restaurant, the well-known eatery, sits between Colaba police station and Esperanza Building. It was particularly popular both amongst locals and tourists for its rich and flavourful *keema*, a spiced minced meat dish typically served with soft, buttery *pav*, which were cube-shaped buns bought to India by the Portuguese and used extensively by their Goan subjects that had become the signature street food of Bombay. The keema was often prepared with a blend of aromatic spices, giving it a distinctive taste that kept the patrons coming back for more. The dish was usually accompanied by sliced onions and a wedge of lime, enhancing the overall culinary experience. Securing a table at Olympia restaurant on a Sunday morning was almost impossible because the demand for seating was exceedingly high. This was due to the fact that the entire Goan community of Colaba would finish the 8 am mass at the Holy Name Church and would then descend on Olympia restaurant for keema pav and chai. It gave them a chance to show off their Sunday best, and it was a chance for potential match-ups between aspiring youngsters looking to settle down in holy matrimony.

'Lesley lived in the Esperanza Building and was a regular at Olympia. Much to the disappointment of the male population that thronged to Olympia restaurant, she wasn't looking for a mate. She had already given her heart to Greg, who worked as an engineer on board a cruise liner. They were not married on paper, but they had been bonded for life from the moment they first set eyes on each other. They lived together in Greg's apartment, and when Greg was away at sea, her sister Daphne stayed with her.

'Shyam Tandel rarely left the comfort and safety of his little kingdom, unless it was for meetings with political leaders who needed uncomfortable issues dealt with. Businessmen who needed his favours were required to present themselves at the border of Sudam Jhopadi and request an appointment, which could or could not be given, all depending on the mood of the moment and the reputation of the one asking for the appointment. For his pleasure, which was not so frequent, women and alcohol were sent to the village. So one Sunday morning, when he woke up and informed his bodyguards that he was feeling like some keema pav at Olpympia's, there was a flurry of activity as preparations were hastily undertaken to make sure the king of the fisher people was properly welcomed at the restaurant in question.

'The universe moves in mysterious ways, and the fates of kings are often decided in a cosmic throw of the dice. The chaos theory deals with the "butterfly effect", where small changes can lead to vastly different outcomes, making predictions practically impossible. All of the above were in play that fateful Sunday when Shyam Tandel broke his normal operating procedures that were in place to ensure his safety, and decided to indulge an unusual desire to eat keema pav at Olympia restaurant. If he hadn't done that, he wouldn't have met Lesley, and the events that followed wouldn't have occurred, and all would have been well in the state of Denmark, to loosely paraphrase Shakespeare. But he did, and what followed brought about the end of a dynasty. I believe we could all use a break,' said Arjun, standing up as he left the great hall.

Shinde stared contemplatively at the departing back of the leader of the fisher folk, drained his glass, stood up, and followed the entourage. They all stepped out into the cool, damp sunset.

*

## *1985, Sundernagari Village*

As usual, the sunset over the Arabian Sea was a wonder to behold. The sun had begun its gradual, but inexorable descent towards the horizon, transforming the sky into a breathtaking canvas of colours. Hues of deep orange and fiery red blended seamlessly with soft pink and purples, creating a stunning gradient that stretched across the vast expanse above. The sun had become a soft, glowing orb, hanging low in the sky, casting a warm golden light that danced across the water.

The gentle waves of the Arabian Sea reflected the canvas of vibrant colours above, shimmering like molten gold as they lapped against the shore where Arjun, Shinde and the entourage stood, each one revelling in the beauty. Each wave carried the whisper of the sea, a soothing sound that was one with the visual spectacle they were beholding. In the far distance, the flames of the Mandwa oil refinery lit up the hills behind, adding to the splendour. Seagulls coasted gracefully above, and in the distance, the sea was dotted with the lights of the fishing boats that became brighter as twilight approached. The colours deepened, and the first of the stars started to twinkle in the emerging night. The air cooled, and a moment of tranquillity descended, but everyone present knew it was a temporary cover for the insanity that had become the new normal.

They were at the entrance to a cove, and in the distance, the lights of Lovedale Apartments, that was on the other side of the cove, came on, one by one. Kalidas had disappeared for a while, and he reappeared with a couple of helpers carrying plates of food. They all sat down in a circle, and one of the helpers went around with a small bucket of water, and everyone washed their hands.

'I trust you have no problem eating with your hands?' asked Arjun. 'If you do, I can arrange for cutlery.'

Shinde shook his head and said, 'I have no problem eating with my hands.'

The fish curry and rice were delicious, and Shinde found that he was starving and wolfed down his food in record time. He accepted a second helping and ate more slowly. Arjun ate sparingly, unlike the rest of the group that matched Shinde in appetite.

He continued. 'Shyam Tandel was given a welcome by the owner of the Olympia restaurant befitting a visiting dignitary or celebrity that he was. He was given a table in the far corner that gave him a clear line of sight of all the patrons and of those coming into the bar. Of course, he did have his bodyguards, but Shyam believed it was better to be safe than to be sorry. The fisher folk didn't have any enemies, at least none that would dare to risk death by attacking the king of the fisher people. But one could never be too safe. Many a king has died due to complacency. The aroma of delicious food filled the air, and Shyam Tandel's eyes wandered around the room. No one made eye contact, either because they were occupied with their own conversations or the sight of the bodyguards was enough to turn curious eyes away.

'Lesley walked into the Olympia restaurant at around nine-fifteen, just after attending the church's 8 am church service. Her sister Daphne was with her. Daphne was very pretty, but there was something ethereal about Lesley that made all heads turn. She made her way to an empty table near Shyam and his bodyguards. Daphne said something which Shyam could not hear, and Lesley laughed, her smile brightening the room as though a bright light had been turned on. Shyam Tandel, head of Tandel House and ruler of the fisher folk, felt an unfamiliar flutter in his chest. He was captivated.

'A waiter came to their table, and Daphne ordered for both of them. Shyam Tandel watched for a while and then did something his unsuspecting bodyguards were not prepared for. He stood up and very quickly went over to Lesley's table.

'"Good morning. I'm Shyam. I couldn't help but notice you from across the room. You have the most beautiful smile."

'Lesley looked up at him, her expression warm and friendly. "Thank you, kind sir. That is very nice of you. I'm Lesley, and this is my sister Daphne. It's our pleasure to meet you."

'Shyam felt a spark of hope. "I was wondering if you would like to come to my table and have some coffee and some breakfast with me. It would be an honour to have you and your sister grace my table. I would like to get to know you better."

'Lesley's smile softened, and she shook her head. "It is very kind of you, Shyam, but I'm afraid I must decline your offer. I'm not looking to date anyone. I am already taken, you see?"

'Shyam felt the bitter stab of disappointment deep in his soul, but maintained his composure and said, "Of course, I completely understand. Please accept my apologies, and breakfast is on me."

'Lesley smiled again and said, "We pay our own bills, but thank you. Enjoy your breakfast."

'As Shyam walked back to his table, he felt a mix of emotions. While disappointment was the powerful ingredient in the mix, he respected her honesty. He took a deep breath as he sank into his chair. He reminded himself that things did not always go as planned and new days brought new opportunities. The lively atmosphere of Olympia restaurant continued, unabated.'

Arjun finished his plate of food and washed his hands. Shinde asked, 'Is there any more beer?'

Arjun smiled and said, 'Of course.' A large jug of beer and a mug appeared, and Shinde poured himself a generous dose and took a big swig. In the years to come, his drinking prowess would become legendary, but that evening, the small group gathered by a cove in the fisher village were getting a first-hand demonstration of that prowess.

Arjun continued, 'Now, if that had been the end of the matter, we might not be gathered here today. At least, definitely not in Tandel House.

'Shyam Tandel always had a retinue of bodyguards handling his security when he left the fisher village. That Sunday morning was no different. Two were stationed outside the Olympia restaurant. They looked for potential threats that might enter the restaurant. They would then engage with the enemy, giving Shyam and the two bodyguards watching his table the option to either fight or, if the attackers were an overwhelming force, to exercise the flight option through the kitchen at the back. That day, it was Raj Gaikwad and Nitin Bhonsle who had been tasked to watch the table that Shyam was sitting at. As Shyam walked back to his table, they witnessed the entire interaction. They exchanged glances, barely able to contain their laughter at the sight of Shyam's hopeful demeanour quickly turning to disappointment.

'They didn't say anything, but Shyam felt their derision and cursed himself for being overconfident. At the same time, he felt a surge of anger rise within him. He had just been rejected in front of them, and their amusement felt like a knife being mercilessly turned in a deep wound. He turned to face them, his expression darkening.

'"Are you two done?" he snapped at them, his voice low and tense. "Would you two like to go a couple of rounds with me at the sparring arena? After I've finished with you two fucking idiots, you'll be smiling a lot less. I guarantee it."

'Raj and Nitin blanched. Everyone knew Shyam Tandel had been trained under several different martial arts instructors. He had spent some time in Japan and had fine-tuned his fighting skills under the famous Shihan Shintaro Ito, and had even bought two *isshin ryu* black belts back with him to keep him in fighting shape. Everyone was aware of Shyam's fighting skills and also his ruthlessness in combat. No one wanted to be in the ring with an irate Shyam Tandel. Chances were bright that you could end up in the hospital. Raj raised his hands in mock surrender, an uneasy smile on his face. "Sorry, boss, we didn't mean to upset you. We were just sort of taken aback by her refusal to sit with you. I mean, it's not like you asked her to marry you or anything."

'Shyam's eyes went blood red with humiliation. "You are absolutely right. All I did was to invite her for a meal, and then I offered to pay for hers, and she refused me both times. She doesn't get to treat me like that and just walk away! I'll show her."

'Raj and Nitin exchanged worried glances as Shyam's anger transformed into a dangerous determination. "What are you talking about?" Raj asked cautiously.

'"I'm going to take her," Shyam said, his voice steady, but filled with intensity. "We are going to kidnap and take her to the fisher village. She doesn't know who I am. Once she sees the twin villages and realizes who I am, things will change. She'll see what she's missing."

'The bodyguards stared at him, taken aback by the sudden shift in his demeanour.

'"Boss, you can't be serious?" said Raj Gaikwad, his tone urgent. "That's insane! You can't just force someone to like you."

'"Watch me," Shyam replied, his eyes narrowing. "She needs to understand who I am and what I can offer. I'll make her see."

'Raj stepped forward, trying to reason with him. "This isn't the way to handle things. You're better than this. Think about the consequences!"

'"Consequences?" asked Shyam. His tone had become very calm. "Come outside with me, Gaikwad bhai."

'Shyam and his two bodyguards stepped out of Olympia restaurant onto Colaba Causeway. The two bodyguards watching the streets came to join them. Shyam turned around and looked at Ram Gaikwad, who, at six feet two inches, towered over the fisher king.

'He said, "I am the king. There are no consequences for kings." And before the words were out of his mouth, he jumped and spun in the air, his left leg whipping around at a deathly speed. It caught the bodyguard on his jaw, dislocating it. As the bodyguard dropped unconscious, Shyam Tandel dropped on him with an elbow that caved in his cranium as though it had been hit with a hammer. The whole encounter lasted not more than four seconds, and Ram Gaikwad lay extremely dead on Colaba Causeway.

'Someone screamed, and people started running helter-skelter in all directions. The remaining three bodyguards instinctively drew their weapons to protect their king, which added to the panic. Shyam Tandel looked around, totally unruffled. He then looked at his three bodyguards, who looked back at their king with a mixture of bewilderment and fear.

'"You see? No consequences. I will be walking back to the village. You three idiots get the car, and I will meet you back at the village.' He raised his hand, stifling any dissent. "I don't want any protection, and I don't fucking need it. Go on! I will see you back at the village."

'With that, Shyam Tandel turned and walked through the stampeding crowd. He walked past Colaba police station, which coincidentally happened to be remarkably deserted at the time. No one called out his name, and no one tried to stop him. But Shyam didn't notice anything. He was already lost in his thoughts, envisioning the plan in his mind. The thrill of the idea consumed him, drowning out the voices of caution. He felt powerful, and the prospect of taking control of the situation was intoxicating.

'As he plotted, a small part of him wrestled with the morality of his intentions, but the anger and humiliation he felt overshadowed that voice. He was invisible to Lesley. He was determined to make Lesley see him, no matter the cost. The line between right and wrong blurred in his mind, and he was ready to cross it.'

Arjun took a deep breath as he uncharacteristically got caught up in his own emotions. He shook his head and said, 'The most fragile part of the male human being is his ego. It is the most difficult part of the male make-up to control. It is easily wounded, and more kingdoms have fallen because the rulers could not get over their egos. Shyam Tandel was no different. And the truth is that he might have just got away with it. He was an unchallenged ruler. He had a platoon of stormtroopers led by a giant who had sworn an oath of loyalty to him. He was untouchable. But it is that moment when a person thinks himself to be completely safe that he is at his most vulnerable.'

Arjun looked at Shinde, who had emptied the jug of beer, and smiled. 'You really are quite remarkable. Would you like some more beer? And I see you have exhausted your supply of cigarettes. I will order another packet of Gold Flakes for you.'

Shinde nodded in the affirmative. In the background, the flames of the oil refinery at Mandwa glowed in the distance.

***

# Chapter Nineteen

Back in Tandel House, Shinde found that a large jug of beer and a packet of Gold Flakes had been placed on the table next to where he was originally sitting. The table was large and oblong, and as they sat around it, Shinde was reminded of King Arthur and the Knights of the Round Table. He thought about Lancelot and his betrayal of his king. He looked around and saw Ghaniya, Namdeo, Kalidas, Nagaya, and the giant Lhoncha, all sitting around. They would all give their lives for the teenager—that was a given. But as Shinde's eyes wandered around the group, he wondered if there was a Lancelot there. Years later, he would realize there was no Lancelot. But there was a Mordred. He just wasn't there that day at Tandel House.

Shinde poured himself a glass of beer and lit up a Gold Flake. He looked around the table. No one was drinking anymore. And there was definitely no smoking. He smiled to himself. Arjun caught the smile and smiled in return.

He continued. 'One morning, a few months after the Olympia incident, Lesley came down from her apartment and stepped out onto the pavement bordering the Colaba Causeway. There were flower sellers, and a familiar face was selling sugarcane juice. She smiled at the son of the building watchman and said, "Arey, Ashok, how are you?"

'"I'm fine, *didi*. Would you like some sugarcane juice? It's very fresh."

'"No, thank you. I'm on my way to the airport to pick up Greg. We will have some when we are back."

'Lesley stepped out onto the Colaba Causeway and looked for a cab. A passing black and yellow Fiat taxi did an illegal U-turn and came to a halt in front of her.

'Lesley smiled at the driver and asked, "Bhaiya, will you take me to the international airport?"

'The driver, a young man in his twenties, smiled and said, "Of course, madam. But I need to stop at the Hanuman Mandir petrol bunk. You are the first customer this morning."

'Lesley nodded understandingly. Taxi drivers normally didn't have much money in their pockets early in the morning. Most days' earnings went either to the wife or to the owner from whom the driver was leasing the vehicle. They would wait for a couple of the usual short fares and fill up their gas tanks. The international terminal was a long-distance drive. He would have to have a full gas tank before he began the journey.

'"Of course, bhaiya. There's no rush," said Lesley as she got into the cab. They headed south on Colaba Causeway and reached the petrol bunk. They drove in, and the driver brought the car to a stop near one of the filling stations. The driver got out and went to connect the hose to the car.

'After a while, he came back and said in a very apologetic tone, "Madam, I am very sorry, but the two tyres at the back are flat. I'm not sure if it's just a leak or if the tyres are actually punctured. I have spoken to a friend of mine, and he will take you in his taxi. I do apologize, madam."

'Lesley smiled and said, "Of course, it's not a problem. I'm grateful you were able to arrange an alternative for me. You are a very kind man. Thank you."

'For some reason, the taxi driver was unable to meet her eyes. He just looked away and pointed to the other taxi that had arrived. Lesley didn't think much of it as she got into the replacement taxi. Another bright smile greeted her.

'"Welcome, madam. Shall we take the route via Radio Climb and the Taj Hotel? There will be less traffic, and you are already a bit delayed. My name is Nitin Bhonsle, and I will take you safely to the airport. I can wait for you if you like."

'"That is very nice of you. Thank you, that will be lovely."

'Lesley settled back into her seat and closed her eyes. She was very relaxed by the extremely hospitable behaviour of both taxi drivers. So, when the taxi stopped and the car doors opened, she wasn't quite sure what was happening. There were four men in the car now, including the driver, who suddenly wasn't smiling. Lesley looked out of the window and saw that while she had closed her eyes, Nitin Bhonsle had driven the taxi to the edge of what she knew as Sudam Jhopadi. For Lesley, this was a settlement of slums. This was not a place that she would ever think of coming to. But as the taxi made its way through the teeming crowds that parted like the Red Sea before Moses, she realized that this was what a kidnapping looked like. She felt a moment of panic combined with terror, and fought it back with an effort that was almost physical. She looked around her and tried to take stock of her situation. She was stuck in the back seat between two rather unsavoury characters, and Mr Bhonsle had been joined in the front by yet another very dangerous-looking individual. It would be a fair summation that her situation did not look good.

'Waves of panic inundated Lesley again, and she had to stop herself from screaming. Instead, she asked in a very calm tone, "Please, bhaiya, what are you doing? I need to get to the airport. Where have you brought me? Please let me go."

'There was no reply from the men in the car, and the atmosphere got even more tense as the taxi went further into the village. Lesley began to scream, but one look from the scarred man on the right silenced her. It was pure terror. The crowds suddenly cleared, and the taxi came to a halt in a huge clearing.

'"Get out," said Nitin Bhonsle.

'As they all got out of the car, Lesley squinted into the sunlight as a figure approached her. It was Shyam Tandel. Of course, Lesley didn't know what he was doing there, but she began to understand that this Shyam guy who had approached her in Olympia was behind her abduction.

'"Welcome to my humble abode, Lesley. Please forgive the manner in which you were brought here. But I had no choice. You are very special to my heart, and I would like to spend some time with you unfettered by outside influences."

'"Are you crazy?" said Lesley. "I have a boyfriend, and we are going to get married. I already told you this in Olympia."

'"There's many a slip between the cup and the lip, and I'm working on all the slips." Shyam laughed. He was an attractive man with clean white teeth. But all Lesley saw was a crazy sociopath who had kidnapped her. Lesley was not stupid. She decided that in order to be free, she would have to play the game. This crazy fucker might just kill her if she rejected him again.

'She smiled a small smile. "We don't know each other very well. Why don't you let me go? Then come to my home, and ask me out on a date like a normal guy."

'Shyam's smile disappeared. "How stupid do you think I am? You'll just run to the police. But let me remove any illusions you might have. The police fear me. I am Shyam Tandel. I am the Fisher King. No one is coming to get you, least of all your idiot boyfriend. Now, Savitri here will take you to your lodgings. Rest a bit, and we will talk later. I have some business to attend to."

'Lesley began to weep loudly, and Savitri, an attractive lady dressed in the classic outfit of the fisher people, stepped forward and slapped her. Shyam Tandel roared in a rage.

'"Don't you dare touch her in anger. I will have you publicly flogged. She is a queen and you are to serve her."

'Savitri lowered her gaze and bowed in supplication before Shyam Tandel, but when she looked at Lesley, it was with pure hatred. But she obeyed her master without question and led Lesley away to her luxurious lodgings inside Tandel House.'

*

For once, Shinde had paused his drinking and smoking. He was completely held in the thrall of the story. Arjun took a sip of water and continued.

'If I hadn't been walking back from college at the exact time Greg stepped out of his cab, maybe it would have been a while before I would have learned of the abduction. But as I have said, we cannot understand the universal plan. It's like trying to explain the concept of an airplane to a caveman. It's beyond our ability to comprehend it. As it happened, I was walking back from college down Colaba Causeway when I saw Greg getting out of a cab, looking distraught.

'"Hey Greg, how are you? What's the matter?" I asked him.

'Greg looked at me, and a small smile danced around his lips briefly before clouds of worry took over. I knew that Lesley and he adored their tennis player. We had history together.

'"Hey, Arjun. Lesley was supposed to meet me, but she never came to the airport. And that's really strange, because that silly girl loves to be there to pick me up. She says it gives her an extra ninety minutes with me. I tried calling the house, but her sister Daphne said she left at around ten in the morning for the airport."

'I knew for certain that Lesley would have never left Greg waiting at the airport without a damn good reason. There was no way. Maybe she had been in an accident! Oh God, that would be absolutely devastating. I didn't show my concern to Greg, who was already close to tears.

'"You need to file a missing person's report with the police, Greg. That's the first thing you need to do. Let them coordinate with the police stations along the way to the airport and see what turns up."

'Greg went pale. The thought that Lesley might have been in an accident had already crossed his mind, but my talking about it brought the whole thing into an unpleasant perspective. Without a word, he set off down the road to Colaba police station, and I set off towards Strand. There was nothing to do but wait.'

Arjun continued as Shinde finally took a sip of his beer, 'As I walked down Colaba Causeway, I was invisible to the people around. I was simply inconsequential and didn't blip on anyone's radar. It was also my greatest strength. People let their guard down when they think the coast is clear. Their tongues become loose, and I hoped that maybe, just maybe, someone would talk. All I could do was hang around and hope for the best.

'The whole day passed with no joy. I hung around Strand Coffee House, Colaba Market and Janata Stores. I walked around the bylanes of Mereweather Road, where all the drug addicts hung out. I walked around the Taj Hotel and the Gateway of India, and listened to the chatter of the hawkers. But there was no information forthcoming. I was a little disheartened, but I was professional enough to know that patience was the key. Someone always talks. I went to meet Greg in the evening at his apartment. He seemed to have aged suddenly. Extreme grief will do that to a person.

'"The police have checked. There are no reports of any accidents from here to Santa Cruz airport. She's just disappeared. Ashok, our building watchman's son, who has a sugarcane juice stand outside our building, saw her get into a taxi around ten in the morning. The strange thing is that the taxi went south towards Strand instead of taking the right at the Causeway traffic lights and heading towards Marine Drive."

'"Did the juice boy get a look at the taxi driver?"

'"Unfortunately, no."

'I took a deep sigh and settled back into the comfortable sofa in Greg's house. The place was very familiar to me. I had spent a very pleasant two weeks there when I was much younger. I contemplated the new information. So Lesley had headed towards Strand. Why? It must have been the driver who had either coerced her or tricked her into taking that route. But I had no clue how to find out about the taxi driver who had picked up Lesley. But most important of all, I had no idea why anyone would want to kidnap Lesley. The normal motivation of the average kidnapper is money. Greg and Lesley lived a comfortable life, but they were not rich by any standards. So it wasn't money. Something else had happened that had inspired this crazy abduction, and for the life of me, I couldn't figure out what.'

Shinde lit up a Gold Flake and took a long, large swig of his beer. It had been a while now, and he was parched. An owl hooted in the darkness, and this was followed by a lonely howl of a dog in the distance. The entourage sitting around the table shifted uncomfortably in their chairs. Only Arjun looked unperturbed and said, 'My brothers here feel there are evil spirits abroad tonight. My belief is that they are always around. But they can only harm you if you let them. They thrive on fear, hatred, malice and greed.'

Shinde laughed. 'All the fine emotions, you mean?'

Arjun smiled and said, 'Yes, the fine ones. The ones that drive most men are the ones that empower them.' He looked at the guards at the entrance of the hall and said, 'Get us some food. Our guest must be hungry.'

***

# Chapter Twenty

***May 25th, 1985, 1930 Hours, Indian Standard Time***

*Jhinga masala* made in the traditional Malwani style and *chappatis* arrived, and there was silence for a while as everyone at the table dug into the delicious prawn preparation. Shinde sat back and lit up a Gold Flake, refilled his glass, and waited.

Arjun continued, 'It was late in the evening at Gokul Wines that I got my first break. Nitin Bhonsle, an enforcer for Shyam Tandel, the fisher king from the fisher village, arrived at the wine shop with three cronies in tow. They were already a little drunk and were talking about the great operation they had undertaken that day.

'"Of course the police know," slurred Nitin Bhonsleas as he went past me, not seeing me at all. "But do you think they will do anything to the boss? He is the king. Although I still don't understand why he is so besotted with that green-eyed Goanese."

'They went into the bar and went to a corner table where they could drink and talk with relative privacy. I waited for them to have a few more drinks, and then went in, taking a rag and pretending to clean their table. There was an overflow of customers, and the noise inside the bar was deafening. Neither the manager, nor the waiters, nor the drunken trio noticed the relatively well-dressed kid cleaning the table. I was close enough to hear the end of their conversation.

'"Arey, that Savitri gave that poor girl such a slap. But then Tandel Bhai really lost his temper. He told her that the Goan was a queen and was to be treated as such. I think he is losing his mind a bit. No one will accept that Goan girl as a fisher queen. It's absurd," said one of the cronies wisely, and got a slap from Bhonsle.

'"Hey chutiya, you just be a soldier and keep your fucking mouth shut. If you feel so strongly about this matter, then why don't you take it up with our king? I'm sure you are strong enough to challenge him to single combat. I could pass on the message for you if you like?"

'Nitin Bhonsle and the other soldier laughed, and the concerned crony put up his hands in fear. "Sorry, Nitin Bhai. I didn't mean any disrespect. It's the alcohol talking. I'm loyal to Shyam Tandel with my life."

'Nitin Bhonsle laughed even louder, "It's okay, *gaandu*, drink up and let's go the Kamathipura. I heard some maal has come from Assam. Let's taste some north-eastern delicacies. I heard they like it rough."

'I had heard enough, and I left the bar before Nitin Bhonsle and his friends. Now I knew enough to piece together what had happened. Lesley had been taken by Shyam Tandel, the king of the fisher villages of Sunderngari and Geeta Nagar! I was not able to wrap my head around the unbelievable news. What had happened to set off such a chain of events? Shyam Tandel was not an unreasonable man. He was not given to bouts of megalomania. He was a good enough administrator. What had happened to derail his judgment?

'And then I realized something else. It didn't matter what had transpired. Lesley was a prisoner inside the Fisher village, and no one would be able to get her out. The police, totally unreliable at the best of times, would do nothing. And truth be told, they could do nothing. There was too much business going on in and out of the fisher village. Too many people owed the Tandel clan, not to forget the big wads of cash reaching the desks of the local inspectors with clockwork regularity. Desperate times call for desperate measures! While I adored Lesley, the last thing I needed was to get involved in a war with a king and his warriors.

'I decided to think out of the box. Sometimes it's best to rip the band-aid off. One gets to see the true character of a man, when he is faced with an impossible option. I went to Greg's apartment and knocked. Lesley's sister Daphne opened the door with a look of expectation, which died when she saw who it was.

'"Who is it, Daphne?" Greg's voice sounded very frail, and my heart broke. I was going to ask a good-hearted, but not a very courageous man, to do a very courageous thing. I didn't waste time sugarcoating anything. I went straight to the point.

'"Lesley has been kidnapped by Shyam Tandel. He is the ruler of the fisherfolk. A dangerous man. I don't know how their paths crossed, but they did."

'"Shyam Tandel? I know that name," said Daphne. She then recounted the whole encounter that had taken place in the Olympia restaurant. "He seemed to take the rejection quite well, actually. Lesley was charming as ever. You know she can reject a man, and he would leave feeling exhilarated. It's a natural gift. There was no bad blood when this Shyam guy left the table, so I don't know what happened to make him take such an extreme course of action. Anyway, I think we should go to the police immediately."

'I shook my head and said, "That's not going to work. Firstly, the police would never believe you with no proof. Secondly, even if they did, no sane policeman would have the moral fibre to breach the village borders and conduct a search. That would be professional and economic suicide. Have you seen the car the chief inspector of Colaba police station drives? He didn't buy that Toyota on a policeman's salary."

'"So what do we do? I'll do anything to get her back." Greg sounded desperate, and I needed him to be desperate. It's easy to convince desperate men to do desperate things. Like alcohol, desperation impairs judgement.

'I delivered the punchline, "The only thing that may get her back is if you go to the village and plead directly to Shyam Tandel yourself. There is no other way. Maybe when he sees you, he will relent and release Lesley, and we can all go our own ways with no harm and no foul. But I have to be perfectly clear, Greg. This is an extremely dangerous gamble. I think that you are risking your life."

'Greg didn't even blink. "Let's go," he said, looking straight at Daphne, daring her to say anything.'

*

'Moonrise over the fisher villages was always a beautiful sight, especially when it was a full moon night. As the first stars began to twinkle in the deepening sky, a silvery glow emerged on the horizon. The moon, full and luminous, rose gracefully from the sea, its reflection shimmering across the water like a path of liquid silver. It bathed the village in a soft, ethereal light, illuminating the outlines of the boats bobbing gently in the harbour and casting long shadows across the beach.

'It was spectacular enough to make the most hardened fisherman pause in his evening routine to admire the moonrise, a nightly spectacle that never lost its magic. Conversations softened, and a sense of calm and wonder enveloped the community. The moon's gentle light revealed the intricate patterns of fishing nets hung to dry and highlighted the glistening scales of the day's catch, now resting in crates along the docks.

'As the moon ascended higher into the night sky, it became a silent guardian over the village, watching over the soon-to-be slumbering homes and the tranquil sea. The moonrise, a timeless and serene moment, reminded the villagers of the natural rhythms that guided their lives, offering a sense of continuity and peace in the ever-changing world. That, of course, was for the folks not involved in the day-to-day business of violence and death. For the predators of the villages, the full moon was a curse, because their ships were lit up and were nice shiny targets for the coast guard that was always around. Many a ship had gone down with all hands on board after unsuccessfully trying to first outrun, then outshoot the sleek, heavily armed cutters. It wasn't a walk in the park for the criminal underworld in the city either. It just wasn't the same conducting a robbery or a rape under the full light of the moon. Faces had been seen, later identified in line-ups and were now sitting in jail. So not everyone was thrilled about a full moon night. Arjun accompanied Greg to Sudam Jhopadi, which marked the buffer zone between the civilized world and the fisher villages.

'"You'll have to go on your own from here, Greg. I don't want them to see me just yet. You'll run into the border guards. Be respectful, even if they get rough with you. Don't change your demand to see Shyam Tandel, however threatening they get. Once you're in front of him, ask him to release her. Don't show any fear. I know it's hard, but you must try, Greg. These are predators, and they can smell fear. I don't have time to train you. I can only tell you what to do, and pray that you remember it."

'In spite of the developing situation and the fear that came with it, Greg had a moment of clarity as he departed towards the buffer zone of Sudam Jhopadi. "What the hell had happened to the tennis brat they loved? He was still a kid, not much older than when they had rescued him from the streets. But now he spoke like a man. Like a man who knew about violence and life. Definitely had to have a sit-down with the kid when he got back."

'Kalidas appeared next to me and we both looked at Greg's receding figure in the darkness.

'"How do you think this is going to end?"

'"I can only hope for the best, and prepare for the worst." Arjun was not able to see a reasonable way out of this quandary that was not of his making, which had put him in a situation that would bring me out of the shadows. "Stay here, Kalidas. I don't want to tip our hand as yet," he said. "I need to go and get something."

'Kalidas' eyes widened with wonder and reverence. "Are you going to go and get it now? Are you going to use it?"

'Arjun grinned and Kalidas, recounting the event to a bunch of young bucks much later on, said that he looked like an avenging angel in the darkness.'

*

'The first of the border guards accosted Greg near Dhobi Ghat, where the launderers for the masses did their jobs of washing a million clothes a day at least. It was a miracle they were able to connect the numerous batches of laundry with the correct owners. One would expect several disasters to occur every day, and in that assumption, one would be dead wrong. Rarely was a mistake ever made.

'"Hey *chooth*! Fuck off from here!" said the guard aggressively.

'Greg folded his hand and said, "Please, sir, I need to speak to Shyam Tandel about a matter of great importance."

'The guard laughed drily and said, "Oh, you wanted to see Shyam Tandel? Why didn't you say so in the first place? Of course, you can meet him. Wait, let me get him."

'As Greg started to smile in relief, the guard punched him in the solar plexus, and Greg hit the ground like a stone. He gasped in agony.

'"Want to meet Shyam Tandel, is it?" asked the soldier again as he kicked the face of the now prone Greg. There was a wet crunching sound, and Greg grunted in agony as he lost some teeth, his body arching momentarily and then relaxing as he lost consciousness. The guard raised his leg to stamp on Greg's head. It was a killing blow. Greg's head would have been crushed like an eggshell. Something stopped the guard in mid-strike. He lowered his foot and looked around. The feral part of his brain told him danger was close by. Really close by!

'Before he could realize what was going on, Arjun came out of the darkness Ike an evil desert spirit, and the guard was locked in a vice-like rear-naked choke. He tried to struggle, but the choke was tight, cutting off the blood flow and oxygen to his brain. He went limp. Arjun dropped the body and turned to look at Kalidas.'

Arjun said, 'I couldn't just stand back and let him kill Greg.' He wasn't justifying his actions, merely explaining them.

'Baba, you cannot go in and ask for Lesley. You have already broken protocol by disabling a perimeter guard. He will have you killed. I think you are a very good fighter, but no one is good enough to take on all the Visarjan troops and the other ground troops. And please, let's not forget about that giant Lhoncha.'

Everyone at the table laughed, but the mood suddenly turned sombre as everyone recalled the events of that fateful night. The only one who was unaffected by the ebb and sway of everyone's mood and the evening conversation was Shinde. He lit up another Gold Flake and took another large swig of his beer. He refilled his glass and then pointed to the empty jug. More beer appeared almost immediately. Arjun continued.

'Suddenly, everything came into perspective. Slightly late but better late than never. Sending Greg was my way of trying to stay out of things that didn't concern me. The problem was that it did concern me. There was no way to reason with Shyam Tandel. I had figured that out. For some reason, he was besotted enough with Lesley to have kidnapped her and spirited her away into the village. I have always blamed the Hindi movie industry for all that. It has glamorized criminal acts against women and allowed men to legitimize these acts in their heads as acts of romanticism. Maybe Shyam Tandel saw one too many Hindi films. I don't know.'

There was silence in the room as everyone travelled back in time in their minds, and Shinde took a long drag of his

Gold Flake, followed by a sip of his beer. Arjun sighed and continued.

' It was a vain hope that Shyam Tandel would respond positively to a plea to return Lesley. I saw that with great clarity. He wasn't going to give the girl back. He would rather kill her than return her to Greg. Therein lay the danger. But he would have no choice if someone challenged him for the throne of the twin villages. He would have to fight, and it would be to the death.

Shinde stopped in mid-swallow. Suddenly, things were beginning to make sense.

Arjun said, 'And you have to remember that I owed both Lesley and Greg big time. The choice to stay away was removed from me."

***

# Chapter Twenty-One

There had been a bit of a break as Shinde had requested the use of the facilities.

'Frankly speaking, boss, it's not only his capacity to drink that is amazing, but he also has a very strong bladder. I don't know anyone like him,' said Kalidas, and Lhoncha nodded with grudging agreement.

'He is a very unusual man. I like the fact that he is not intimidated by you reprobates,' said Arjun to a round of laughter. Shinde returned, accompanied by a bodyguard, and settled into his seat. He lit a Gold Flake and took a look at his beer, weighed his options, and topped off his glass.

'Your facilities are excellent, I must say,' said Shinde. 'Top notch. I felt I was at the Taj Hotel.

'I would love to take credit for it, but it was way before my time.' Arjun shrugged, removing the need for any further discussions. He continued. 'There is a tradition in the village. The strongest one sits on the throne. Anyone can challenge the king for the throne. But once a challenge is made, the king has to accept it, or abdicate the throne immediately. If he accepts the challenge, then it is to the death, or until quarter is asked. In three hundred years, no king or challenger has asked for mercy. It has always been to the death.'

Arjun raised his hand, snuffing out the chances of a question he saw coming from Shinde. 'Patience, doctor. I will give you all the answers shortly.'

*

'The Iranians had hired Indrajit to supervise the training of their assassins.'

Shinde took a drag of his Gold Flake and then nourished it with a large swig of his beer. He looked mildly confused at the sudden change in direction of the story.

'Patience, doctor,' Arjun said again. 'It will all start to make sense.'

As Shinde took a drag, Arjun continued, 'In the annals of history, where legends intertwine with reality, the story of Indrajit, the renegade warrior from the south of India, stands out as a testament to the confluence of cultures and the art of warfare. Known for his unparalleled skills in weaponry and combat, Indrajit was a master tactician, revered and feared across the Indian subcontinent. His journey from a rebellious youth to a sought-after military trainer for several governments before finally inexplicably choosing the Iranians is a tale of intrigue, strategy, and the relentless pursuit of excellence.

'Indrajit was born in the lush, verdant landscapes of Kerala, a region known for its rich cultural heritage and martial traditions.

'From a young age, he was drawn to the ancient martial art of *Kalaripayattu*, a discipline that combined physical prowess with spiritual enlightenment. Under the tutelage of seasoned masters, Indrajit honed his skills, mastering the use of traditional weapons such as the *urumi*, a flexible sword, and the spear, as well as developing expertise in hand-to-hand combat.

'Despite his prodigious talent, Indrajit was not content with the confines of his village.

'His spirit yearned for adventure and the opportunity to test his skills against the best warriors of his time. This restless ambition led him to become a renegade, a warrior without allegiance, who roamed the country challenging and defeating the champions of various disciplines.

'His reputation as an invincible fighter spread far and wide, earning him both admirers and adversaries. It was during this period of wandering that Indrajit's fame reached the ears of the Iranians. The Iranians, known for their strategic acumen and appreciation of martial prowess, were embroiled in a conflict that required innovative military strategies and superior combat training. Recognizing Indrajit's potential, they extended an invitation for him to join their ranks as a military advisor and trainer.

'Indrajit did his due diligence and was intrigued by the Iranians. He admired the way they were holding out against more highly funded Iraqis. He was also intrigued by the prospect of exploring this new land and learning new techniques. Much to the dismay of the British, who were wooing him in the hopes that he would be able to train their famed SAS, Indrajit accepted the Iranian offer. His journey to Iran marked the beginning of a new chapter in his life, one that would see him blend the martial traditions of the East with the strategic innovations of the West.'

Arjun continued, 'It was during his tenure in Iran that Indrajit met me, a young warrior with a broken heart and extraordinary potential. I was famous because I was the only one to survive "death camp", and Indrajit's reputation as a master trainer made him the ideal mentor. The meeting was a turning point, not only for me, but also for Indrajit, who I think saw me as a reflection of his own youthful ambition and drive.

'I was eager to absorb all that Indrajit had to offer. Under Indrajit's guidance, I learned the intricacies of close combat, the art of stealth in urban environments, and the strategies for navigating the dense jungles that characterized much of the Indian subcontinent. Indrajit also imparted lessons on the philosophy of warfare, teaching me that true mastery lay not just in physical prowess but in understanding the mind of the opponent and the dynamics of the battlefield. It was he who gave me the sacred black sword of the Cholas.'

Shinde stopped in mid swallow and said, 'What is the black sword of the Cholas?'

*

Namdeo took over the role of narrator and brought the listeners back to the last night of a king. But the time anyone realized something was amiss, most of the perimeter guards had been disabled. Baba didn't kill them. They were innocent of Tandel's crime and were only following orders. They did not deserve to die.'

'That is true,' said Arjun. 'There was no need to kill them. I just needed them out of the way.'

'"SHYAM TANDEL!" The name rang out in the darkness, shattering the silence. Lhoncha, supervising the offloading of some television sets that had been acquired from a Korean liner out in the bay waiting for docking instructions, heard the voice crashing through the darkness. Without a word, he turned and ran towards Tandel House. The king was in trouble! Several Visarjan fighters loped silently behind him.

'When they reached the big square in front of Tandel House, they found it ablaze. Someone had set fire to the ceremonial yacht that adorned the entrance of Tandel House.

'"SHYAM TANDEL!" Someone shouted his name again. Lhoncha searched through the shifting light for the source of the voice. He saw a figure standing in the centre of the main square in front of the fire. Lhoncha looked around for hidden soldiers. There were none. The person standing before the fire was alone. Admittedly, he was dressed in some weird sort of black flowing garb. But he was alone.

'A key component of the stranger's outfit, Lhoncha noticed, was the hood, which Lhoncha didn't know at the time was known as a *zukin*, concealing the stranger's identity. It also protected the wearer against the elements, although in the full spirit disclosure, Lhoncha didn't know that either. It covered the head and neck, leaving only the eyes exposed, allowing the stranger to maintain a wide field of vision, taking in the fighters that rushed into the square while remaining anonymous. They surrounded the stranger, who was oblivious to them. His eyes were fixated on the door that was the entrance to Tandel House.

'"SHYAM TANDEL!" The voice of the stranger cut through the night, harsh and implacable.

'The door of Tandel House opened, and Shyam Tandel came out. He looked confused, but he was fully dressed in fighting gear, not unlike the outfit the masked stranger was wearing. He was surrounded by a retinue of Visarjan soldiers. He stepped into the main square.

'"Who are you, stranger? Only fools go daringly where wise men think a thousand times before putting forth a single foot. Are you a fool?"

'"You have committed a crime. You have kidnapped a young girl from Colaba and are holding her in the village against her will. You have violated your code as king and deserve to be ruler no more. I challenge you for the throne of the twin villages."

'A ripple of shock ran through the bodyguards present. But there were also local villagers who came to investigate the cause of the disturbance and heard the challenge issued to the king. Shyam Tandel looked around and weighed his options. He wasn't too concerned with the stranger. He knew his combat skills were par excellence, and he was fairly certain of the outcome. What concerned him was that everyone present now knew he had kidnapped a girl, and she was a guest inside a Tandel House. He had not wanted his actions to be public knowledge until Lesley had accepted him as her man. Smaller things than this had burnt down great houses in the past. He wondered now, perhaps a little too late, whether her had overstepped his limits.

'Lhoncha stepped forward and said, "Do not bother yourself with this stranger, my lord. Let me deal with this upstart from the city." He looked at the stranger in the hood and said, "You do not have fisher blood and cannot challenge the king for the throne. However, I will enjoy ripping your arms from your body."

'And then, a shocked silence enveloped everyone present as Kalidas stepped out of the darkness.

'"I am of the Koli clan. Everyone knows me. This here is my brother." He pointed to Arjun. Everyone knew Kalidas. He came from a royal bloodline, and his forefathers had ruled the twin villages a few generations back. He was highly respected, and if he was vouching for the stranger, then it was as though it were carved in stone. The stranger had the right to challenge Shyam Tandel for the throne.

'"As brother to Kalidas Lingayat, I have the right to challenge you,' said the stranger, removing his hood. Everyone, including Shyam Tandel, gasped. He was so young. Could not be more than sixteen or seventeen.

'Someone in the crowd surrounding Arjun said, "Arey, it's that tennis player from Lovedale Building. What the fuck does he think he is doing? He gets his ass handed to him regularly by the Building Boys. He has no chance. Our king will kill him."

'Shyam Tandel felt a moment of uncharacteristic pity. "Go away now, and I will consider the challenge withdrawn. I don't want your mother to be without her son," he said.

'And then he looked into the blackness of the young man's eyes, and although Shyam was without a peer when it came to courage, a shiver ran down his spine. This was no ordinary teenager.

'Lhoncha stepped forward again, slightly ahead of his king, and said again, "This is not for you, my Lord. Let me deal with this upstart."

'Shyam Tandel shook his head and said, "A challenge has been issued, and as blood brother to a Koli, this young man is within his rights. I will fight him, as is the tradition." He looked at Arjun and said, "You should not have come here, and you should not have bought up Lesley. She is mine and will reign as queen by my side. For this affront, I will have no choice but to kill you."

'Arjun looked expressionlessly at the fisher king and said, "You bought her here against her will. I am here to take your throne and take her back to her home and to the life she lives. I will not give you quarter and ask none for myself."

'A ripple of laughter rolled through the soldiers. The general opinion was that this was going to be over really soon, and everyone could go back to sleep. Even Lhoncha allowed himself a small smile.'

*

Namdeo continued the role of narrator. He had a glass of whiskey and took a sip and began, 'Shyam Tandel spoke, "What is your weapon of choice, young master? Maybe it's your tennis racket? I have heard you are a pretty good player." Again, there was a ripple of laughter. But it came to an abrupt halt as Arjun unsheathed his weapon, which had been strapped to his back. Shyam Tandel's breath caught in the back of his throat as he recognized what Arjun was holding in his hand.

'And to be honest, at that moment in time, I had no clue. But before that, let me tell you about Shyam Tandel's weapon,' said Namdeo.

'The katana in Shyam Tandel's hand was a masterfully crafted weapon, its blade gleaming with a polished sheen that reflected the light in a mesmerizing dance of shadows and highlights. The steel had been folded with expert precision, creating a subtle, wavy line that spoke to the skill of the swordsmith who forged it.

'But what truly set this katana apart, however, was the intricate inscriptions etched along the length of the blade. These inscriptions were not merely decorative; they told the storied history of the sword through the names and deeds of its previous owners.

'Each name was accompanied by a brief account, written in elegant *kanji* characters, detailing the significant events in which the sword played a role.

'The first inscription near the hilt was that of the original owner, a legendary samurai who commissioned the blade during the Sengoku period. His name was followed by a short tale of his valour in battle, where the katana was first baptized in the fires of conflict.

'Further down the blade, another name appeared, that of a renowned ronin who acquired the sword after the samurai's death. That inscription told of his wanderings and the duels he fought, each victory adding to the katana's legacy.

'There were more inscriptions revealing a lineage of warriors, each of whom had added their own chapter to the katana's history.

'Some inscriptions were more elaborate, recounting tales of honour and sacrifice, while others were simple, marking the passage of the sword from one hand to another.

'The final inscription, closest to the tip, was that of the current owner, who had vowed to uphold the traditions and honour of those who wielded the katana before. This promise was etched with a sense of reverence, acknowledging the weight of history that the blade carries.

'Together, these inscriptions transformed the katana from a mere weapon into a living chronicle, a testament to the enduring spirit of the warriors who had held it. The blade was not just a tool of war; it was a keeper of stories, a bridge between the past and the present, and a symbol of the unbroken chain of honour and duty.

'Arjun looked at the blade with reverence. He was well-versed in several martial arts and had spent two years at the great Shihan Mitsuogi. He spoke with a respectful tone.

'"You have Shinatro Ito's blade! He must have been extremely pleased with you to have given you his blade."

'Shyam was uncharacteristically humble "He was. It was handed down from master to student, and I was supposed to have handed it down to my best student. But I am not a master, nor do I intend to be. I will not hand this blade down to anyone. The inscriptions on the blade will end with me. If I am to die here, please preserve my weapon. Someone eventually will come for it. It may take some time for news of my death to reach Shintaro san's ears. If he is still alive, he will come for it. If he doesn't," Shyam shrugged, "Then I guess it is yours."

'Shyam Tandel smiled. "But don't start making any plans just yet, young sir. It will take a stronger-willed man than you to separate me from my blade." Shyam Tandel smiled and thought to himself, *This shouldn't take long*.

'"What weapon will you be using?"

'Then there was a gasp as Arjun unsheathed his weapon that had been wrapped in a woollen blanket.'

*

Now it was Arjun's turn to take over as storyteller. Shinde had exhausted the supply of cigarettes, and as everyone waited for a new packet to arrive, Shinde drained his glass and refilled it immediately.

'The legendary black sword of the Cholas is a fascinating tale interwoven with history, mythology, and the grandeur of one of South India's most powerful dynasties. The Chola dynasty, which reigned from the 9th to the 13th centuries, is renowned for its remarkable contributions to art, architecture, and governance. Among the many legends that have emerged from this period, the story of the black sword stands out as a symbol of power, mystery, and divine intervention.

'According to legend, the black sword was forged by a master blacksmith under the guidance of the Chola King himself. It was said to be made from a rare meteorite metal that had fallen from the heavens, giving the sword its distinctive black hue and otherworldly properties. The sword was not only a weapon of war but also a symbol of divine right and the king's unyielding authority.

'The Cholas believed that the sword was blessed by the gods, particularly by Lord Shiva, who was a central deity in their religious practices. It was said that the sword could cut through any armour and was imbued with the power to protect the kingdom from invaders. The blade was reputed to be unbreakable, and its sharpness was unmatched, making it a formidable weapon on the battlefield.

'The black sword was passed down through generations of Chola rulers, each of whom wielded it with reverence and respect. It was often used in ceremonial functions and was a central part of the coronation rituals, symbolizing the continuity of the Chola lineage and their divine mandate to rule.

'The legend also speaks of a prophecy associated with the sword. It was foretold that as long as the sword remained in the possession of the Cholas, their dynasty would flourish and their empire would remain unconquered. However, if the sword were ever lost or stolen, it would signal the end of their reign and the decline of their empire.

'Throughout their rule, the Cholas expanded their territory across South India and beyond, establishing a vast empire that extended to parts of Southeast Asia. The black sword was a constant companion in their military campaigns, and its legend grew with each victory. However, as with many legends, the fate of the black sword was shrouded in mystery. Some stories suggest that it was lost during a battle, while others claim it was hidden away to protect its power from falling into the wrong hands. Despite its uncertain fate, the legend of the black sword endured through the ages, a testament to the Chola dynasty's enduring legacy and the rich tapestry of Indian history.'

Shinde found that he had stopped drinking and smoking, and was holding his breath without realizing that he was doing so. He exhaled slowly and said, 'I must admit that I did not expect to be on such a roller coaster ride when I woke up this morning. The legend of the black sword of the Cholas isn't common knowledge. You have to be a student of ancient indian history to know about it. How I know about the legend is not important. The million-dollar question is, how is something that priceless in your hands? What did you do to deserve to be the keeper of such a precious treasure?'

'Have a drink, doctor.' Arjun smiled and thought about Indrajit. He wondered where his master was. Was he even alive?

'We still have a long way to go, doctor. You will know everything before the cock crows thrice. But the sword, and how it came into my hands, is not a story for you as yet.'

*

'As the two warriors faced each other, the atmosphere crackled with tension. The spectators, a mix of locals and soldiers drawn by the promise of bloodshed, held their breath in anticipation. Not everyone got to witness a battle to the death for the throne in their lifetime. Everyone knew of ShayamTandel and his formidable skills. His boat had once been captured by the coast guard, and he had been taken as a prisoner to INS Kunjali, a naval base near Sasoon dock. The naval base had some of the famous "black cat" commandos on site, going through some training drills. Shyam Tandel saw them and recognized them for who they were, and challenged them to a fight to the death with the condition that he would go free if he won. The base commandant, a bit of an action junkie, agreed to the terms. Rumour had it that Shyam Tandel fought three black cat commandos of the Indian army and killed two of them, letting the third one live. The commandant of the base had been so impressed that he kept his word and released Shyam.

'The youngster was an enigma. Most people had seen him with his tennis racket going to the tennis courts at Cooperage or coming back. It was quite unbelievable that he was there in the middle of the night, outside Tandel House, challenging their king to battle for the throne. Of course, the youngster had no chance. That was quite obvious. But would their king show mercy when the time came? That was the only question preying on all the spectators' minds. The moon rose higher, casting a silver hue over the arena, as if nature itself was holding its breath for the impending clash.

'Arjun took a deep breath, centring himself. This would be different to his previous kills. There would be no camouflage, no sudden attacks on an unprepared enemy. Here, the enemy was prepared and obviously extremely capable. This would be a battle of skill and endurance. He wasn't sure if he was ready, but that was moot. He was in the middle of it all now. There would be no prize for coming second.

'Shyam Tandel, Keeper of the Shintaro Ito Katana, stood with a calm demeanour. His stance was low and balanced, his feet planted firmly on the ground. The katana, known for its razor-sharp edge and perfect balance, was an extension of his arm, held with a relaxed grip that belied the lethal precision he was capable of. His eyes, sharp and focused, met Arjun's with a silent acknowledgement of the challenge before them.

'Arjun, wielding the legendary Chola black sword, exuded a formidable presence. The sword, with its dark blade that seemed to absorb the light around it, was held in a two-handed grip, its weight and authority evident in Arjun's stance. His posture was upright and commanding, his gaze unwavering as he prepared to engage in a duel that would test his skills to the limit.

'A dog howled in the darkness, an eerie sound laden with menace wafting through the night air. Shyam attacked first with no warning, his katana slicing through the air with a whisper. He employed a technique known as *laijutsu*, a swift, fluid draw and strike that aimed to catch Arjun off guard. The blade flashed in the fading light, a blur of motion that was beautiful in its viciousness and intensity.

'Arjun, it seemed, was effortlessly prepared. With an almost lazy movement, he brought the black sword up in a defensive arc, employing a high guard position that allowed him to absorb and redirect Shyam's attack. The clash of steel rang out, echoing across the water like a violent symphony.

'The fight was a contrast of styles. Shyam's speed and agility were countered by Arjun's incredible anticipation and strategic mind, which made Shyam seem slow. Shyam employed samurai techniques, using quick, precise strikes aimed at Arjun's vital points, while Arjun responded with Indrajit moves that Shyam did not recognize, utilizing powerful, sweeping cuts that leveraged the full weight of the black sword, pushing the fisher king back on the defensive every time.

'Despite Shyam's skill and determination, he was hit with the sudden realization that he was totally outmatched. Arjun's mastery of the black sword was overwhelming. Within minutes, the tide of battle shifted decisively in Arjun's favour. He executed a technique which Shyam recognized too late as *Makiuchi*, a winding strike that entangled Shyam's katana, creating an opening for a decisive blow. How did this kid know an ancient isshinryu technique? He was combining Japanese sword fighting techniques with something else that Shyam did not recognize. He did not have any time for an answer, as the end came swiftly.

'With a series of powerful, calculated strikes, Arjun broke through Shyam's defences. He used *Kiriotoshi*, a downward cutting technique that combined offence and defence. There was a surge of endorphins through his bloodstream, and Shyam felt no pain as his katana fell to the ground, his sword hand severed above the elbow, hung loosely, connected to the arm by a piece of flesh. Arjun did not stop. He stepped back slightly and then plunged the Chola black sword into Shyam Tandel's heart. Shyam Tandel's eyes widened with pain, and before anyone could blink their eyes, Arjun had swivelled around counterclockwise, sword flashing, and separated Shyam Tandel's head from his body. Everyone present gasped in shock and disbelief as the king of the twin fisher villages lay dead. The entire encounter had taken no more than three minutes. Arjun straightened up and stood over the body of the fallen king. He looked at Lhoncha, who was face reflected the shock that everyone around felt.

'"Leader of the Visarjan warriors! Do you question my right to the throne?"

'Before Lhoncha could speak, a ripple ran through the crowd. Lhoncha stopped what he was about to say, looked behind Arjun, and growled in a loud voice, "NO!"

'Arjun turned around. Eight members of the Tandel clan stepped out of the crowd, weapons in hand. Arjun looked at them and then looked back at Lhoncha.

'"Are these your troops?"

'Lhoncha shook his head and said, "They are kinsmen to Shyam Tandel. They are not Visarjan."

'Unbidden, the words came out of Lhoncha's mouth before he knew what he was saying, "Lord, let me take care of them. They know not what they do."

'Arjun raised his hand, silencing Lhoncha. He turned and faced the eight warriors and said, "You can still leave here alive. No one will think you guys are a bunch of fags. I strongly suggest you run and run quickly."'

Namdeo spoke, 'At that time, no one understood what the boss was doing. All we saw was the eight Tandel fighters being humiliated in front of us all. It was obvious that they would have no choice but to respond with violence.'

Arjun spoke, 'If you kill a king, you must destroy any potential challenges to the throne that could come from survivors of his clan.'

Shinde nodded, understanding unambiguously. He took a drag of his Gold Flake and finished his glass of beer, and then proceeded to top his glass off.

'I think we may need another jug of beer,' said Arjun with a smile, and another jug magically appeared.

Namdeo continued the story. 'Each fighter was skilled and determined, their loyalty to Shyam unquestioned and deeply ingrained in their DNA.

'They moved with a unity born of years of training together, their intent clear as they surrounded Arjun, ready to avenge their fallen leader. Arjun took three deep breaths, oxygenating his system as he steeled himself for the challenge ahead. The Tandel clan fighters struck, hoping to draw first blood, attacking with a coordinated ferocity, their movements synchronized and their strikes relentless. The clearing became a whirlwind of motion, the clash of steel ringing out as Arjun fought to hold his ground.

'The first of the Tandel fighters lunged at Arjun, with a thrust aimed at Arjun's midsection. Arjun parried the attack with a swift deflecting move that redirected the blade away from his body. He countered with a diagonal cut that sent his opponent reeling. Another fighter closed in from the side, with a horizontal slash aimed at Arjun's torso. Arjun anticipated the move, turning to meet the attack with a powerful *Kaeshi-waza*, a counter-technique that transformed defence into offence, forcing his adversary back. The Tandel fighters attacked from all directions. Surely one of them would be able to get through. They were sadly mistaken. This tennis player seemed to see the whole board and seemed to be able to anticipate every move by every attacker before it was made.

'The Tandel fighters found themselves struggling against Arjun's skills and the legendary power of the black sword. Arjun moved with the fluidity and grace of a ballet dancer, coupled with the ferocity of a rattlesnake, each strike calculated and precise, drawing blood almost every time before moving out of striking range.

'"Death by a thousand cuts! So I guess it's safe to assume that tennis is not the only thing he's good at," said Lhoncha to Kalidas.

'Kalidas grinned, not letting his worry show and said, "You have no idea."

'As the battle raged on, the villagers, remnants of the Tandel clan and the Visarjan troops watched in awe and fear. The Tandel fighters began to falter under the relentless assault, their unity and will tested by Arjun's prowess.

'In the midst of the chaos, a moment of clarity for all present emerged. Arjun was not what he seemed. He held the black sword. No one but a true king could wield the legendary weapon. And as everyone watched, with a decisive series of strikes, he broke through the Tandel fighters' defences, turning the tide of battle in his favour. He employed *Tsubame Gaesh*i, a swift, unpredictable technique that involved a rapid change of direction, catching his opponents off guard, slipping and sliding amongst them, moving out of range just as they struck, striking back with precision. One by one, the Tandel fighters died, their resolve no match for Arjun's skill and determination. If it wasn't so horrific, it would have been a thing of beauty.

'The clearing, once filled with the sounds of battle, grew silent as the last of the Tandel warriors died, his head flying off his torso and landing at the feet of Lhoncha, leaving Arjun standing amidst the fallen. His breath belied his fatigue, and his body was relatively unmarked by the struggle.

'As the dust settled and the reality of the battle set in, the villagers of Sunder Nagari and Geeta Nagar faced a new dawn. The loss of Shyam Tandel and the defeat of the Tandel clan fighters left a void, a sense of uncertainty that hung over the villages like a shadow. Arjun, though victorious, bore the weight of his actions. The battle had been a test not only of skill, but of character, a reminder of the cost of power and the burden of legacy. As he sheathed the black sword, its dark blade gleaming in the moonlight, he reflected on the path that had brought him here and the choices that lay ahead. There was a sound of pattering feet, and he turned around, preparing for yet another battle. He was surprised. Lhoncha and all of the Visarjan warriors stood in battle formation in front of him.

'"VISARJAN!" Lhoncha yelled, and five hundred men dropped to their knees and paid homage to the new king. Arjun unsheathed the legendary Chola black sword once more and pointed it to the sky.

'One thousand fists drummed the earth, and a roar emerged from the soldiers as Arjun rent the sky with the famous war cry, "Raja Raja Chola!"'

***

# Chapter Twenty-Two

'I cannot be sure when it happened. Maybe he saw me kill Shyam, or maybe he arrived later when the Tandel clansmen fell to my sword, but Kevin Rozario, prized *sicario* for the Building Boys, came to visit Shyam Tandel, who was like a brother to him, and instead witnessed something rather unexpected. Can you imagine the shock to his system when he came upon the scene in the twin villages? His friend and a large number of Tandel clansmen were dead. The legendary Visarjan bowing to my outstretched sword?'

Shinde felt the hairs on his arms rise as he drained his glass. He tried to keep a cool demeanour as he refilled his glass and took a long drag of his Gold Flake, but it was impossible not to be infected with the excitement of the story. Arjun continued.

'There was no question about what needed to be done. Kevin could not be allowed to live. The secret of the new ascension to the throne needed to be kept under wraps until there was a clear consolidation of power and all threats to the throne were wiped out. And as I saw Kevin, I realized that the Building Boys needed to be removed from the board.'

Shinde filled in the blanks. 'And being the chess master, you set a plan in motion that would result in the elimination of the upper echelon of the Building Boys. Let me traverse the rabbit hole, and tell me if I'm on the ball. You decided to kill Kevin. Now, that would enrage the Building Boys and make them come hunting for you. You pass on information that you will be at a particular location. Their desire for revenge makes them blind to the obvious—that they are being set up. And voila! You have led them into your kill box. And no one will escape.'

'Very, very good, doctor,' said Arjun. 'I'm most impressed by your powers of deduction. Do go on.'

Shinde took a drag of his Gold Flake, blew out a smoke ring, and said, 'Well, I guess it's safe to say these Building Boys are no longer a threat. To the world, there has been a power shift, and Shyam Tandel has been toppled. This is the fisher way. No one will question that. But you have not declared yourself king. No, that would raise too many questions about you, and you are most comfortable in the shadows. And anyway, the true power lies behind the throne.'

Shinde frowned as he tried to do the math. He brightened up and said, 'The smart thing to do would be to install someone you trust on the throne. That's what you would do.' And then Shinde almost shouted out the name, 'Kalidas! That is why Kalidas sits on the throne. He is of royal blood and will be widely accepted. But that would require the Visarjan troops and Lhoncha to be complicit in this plan.'

Shinde took a swig of his beer and looked around at the table, total comprehension dawning on him. 'All of you are part of this. You are the inner circle. I think I will refer to you as the inner circle chiefs from now on.'

Namdeo guffawed, not realizing how prophetic Shinde was and said, 'That's a good name. Alright then, story time is over. Are we in agreement about Baig?'

Arjun stood up and looked around at his war council, and said, 'I think that Doctor Shinde has proved tonight, if nothing else, that he can drink us all collectively under the table. That having been said, I believe he adds value to our organization. I propose that he now acts as our eyes and ears on the streets and joins us in the search for this butcher called The Plumber. And if he says we can use Baig, then I believe him.'

Namdeo came across and slapped Shinde on the shoulder and said, 'Bhai, you are an animal. I cannot believe you drank so much and are still cold-cocked sober.'

The rest of the group gathered around Shinde, congratulating him on being accepted into their brotherhood.

No one in the room, not even Arjun, ever imagined that this little group gathered together in Tandel House would become an integral part of a much bigger organization in the not-so-distant future.

*

It was late in the afternoon when his doorbell rang. Inspector Baig was still feeling the effects of the all-nighter from the previous evening. It had been an eventful night, to say the least. There was never a night without an incident in Colaba. It seemed that all the crazies came out to play after dark, with most of the really violent incidents occurring between one and four in the morning. However, the previous night had been nothing short of groundbreaking.

Najma, one of the local prostitutes, was walking her beat as usual down Mereweather Road behind Electric House. She had just finished servicing a fat Gujarati businessman in the back seat of his Mercedes-Benz and the *gujju* had been uncharacteristically generous with his payment, adding a large tip, which had earned him a freebie blow job. Suffice it to say, Najma was in fairly good spirits as she walked down Mereweather Road. She contemplated calling it quits for the night. It was still fairly early, she had a large wad of cash in her pocket, and if she left immediately, she would be in time to tuck her little boy into bed and maybe get to snuggle up and sleep with him. Most nights, he stayed with Najma's mother, an ex-street walker herself.

As she contemplated her next move, a large black Mercedes drew up next to her. It seemed to be a night for Mercedes-Benz owners to be trolling the streets for a quick one. Najma could never understand how guys who were so rich and could afford the most expensive call girls liked to slum it with the lowly street walkers. She stopped and bent down, and placed her elbows on the now open window, and was pleasantly surprised by the handsome young man behind the state-of-the-art steering wheel smiling back at her. The young man didn't haggle about the rather exorbitant price Najma quoted. He even promised a good tip, and Najma slipped into the plush passenger seat, and the Mercedes-Benz headed towards Chandni Guest House in Fort.

Chandni Guest House was one of those establishments where you did not have to provide your bona fides upon check-in and rented rooms by the hour. Najma and her *Giraak*, or customer, were shown to a room on the second floor by a grubby little waiter who provided them with a condom on the house. Chandni Guest House believed in safety first and repeat customers. The foreplay was intense and much against her code, Najma began to feel the fires of passion burn in that pit of her stomach.

The handsome young man gently placed her on the bed and rolled her over so that she was on her stomach. He got on top of her, gently nibbling the nape of her neck, and Najma moaned in pleasure. As the thought that this was a wonderful way to top off the night crossed her mind, there was a moment of flashing violence as the handsome young man knocked her out with a blow to the back of her head with a leather cosh that he had produced while Najma was in the throes of ecstasy.

Najma wasn't sure how long she had been unconscious, but when she came to, she was still on her stomach, but now she was spread-eagled and tied to the bed. Najma craned her neck, looked around to take stock of her situation and became horribly aware of three things. First, she had a throbbing headache that showed no signs of receding. Second, they had been joined by a beefy, not entirely unpleasant-looking older man. The third very confusing thing was that there was a small camp stove connected to a plug socket on the wall.

Then Najma saw the knives appear in the hands of the beefy, older, not entirely unpleasant-looking man, and before she could scream, the handsome young man shoved a gag into her mouth. They both smiled at her and then looked at each other, and the older man said, '*Chalo* yaar, let's have some *raand makhani*.' Both men guffawed at what was obviously a private joke. The older man fired up the stove, and Najma began to scream into the gag as she realized what was about to happen.

The gluteus max is a very sensitive part of the human body on account of the number of nerve endings, including the sciatic nerve, that are housed there. So, when the older man stuck a fork in Najma's shapely behind, she screamed in agony. What happened next made her vomit into the gag. The older man cut out a piece of Najma's ass and used the fork to deposit it on the stove. As the meat began the sizzle, the smell of roasting flesh filled the air, and Najma vomited again. She began to choke on her vomit, and the handsome young man hastily removed the gag as the older man shouted, 'Don't let her die. Her meat will taste much better while she is still alive.'

Najma spat out her vomit and began to scream. She'd gotten a few loud ones out before the duo gagged her again. But her screams had penetrated the thin walls at Chandni Guest House, and several neighbours came out of the adjacent rooms. Someone yelled for the manager, who was having himself a free blow job from a hooker who wanted a free room for the night, and had promised anything he wanted. The manager had insisted on a preview and was in the middle of testing the merchandise when the commotion on the floors above got his attention. He hastily removed his penis from the hooker's mouth and rushed out of the door, zipping up his pants. When he got to the second floor, there was a small crowd gathered, and someone pointed to the room in question.

The first thing that assailed the manager's nostrils was the smell of cooking meat. He banged on the door and shouted, 'Abey, chutiya, there is no cooking allowed on the premises. If you want something, we can ask for take-out delivery.'

There was a reverberating silence all around as everyone waited with bated breath for an answer from the room. Najma began to scream through the gag, and the manager picked up her muffled screams when he pressed his ear to the door. He was experienced enough and had witnessed way too many horrors to not recognize that there was something terrible happening inside the room. He placed a call to the police emergency hotline and also called the police station.

By the time the police arrived, it had been half an hour, and by the time they broke down the door, a third of Najma's shapely left ass cheek had been well received by the handsome young man and the older, not entirely unpleasant-looking older man. The interruption by the police wasn't so well received, though. Inspector Baig was the first through the door and had almost puked at the sight of Najma's butchered behind and the two men sitting next to her and chewing on well-done pieces of her. With a wild bellow of rage, the handsome young man launched himself at the intruding inspector, knife in hand. Baig dropped to his left knee and punched the flying cannibal in the testicles really hard as he flew over. The handsome young man screamed briefly in agony and was unconscious as he hit the floor. His older partner stared down the face of four Lee Enfield 303s and did not put up any resistance. He did give Najma one last lingering look as he was led out. By the time they got the cannibals to jail, made sure Najma was taken to St George's Hospital, Baig made out his report, filed it, and then got home at eight in the morning. It seemed like he had barely closed his eyes when his doorbell rang. He stumbled out of bed, swearing by all that was holy that if it was not god at his doorstep, somebody was going to die.

'Good morning, Inspector.' It was the medical examiner.

'What the hell are you doing here? And how do you know where I live?' snapped Baig, barely hiding his irritation.

'Well, it's not really a state secret. I just asked around at the police station. Namaste, bhabi!' Shinde joined his palms in greeting as Inspector Baig's wife appeared behind.

'Salma, this is Eknath Wadekar. He is the medical examiner attached to Colaba police station. Although I have no idea why he is here.'

Salma Baig was fair, tall, and extremely pretty. With a radiant, welcoming smile. 'Please excuse my husband's bad manners, bhaiya. Come in and have some tea and *pakoras*.'

'No, no, bhabi, I am sorry to intrude so early in the morning. I just need a word with Inspector saab. It won't take even five minutes.'

When they were alone, Shinde spoke, 'It's about The Plumber.'

Shinde closed his eyes in controlled anger. 'What happened? Has he struck again?'

'No, Inspector, but you remember I told you that you need help from outside the police force?'

'Yes, I remember. I also remember you being rather disparaging when it came to my colleagues.'

'Guilty as charged. But I come with some good news. I have gone to someone who can help us.'

'Well, bring him to the police station this evening.'

'It doesn't work that way with this guy. We will have to go to him. And I need to warn you to keep an open mind. You're really going to need your mind to be as open as possible.'

'What do you mean? What have you got yourself into?'

'Something good. You have to trust me, Inspector. It will all become clear to you. But just to let you know that we will be going somewhere you have not gone before, and you will have to come alone.'

***

# Chapter Twenty-Four

It was with great difficulty that Inspector Baig remembered that Eknath Wadekar had told him to keep an open mind. He had been taken from his apartment in the police chawl to Strand Cinema. There had been a taxi waiting outside his house, and it irritated Baig that everyone seemed to know where he lived. They sat in Strand Coffee House and ordered two chais with pav. Their chais arrived piping hot along with the traditional warm buns, and as they sipped on the tea and chewed on the delicious bread, Baig found his irritation retreating in the face of Eknath Wadekar's irrepressibly strong personality.

They talked about the Building Boys and how their reign seemed to have come to an abrupt end.

'It all started with us finding the bodies of Catholic Niggger Boy and Bobby "Shiv" Kathuria on the side of the road near the Fariyas Hotel,' explained Baig. 'They had been really beaten to a pulp. Of course, there were no witnesses. And don't get me wrong, I totally understand. Who the hell wants to give a *panchnama* and then be tangled with the likes of the police? I get that. Still, it was all really weird. I mean, those two guys were hard as nails and twice as mean as a cobra. Killing them must have taken a lot of planning and a lot of men. And it happened right near the fisher villages. There was no reaction from Shyam Tandel and his men, which was pretty weird. Then there have been rumours of Shyam himself being removed from power, and I heard that Kalidas Lingayat sits on the throne of the twin villages.'

Baig shrugged his shoulders, sipped his tea, took a bit of pav, and continued, 'Of course, I'm just a lowly inspector. No one tells me anything, but I can tell you this much. If I knew someone in the village was responsible for the deaths of those two lowlifes, I would go in, regardless of the consequences.

My future is forewritten, and I will not hide in the shadows. I've taken an oath, and once I put on my uniform, I will stay true to that oath. By the way, you have to tell me why you like to be called to called Shinde. I mean, your real name is Eknath Wadekar.'

Shinde laughed, and as he began to explain the story of Shinde, the fox, two taxis drew up in front of Strand Coffee House. Shinde finished off the last of his pav, drained his glass, got up and said, 'To be continued later, Inspector. We need to go. Our transportation has arrived.'

Baig peered out and saw that the lead taxi was empty and the one following had four tough-looking passengers who had gotten out. He thought he recognized two of them, but couldn't be sure. He sighed, pushed back his chair, and walked out into the warm sunlight. *What the hell had this crazy medical examiner got him mixed up in?* He did not resist the pat-down he was given. One of the tough guys smiled a dangerous smile and said, 'It's for your own safety, Inspector saab. Better you don't give in to temptation.' And he didn't resist the hood that was put over his head. As everything turned dark, Baig's last thought was that it was turning out to be a beautiful day in Colaba.

*

Baig was blinded, but he kept his wits about him and made use of his remaining senses to try and orient himself. He listened to the sounds around him and figured they were in Colaba market, judging by the cacophony around him. The taxi transporting him was moving slowly, and after about ten minutes or so, the sounds of the market reduced considerably. Then he heard shouts and orders being given. An engine started up and then another. The taxi halted momentarily and then carried on. By the time the taxi came to a halt, Baig estimated it was about fifteen minutes. Which meant he was still in Colaba. Then came the smell of drying fish, and much before Baig was led out and his hood removed, he knew he was inside the fisher village. Whether it was Sundernagari or Geeta Nagar, it didn't matter. Baig felt the briefest stab of apprehension. Had he pissed someone off? Had that fucking doctor been sent to lure him to his death? He wished he had hugged his wife instead of being so abrupt with her when he had left. *Fricking hindsight was so fucked up*, thought Baig as the hood was removed, and he squinted into the sunlight.

Five men stood before him, and as Baig's vision adjusted to the light, he saw that the man standing to his right was a giant. He must have been seven feet!

*That has to be Lhoncha*, thought Baig. *Fuck me, it's not some old wives' tale! The fucker really is a giant.*

He looked for Shyam Tandel and couldn't see him anywhere. Shyam Tandel he knew. He had seen him a couple of times with Billimoria. Where was the Fisher King? Were the rumours true? Had he been knocked off the throne? If that was true, then who sat on the throne of the twin villages? His gaze was drawn to the person standing in the centre of the group. As he looked at Arjun, nothing was making any sense to Baig. This was just a kid. He seemed completely out of place in this group of extremely tough and dangerous fighters. Then the kid spoke, and Baig took a closer look.

'Welcome, Inspector Baig. I hope your journey was comfortable. I hope my men were not disrespectful to you? They had explicit orders to handle you with the respect you deserve.'

Everything started making even less sense. It seemed that the kid was in command. The kid seemed to command a measure of deference and respect that was reserved for a top boss. Or a king! Nothing was computing for Inspector Baig, and then, to add to the confusion, Shinde stepped forward and shook hands with the kid. It seemed that he may have bowed ever so slightly.

Baig was led into a large mansion that stood on the border between the two fisher villages. That was obviously the legendary Tandel House. But where was Shyam Tandel? And why was the giant following the kid with a Doberman feel about him? He was the head of the dreaded Visarjan troops who owed their loyalty to the ruler of the fisher villages. At least this is what Baig had been led to believe. One could never really tell what was going on in the damn villages, which were a law unto their own. But obviously, there had been some sort of power shift that no one was aware of. And then there was the medical examiner chatting with the kid like he was something special.

They entered Tandel House, and the first hammer dropped.

'Welcome to Lingayat House,' said the kid.

Baig had prided himself on being able to be cool under trying circumstances. The fact was that he was actually very calm under fire, and nothing really rattled his cage. So the rumours were true. The king had fallen! But this revelation that the person he thought was the undisputed ruler of the twin villages was no longer the king was not the type of news one got while having a cup of tea. This was high-level stuff, definitely out of his pay grade, and he didn't feel too comfortable being burdened with this knowledge. Baig didn't let his shock show. He stayed ice cool, but his brain was moving at the speed of light. That explained the absence of Shyam Tandel. He was out. Again, from what Baig had discerned over the years, the only way the throne changed hands was through single combat with no quarter being asked or given. When had this happened, and why did no one know about it? Was Shyam Tandel dead?

The kid spoke again, as though answering his unasked questions. 'I know all this must be a lot to digest, but Kalidas Lingayat sits on the throne of the twin villages. Shyam Tandel is no longer with us. The new king is inside, awaiting your arrival.'

They passed through the main hall. Weapons from past rulers hung on the walls. Baig saw the katana of Shyam Tandel displayed, but apart from the fact that while he wondered who had been wielding a Japanese weapon of war, it never struck Baig that the katana belonged to the erstwhile ruler of the twin fisher villages.

They entered the throne room, and everyone stood to attention. Kalidas Lingayat, at twenty years of age, was not much older than the kid who seemed to be the spokesman for the day. But he got up from the throne with remarkable alacrity and stood before the kid, and again, much to the shock of Baig, there was that slight bow. It definitely seemed to Baig that the king of the twin villages had just bowed to the kid. The kid put his arm around Kalidas, turned, and smiled at Inspector Baig.

'Come, Inspector. Let us go to the table and talk there.'

They went through the throne room, and Baig got his first look at the oblong table where several generations of warriors going back five hundred years had held war councils. Baig was no fool. He realized that he was in a world into which very few strangers had set foot. He needed to be very careful; otherwise, chances were bright that Salma would be a widow and no one would ever find his body.

The kid went and sat at the head of the table. 'Come, Inspector. Sit next to me. We have much to talk about. Shinde tells me only good things about you. It looks as though we must team up to catch this butcher that goes by the name of The Plumber.'

Baig sat to the right of the kid. Shinde came and sat next to him. Kalidas Lingayat sat on the left. A bunch of very dangerous-looking men came and sat down in the unoccupied chairs. Baig looked around and figured that there was a good chance he was going home that evening in one piece. He breathed a sigh of relief. The worst was over. Now the next step was to find out who this kid was and what he knew about

The Plumber. Why would the twin villages be bothered with a serial killer? No one, not even The Plumber, would dare set foot there.

'Let me introduce myself, Inspector Baig. My name is Arjun. I speak on behalf of the Kaildas King of the twin villages of Sundernagari and Geeta Nagar.'

Kalidas opened his mouth to speak, but Arjun raised his right hand and shook his head, effectively silencing the king. *Like a parent admonishing a child*, thought Baig. And not for the first time that day, Baig wondered what that damn medical examiner had got him into.

***

# Chapter Twenty Four

It was around midday, and Inspector Baig felt a slight rumbling in his stomach. He hadn't had anything to eat since the pav at Strand Coffee House, and that had been well digested after he had been updated with the change in the power structure in the twin villages and the events leading up to it. It was surreal. The kid sitting next to him was some sort of ninja who had killed Shyam Tandel because he had kidnapped a girl.

'Where is she now?' he asked about Lesley.

'She was taken by Ghaniya and Namdeo back home. Greg had been deposited there earlier. From the time he was kicked unconscious by the border guard, he stayed comatose until he was in his apartment, and therefore had no idea what had transpired. He must have wondered about my sudden disappearance, but with the return of Lesley, he was delirious with happiness and forgot about all the nagging questions that may have taken root while he was sitting in his apartment expecting the worst. He was just glad that she was back. He decided to quit sailing the high seas. I had visited them a couple of times, and he told me that he had made enough to sustain himself comfortably and take care of Lesley. I have a very close connection with that couple, but it is time to reduce my presence in their lives.'

There was a tinge of sadness in Arjun's voice as he continued, 'We have reached a fork in the road and our journeys have diverged. Anyway, my proximity to them puts them in danger. They are my weakness, and I cannot have that.'

Many years later, when the news of Lesley's and Greg's death would reach his ears, Arjun would have cause to remember his conversation with Baig, and would be eaten up with regret. But the future hadn't happened yet.

'Tell me, Inspector, how do you think The Plumber chooses his victims?'

'They are all housewives,' said Baig. 'That's the common denominator. He knows their schedules, so he knows when and for how long they will be alone. But how he knows that is still unclear.'

Arjun and Shinde nodded. They had also reached the same conclusion.

'Does this mean that I am a part of the team?' asked Baig. 'Just want to be sure I'm going home to my family in one piece.'

There was a general round of laughter all around, and Lhoncha said, 'If you weren't, we would probably be going for a sailboat ride into the Arabian Sea.'

Arjun raised his hand and silenced the guffaws that threatened to break out.

'My apologies, Inspector. You are a father and a husband. You are one of the good ones. And even if you weren't, we do not take lives unnecessarily. You would have just been escorted out of the villages with our best wishes if things hadn't worked out. However, I am very glad that it did. I have a good feeling about you, and I am sure we will all work very well together.'

Lhoncha came up to Baig, put an enormous paw on his left shoulder, and said, 'Just kidding, mister policeman. We are brothers now. We will protect you and your family from any trouble. Anytime.'

Baig wasn't sure how he felt about all this, but the good thing was that he wasn't going for any boat rides, and the way he looked at it, it was not too bad having this giant and his platoon of soldiers in his corner. Of course, there was the kid, who technically was his boss, and from what he had heard, having Arjun on your side was also definitely not too bad, euphemistically speaking. He looked at Shinde, who was in earnest conversation with Kalidas. Shinde listened to Kalidas intently and then looked up and said, 'We have an idea we would like to share.'

*

### *May 25$^{th}$, Geeta Nagar Village, 2000 Hours, Indian Standard Time*

Shakuntala Bai was fighting a losing battle against time. But at seventy-five, she still looked beautiful. Her skin still had the glow of a much younger person, and her teeth shone as white as when she was a child. In her younger days, she had been likened to the famous Zeenat Aman, and although she had never left Sundernagari except for the odd visit to her relatives in Nagpur, her beauty was well known. Many men had come to her door with hopes of being the one, but they all left with their dreams in tatters.

Shakuntala had a dark secret. When she was seven years old, she awoke one morning screaming with terror. In her dream, she had seen her father get sucked down into the ocean. She ran out of her cottage and found her father about to sail out into the Arabian Sea on his usual finishing run. She clung to him, weeping, and begged him not to go. He laughed and lifted her up, dried her eyes and told her that she was the love of his life and that he would bring her something special that evening. A gift from the ocean, the giver of life. 'Look,' he said, pointing at the clear blue sky. 'It's going to be a beautiful day.'

He did not return that evening as he was supposed to. Shakuntala's mother was beside herself with worry, but Shakuntala was unnaturally calm. She knew he wasn't coming back. To be honest, there was nothing that Shakuntala's father could have done. Unbeknownst to him, there had been a methane hydrate eruption. A massive release of methane from the ocean's floor had reduced the water's density so much that his ship could no longer maintain buoyancy and sank without a trace. There were no survivors. Shakuntala saw her father that night. He came to her as she slept. He was consumed with an immense sadness. 'I have left you and your mother all alone in this world. Please forgive me,' he said.

In her dream, she spoke to her father with the maturity of a woman. 'It is not your fault, baba. There is nothing to forgive. You were trying to do your best for us. We will grieve for a while, but in the end, we will survive and move on. You need to forgive yourself. If you do not, then you will be stuck in the wastelands between this world and the next. It is an exciting time for you. Your next destination is unknown, and I want you to enjoy the journey. We will all be together, but not just yet. Until then, know that Amma and I will always have you in our hearts.'

She never saw her father again, but the encounter unlocked neural pathways in her brain, and she was suddenly able to see things that were hidden from her before. It was overwhelming and terrifying for a young girl from the village. She was able to predict a devastating storm before it hit the village. The elders scoffed at the young girl, but Ramchandra Lingayat, who sat on the throne, was a man who believed discretion was the better part of valour, and ordered all boats to be hauled ashore and tied down securely. All the homes were provided with tarpaulin to be pulled over their thatched roofs. Not everyone listened to the king. They were the ones who did not survive the decimation of the hurricane that hit the village without warning one summer night. After that, no one made fun of Shakuntala.

One night, she saw the husband of her mother's friend in a dream. He was trying to tell her something, but she couldn't quite understand what he was saying. The next morning, she awoke to the news that he had passed away in his sleep. She didn't tell anyone about the visit, but her husband visited her again that night. The next morning, she went to the recently widowed neighbour and told her that her husband had opened an account in her name at the Citizens Cooperative Bank on the Colaba Causeway, and that there was enough money in that account to take care of her and her two children so that they could have a comfortable life. And then, her fame grew. People came from all over the state to seek out the girl, hoping for a favourable prediction. She saw very few of them, but always made predictions of substance, both positive and some quite devastating.

At the age of eighteen, she fell in love with Surya, a boy from the neighbourhood. And then, she received a message in her dreams. It was quite unambiguous. She had been chosen as a conduit. She had been chosen to help people. She was special, and in order to remain special, it was necessary to be unattached romantically. Forever. She saw Surya walking down a street. She saw him spontaneously combust, bursting into flames. More than the burning, it was the way he seemed to dance in a weird and twisted way, screaming as the flames ate away his flesh, that was terrifying. Shakuntala woke up drenched in sweat. The message was clearly received. Although it broke her heart, she cut herself off from Surya and never saw him again. She later heard that he had gotten married to a girl from a village near Alibaug.

Over the years, she had made many predictions and helped many people. With the passage of time, the throne changed hands, and her mother passed on. She visited Shakuntala several times before becoming a memory. Shakuntala was alone, but she was never lonely because she was always with her thoughts. Once in a while, she thought of Surya and imagined a life with him as his wife and the mother of his children, and felt a deep sadness. But the sadness was always fleeting because Shakuntala was a pragmatic woman. As she became older and the world around her evolved technologically, the number of people seeking her advice slowed down to a trickle. But she wanted for nothing. A long time ago, Ramchandra Lingayat, King of Sundernagari and then of the twin villages, had decreed that regardless of who sat on the throne, Shakuntala Bai would always be taken care of. When the Tandels ascended the throne, they maintained tradition. No one wanted to upset the gods. Now, as the winds of time turned against her, she waited for the next step in her journey and looked forward to seeing her parents again. So when she received a request from Kalidas Lingayat, she was pleasantly surprised. She had no idea that a Lingayat sat on the throne again.

*

They sat on the floor, cross-legged on some surprisingly comfortable *dhurries*. From left to right were Baig, Shinde, Arjun, Kalidas, and Namdeo. Outside the hut, the Visarjan troops set up a perimeter, and Lhoncha stood at the entrance. The dhurries had been a gift from a grateful businessman who had come to Shakuntala's door sometime in the distant past. The businessman had lost his wife to cancer and was finding it exceedingly difficult to bring up his two little boys with just his hired help. On the advice of his friends, he had hired the services of a well-known matchmaker and very soon had zeroed in on a beautiful prospective bride. She came from a middle-class family and brought along with her strong family values. But the most important thing was that she was unable to bear any children due to an attack of cholera when she was a teenager. She was no doubt the perfect choice, and very soon they were married, and the year that followed was one of the most amazing years in the businessman's life. She was an intense lover in bed and took care of the girls like they were her own. Soon, the stepsons had started calling her Amma, and the businessman's cup of joy was overflowing.

And then things started taking a turn for the worse. First, one of the sons started complaining of stomach cramps that wouldn't go away. Then the other son started complaining of the same symptoms. Doctors were called, but no one could find the cause of this ailment that had struck the two boys. And then the symptoms started getting increasingly severe. The boys began to vomit frequently, started looking sickly and weak, and were very soon confined to their beds, and it seemed that the Grim Reaper was knocking on the door. Just as things couldn't get worse for the businessman, his new bride developed the same symptoms. Desperate for a key to solving this impending disaster, and convinced that dark forces were at play, the businessman landed at Shakuntala Bai's doorstep. Shakuntala took the businessman's hands in hers, closed her eyes, and looked for an answer.

Her body convulsed as though wracked with agony, and when she opened her eyes, she looked at the businessman who was looking at her with fear-filled eyes.

'Those poor little boys,' said Shakuntala with anger in her voice. 'You have a new wife and she is the cause of your sons' suffering.'

'But how can that be, Shakuntala Bai? She is suffering from the same malady. And she stands to gain nothing. She is barren and cannot bear any children.'

'My dear sir, you have been deceived. She has lied about her inability to bear children.'

'But she is also suffering! I myself have sat with her all night, for several nights, as she tosses and turns in the throes of agony.'

'She has been dosing your children with small, undetectable amounts of arsenic for a year. And over the last month, she has also been dosing herself so that the finger of suspicion would not point at her. This is all her mother's idea. The girl herself is not to blame but has been forced into this deadly deception. Once your sons had succumbed to the poison and after an appropriate period of mourning, your wife would have had a visit from Lord Krishna in her dreams, and would have had her barren womb blessed by him. She would have been miraculously able to bear children, and you would have been so glad that your line would not end with you, it is quite probable that you would have forgotten about your dead children.'

What followed was straight out of a Hindi movie. The businessman went back home and confronted his wife, who initially denied the accusations, but after the arrival of some very hard-looking bodyguards, she confessed to the crime, completely implicating her mother. The police were called, and both the conspirators were taken into custody and were sentenced to life imprisonment without the possibility of parole. The boys were sent away to live with their aunt in Gujarat, and the businessman visited them every month. It wasn't the most ideal of situations, but it was better knowing that they were safe than having them next to him all the time and worrying about the next attack.

He came back a few days later with a suitcase full of cash. But Shakunatala had no need for money. She thanked him, but graciously rejected his gift of cash.

'I thank the Gods that your little boys are safe, Mr Rhambani, and I am glad I could help. Your boys will grow up and surpass you in business, and you can be rest assured that your legacy is cemented and will live down the ages.'

The businessman then returned the next day with very expensive hand-woven dhurries from the north-west frontier of India.

'For the nights when it gets cold, Shakuntala Bai. May these keep you warm always, and know that I live to serve you if you ever need.'

Decades later, Arjun and his motley crew sat on the dhurries in front of an ageing, but beautiful Shakuntala Bai, and waited for her to speak.

***

# Chapter Twenty-Five

'You are not the king of the twin villages.' It was a statement, not a question, and it was directed at Kalidas, who shifted uneasily. The brown eyes hadn't lost their sharpness as she ran over the group. She looked at Baig and Shinde, who looked back at her expressionlessly. She shook her head almost imperceptibly. Then her gaze fell upon the stoic face of Arjun, and she smiled.

'So the king is not really the king. But you are not more than a child yourself.'

'There was a king called Alexander, Shakuntala Bai,' said Arjun with half a smile.

Shakuntalabai nodded. 'It is said that at the age of thirty, he wept, for there were no more worlds left to conquer. Is that what you seek? A place in history?'

Arjun shook his head while the others listened intently. 'I yearn for peace, mother.'

Shakuntala Bai stretched out her hand and took Arjun's hand in hers. She closed her eyes and everything seemed to slow down to a standstill inside Shakuntala Bai's hut for what seemed an eternity, but actually, it was not more than just a few seconds. And then, she opened her eyes, and time seemed to restart. She looked at Arjun with what seemed to be wonder in her eyes.

'I am an old woman, and many have sat before me like you. Yet none of them have had your darkness or your greatness. You have seen too much blood at too young an age. You are a killer. No, not a killer, a hunter. Happiness will always just be out of reach for you for now. It is possible that you will find it, but not yet. You have an impossible burden to bear. You will carry the hopes and dreams of a fallen king and a defeated people. This will consume you, and I am unable to determine if you will emerge unscathed.'

The silence following Shakuntala Bai's prediction was deafening. Shinde squirmed uncomfortably, and Baig was fixated on a point on the thatched roof as he fought to control his emotions. *What in heaven's name had he got himself into? That damn Eknath! Oh wait! He wanted to be called Shinde. After some fucking fox! And now there was this old lady talking about the kid. What hopes and dreams? Of which people? It was all extremely sinister. Not to forget that this kid had killed Shyam Tandel and put his friend on the throne. Billimoria definitely had no clue about this turn of events.* The cool voice of Arjun brought everyone crashing back to a semblance of normalcy.

'That is in the future, mother. Between now and then, anything can happen. We have come to you with a problem.'

'You seek the killer. The one who is known as The Plumber.'

Arjun nodded and said, 'He has taken my friend's mother from him. It has fallen to me to rid the world of this madman. But I am not able to understand how he chooses his victims and the timing of his killings… he is following a pattern I do not understand.'

'Do you have anything of his? A possession, something he may have touched?'

'I'm sorry, mother, we have nothing.'

Baig interrupted Arjun. 'That's not entirely true. We do have something. Actually, we have twelve things.'

Arjun smiled, comprehension dawning immediately. 'My mistake. Yes, you do.'

'What do you have, Baig?' asked Kalidas, perplexed.

And Shinde completed the conversation. 'Twelve plumber's wrenches to be precise.'

*

By the time Baig got back, an hour had passed. In the meantime, the group inside the hut chatted and drank glasses of a delicious herbal concoction that Shakuntala Bai had prepared. It was served hot and tasted of cinnamon and cloves with a distinctive banana flavour. They filled in the gaps in Shakuntala Bai's knowledge, updating her with the goings on in the world. Shakuntala found their company unexpectedly enticing, and when Baig returned, he could hear laughter from inside Shakuntala's humble lodgings.

Lhoncha just shook his head and shrugged as he opened the thatched door and let Baig in.

"It sounds like a party in here," Baig said. He smiled and took out the wrench from his bag. 'Hope I didn't miss anything.'

'Just talking about police efficiency,' said Shinde, and everyone burst out laughing.

Baig tried to maintain a straight face as he handed the wrench over to Shakuntala.

She took the tool and sat down. She wrapped her palms around it and closed her eyes. Time seemed to stand still again. This time, Shakuntala remained with her eyes shut for about ten minutes, although it seemed longer. She rocked back and forth, humming a strange tune that seemed to come from the pit of her stomach. Suddenly, she stopped her humming and her eyes snapped open. Her eyes were unfocused, and she began to talk.

'He hunts by the stars. He worships the god of war. The women signify uncleanliness. He is trying to purify the world through his killing. He takes their hearts as an offering to his God. I am not able to see his face. It is as though his identity is being hidden from me, and I am not able to see through the veil. I don't understand how this is possible.'

Then suddenly, she gasped and said, 'Not by the stars! He worships a star. He worships the god of chaos and misery. He is not alone. He is protected by a power that has a strength I have not seen before. It will not let me see his true form.'

Kalidas was born into superstition and had grown ashen with fear. But the rest of the group, although taken aback by the unfolding events, kept their wits together.

'What do you mean, the god of chaos and misery?' asked Shinde. 'Who is the Hindu god in charge of all this? I have no idea...'

'It is not a Hindu god that he worships. If you are right, mother, then I know why he worships the morning star,' said Arjun, his voice was strained as though he was struggling to come to terms with his understanding of the situation. Everyone in the little hut, including Shakuntala, looked at Arjun, curiosity rife across all their faces. Arjun took a deep breath and began.

'In the Old Testament of Christianity, the first beings that God created were the angels. And the most favourite angel of God was Lucifer. Then God, for some reason unknown to anyone, decided to create human beings, and then again, for yet another unknown reason, decided to give them dominion over the earth. Humans became his favourite beings over the angels, and this did not sit well with Lucifer who suddenly found his most favourite status put on what seemed to be an eternal hold. So Lucifer led a revolt against God, and there was war in heaven.'

'So it was sort of a gang war going on in heaven,' said Kalidas, and everyone laughed at the simplicity of the explanation.

Arjun smiled and continued, 'Lucifer's gang lost, and Lucifer was cast out of heaven and fell to earth. He is known as the fallen angel, the devil, and Satan. But what most people don't know is that his name is Lucifer Morningstar.'

'So you think this guy is a devil worshipper?' asked Baig.

'What he does is evil, and it is well known that the devil demands human sacrifice, so either he worships Satan, or he is protected by an individual or group of individuals who worship the devil. It can't be anything else. How does he choose the time of his killing? Can you see that, mother?' There was an urgency in Arjun's voice. He wanted to get on with the business of the hunt. But he would have to be patient. He gritted his teeth as Shakuntala wrapped her palms around the wrench and closed her eyes again. Again, the eerie tone emanated from her throat, and she rocked back and forth. When she opened her eyes, she was focused and lucid. Kalidas breathed a sigh of relief. All these supernatural events were getting too much for him.

'All planets follow a predetermined path,' said Shakuntala Bai. 'And so does Mars. It transits through the zodiac signs, beginning with Aries, the sign that rules, and ending with Pisces. It takes six to seven weeks to transit through each zodiac sign. All together, the entire journey through all the zodiac signs takes about two years.'

'So each kill is connected with the transition of Mars through a particular zodiac sign,' said Arjun. 'Now we have a pattern. He killed Homi's mother five days ago. He has killed twelve times in two years, which means he is killing during the transition of Mars through every alternate zodiac sign.'

'Which means we have about fourteen weeks before his next kill,' said Shinde.

A sound similar to a growl escaped from Arjun. 'It's too long. We must catch him now. Help me, mother. Is there any way that you can pierce the veil that surrounds him?'

Shakuntala looked at the group seated in front of her with expressions ranging from fear to frustration. She took a deep breath.

'There is something that I can do. But it is for a much younger person, and I am unfortunately too old. It puts a great strain on the body, and it is almost certain that I will not survive.'

Arjun was immediately contrite. 'Please forgive me, mother. I did not mean to ask you to put yourself in danger. I would never do that. You have helped us enough. We will have to find another way.'

He stood and bowed. 'My deepest gratitude. I know that you have little need for cash. But I will arrange for you to have round-the-clock help. You are living on your own with no help, and at your age, mother, that for me is unacceptable. From now on, you will have two companions who will take care of your nourishment and anything that you might desire. It's the very least I can do.'

He turned to leave and called to Lhoncha. The giant stepped inside the hut, and everything became slightly claustrophobic. But before Arjun could give instructions to the head of the Visarjan troops, he was cut off by Shakuntala.

'I am an old woman and my time draws near. Life has been good to me. Unfortunately, a family was denied to me, but that was the price I had to pay for the power I have. I have been able to do some good, right some wrongs, and make some bad people answer for their sins. But I have never felt a power like this in all my years. I fear that this killer will not stop, and I fear that without my help, you will be clutching at straws in the wind. If this is to be my last act, then I want to do my very best to help you. And if I die…?'

The question left a very pregnant and uncomfortable pause in the room. Shakuntala looked deeply at Arjun. 'Your journey is just beginning, and you have many miles to go before you sleep. I will be gone by then, but I will wait for you on the other side for you to join me and tell me how it all worked out.'

She laughed as she took in the varying expressions around the room, ranging from grim to total panic and consternation, and said, 'Oh, don't look at me like that. It will not be for a long time. Remember that time passes differently in other dimensions. Where I am going, a thousand years is but a blink of an eye. So believe me, young warrior, when I say I will wait for you. But now, I must prepare myself to attempt to pierce the cloak that surrounds this killer. Give me a few moments.'

She got up and went to a darkened corner of the hut, and drew aside some blankets that were covering an old wooden box covered with strange carvings. From inside the box, she took out a long, thin bottle that was filled with a dark blue liquid that seemed to glow with an ethereal light.

Arjun spoke. The rest of the group seemed struck dumb with religious awe. 'What is that, mother?'

'In a hill station in the south of India called Kodaikanal, there is a place called Bear Shola Falls. It is said that deep under Bear Shola Falls runs the river of death that connects many worlds. What I have in this bottle is water from the river of death, given to me many years ago by a businessman whom I had helped. How he came by the water, I do not know, but he was told that drinking this water opens your soul to other worlds and the denizens of those worlds. I drank from this bottle once many years ago as I tried to find a missing ten-year-old girl who had been abducted from her home at night, while the parents slept in the other room. In the absence of any signs of a break-in and unable to zero in on a suspect, the police came to the natural conclusion that it just had to be the parents. By the time the case came to me, the hapless parents had been languishing in jail for five days awaiting a trial date.

'The elderly parents of the wife came to me for help. Initially, I was not able to see anything and understood that the kidnapper was using a shielding force to prevent anyone from discerning his identity. Out of desperation, I drank from the bottle, and it seemed that the clouds opened up before me. I saw the kidnapping as it happened. The priest at a local temple had seen the little girl with her mother when they came every Saturday to do their weekly *puja* and had chosen her for a sacrificial ceremony.'

Shakuntala looked around her and sensed the scepticism. Unperturbed, she carried on. 'Unbeknownst to anyone, the priest had been practising forgotten dark arts, and had invoked a spell that concealed him from discovery in the event anyone decided to use a medium to try and flush him out. But in return, the old gods demanded the sacrifice of a young virgin girl. Suffice it to say, the police were just as mistrusting of my vision then as you modern young men are now.'

She laughed and continued, 'But the parents hired a newly found detective agency called Globe Detective Agency, and put the priest under surveillance. They followed him to a godown in Kandival East.'

'It's a jungle out there,' said Shinde. 'I had to go to the scene of a crime at Borivali, and I can tell you it's the perfect spot if you want to kill someone and dump the body. Kandivali is somewhere in the vicinity, so it can't be too different.'

'That's just great. I've made a mental note of where I should go if the need arises,' said Lhoncha.

'Please let Amma finish her story,' said Arjun quietly.

In the immediate silence that followed, Shakuntala continued. 'They caught the priest as he brought the little girl out from a container in which he had locked her. She was starving and dehydrated, but alive. From what the detectives told the police, the priest, rather than get arrested, had shot himself with a revolver he had been carrying. There were several things, however, that could not be explained. Primary amongst the things that didn't quite add up were the broken teeth and nose. Then, the autopsy, which had been conducted a few hours later, showed extensive internal damage as though the priest had been beaten repeatedly with blunt instruments.

Also, there was no record of the priest having ever owned a gun. In their deposition, the detectives could not offer any explanation as to how the damage, both internal and external, had occurred. They assumed that it happened after the priest blew his brains out and his body hit the ground. In the absence of any witnesses and the fact that they had apprehended the would-be killer red-handed, everyone wanted the story to go away. The detective's story held strong, and the case was closed. Death by suicide.'

Shakuntala continued, 'There are many unhappy souls that travel on the river of the dead. Taken before their time, either due to violence, disease or accidents, they have no desire to go to the other side. They leave behind unfinished business. Whether that is loved ones with whom they did not have time for closure, a book or a poem that would forever remain unfinished, or business matters.' Shakuntala shrugged, 'They are in a state of flux, unable to accept the inevitability that there is no going back, and they are in torment.'

Shakuntala paused and sipped water from a steel tumbler. 'Drinking from the water of the river of the dead allowed me to see and touch these souls. I was able to offer them a modicum of solace, give them some peace to help them in their journey. They gave me messages to give to their loved ones. Something which I have attempted to do, but quite often the people I was supposed to talk to live in foreign countries, and communication was almost impossible. Still, I believe I gave those poor souls peace as they crossed over. In return, they gave me the vision to identify the killer.'

Shakuntala paused and took a deep breath, as though controlling her emotions and continued, 'But there are other souls, evil and old, that have found a way to stay on the river without crossing over to the other side. They wait, draining energy from the souls passing through to sustain themselves, waiting for a chance to return to the world from which they had been snatched. For them, there is no favourable outcome on the other side, and they desperately want to avoid the transition. If they can possess a living being, they are able to stay on this side, but they bring their evil with them. When I drank from the bottle, I was able to pierce the veil, but in doing so, I exposed myself to an old evil soul that tried to take possession of me. I fought back with meditation and prayer, but it was all I could do to keep it at bay. I almost died in the supernatural attack, but I was young then. Young, willful, and strong. Eventually, I prevailed, but after that experience, I have never tried to drink from the bottle.'

Shinde didn't exactly scoff, because that would have been rude. He coughed very loudly, cleared his throat, and said, 'So let me understand all this. Evil spirits, possession, river of the dead. I am a man of science, Mother. You cannot expect me to believe these fairy tales. What about the movie *The Exorcist*? Is that also true? And I also hear there is this new movie out called *The Evil Dead*. Maybe they are also based on true stories.'

'I am sorry,' he turned and looked at Arjun and the rest of the group. 'I find all this very hard to believe.'

Shakuntala looked at the group in front of her, taking in the fearful, incredulous and contemplative looks. She smiled and suddenly put the slim bottle to her lips, and before anyone could object, she had taken a long sip of the blue liquid. She looked around at the shocked faces and said, 'I see that without my help, you may never find the killer and put a stop to this evil. There will always be disbelievers, and I do not have time to allay the doubts of the good doctor. Or any of you, for that matter. The proof of the *gulab jamun*, as they say, is in the eating. The water from the river of the dead is in me now. Hopefully, I will be able to discern the identity of this killer. And you, young warrior, maybe you and your silent army can stop him. But remember, he is not alone. He has his own army, equally silent. As for me, I will deal with the aftermath of my actions.'

She laughed a pleasant tinkle and said, 'Maybe it won't be worthwhile to a marauding spirit to possess an old woman that is about to join them on the same river they travel.'

***

# Chapter Twenty-Six

Shakuntala Bai sat cross-legged, her back straight as an arrow, and Arjun marvelled at her posture. But as the minutes went by, the old soothsayer fell silent and began to hunch over. The group gathered around her, concern on all their faces. She began to mutter incoherently, and suddenly, her head snapped back. Her eyes were open wide, pupils dilated, but unseeing of anything around her. She began to talk. It was not her voice. It was a male voice. The accent seemed Eastern European.

'You seek the killer of the women. Your hunt is unsuccessful because there are forces at play that will not let you see his face. It is hidden even from me. You wish to know how he chooses his prey. That, I can tell you. It is chosen for him.'

The change in the voice coming out of Shakuntala's mouth drew an audible gasp from Inspector Baig. Kailidas looked like he was about to faint, and Shinde stood up, multiple questions on his lips. But before he could begin, Shakuntala cut him off.

'Do not interrupt me. I do not have much time. This group that protects the killer worships the fallen angel. But they also worship an even older God.'

And then abruptly, Shakuntala began to moan—an unearthly sound that made the hair stand on Arjun's back. He had heard these types of sounds before from the mouths of shamans in the deserts of Arabia. And then, several voices started speaking out of Shakuntala's mouth. Violent, guttural, and full of menace, it was in a language that no one in the room understood. Except Arjun. He didn't understand it, but with his keen ear for languages, he knew he had heard this before.

In August of 1983, on a mission for the Iranians in the heart of the Arabian desert, while he had been embedded with the Shamar, a shadowy nomadic tribe fleeing from the oppression of Saddam, he had witnessed a sinister ritual beneath the sky darkening with twilight. The shamans, the mystical priests of the Shamar, were shadowy figures cloaked in tattered robes gathered in a circle, their presence in stark contrast against the desolate landscape, as the sun began to sink below the horizon, casting long shadows, and unsettling stillness descended upon the camp. The shamans had been summoned to invoke the ancient Sumerian god Enlil to wipe out a pursuing Kurdish force that was hell bent on destroying the Shamar. Armed with sophisticated weapons and owing their loyalty to Saddam Hussein, the traitorous Kurdish force had been systematically wiping out the vanguard that the Shamar left in their wake to cover their flight. Arjun had been sent to infiltrate the Kurds with orders to kill their commander and his lieutenants, and sow chaos in the ranks of the Kurds. But the elders of the Shamar had asked him to wait while their shamans tried to stop the pursuers in their tracks. Arjun, tasked with specific orders from his handlers, had been reluctant to hold back but had been talked down and had become a witness to a bizarre ritual not seen by many.

The ritual commenced with a deep guttural growl that seemed to emanate from the very bowels of the earth. It was a primal unsettling vibration reverberating through the sand, as though its aim was to awaken ancient malevolent spirits that had been slumbering for centuries. The shamans, their faces obscured by hoods, swayed in unison, their bodies swaying with a disconcerting fluidity, as if possessed by forces beyond their control. As the growl intensified, it was joined by a cacophony of whispers, a dissonant chorus, many voices slithering through the air like a swarm of venomous serpents.

'Those are the voices of the damned, tormented souls trapped in a forsaken limbo for millennia,' said Sarah, a pretty young Shamar, who cowered in terror next to Arjun. 'You must bow, or be damned along with them.'

Arjun, however, had chosen to remain standing, more curious than afraid. The shaman's chants began to rise and fall. To Arjun's ears, not fully accustomed to the ancient languages of the desert, it was a chaotic incantation, the words a twisted language that seemed to claw at the very fabric of reality.

And then, much to Arjun's surprise, a cold wind came out of the desert. Relentless and malevolent, it howled as it made its way across the dunes, like the wail of a banshee. It was a sound that chilled Arjun to the bone. The wind tore up the sand, whipping it into frenzied spirals, creating a vortex of swirling shadows and grit. It seemed as though the desert had come alive, and that a sentient entity was writhing in the depths of the vortex, screaming in agony. The shaman's voice rose to a fevered pitch, invoking the ancient demon, and in response, the vortex came at breakneck speed across the sands and hovered over the cowering tribe.

Arjun, his face covered, looked up at the vortex. The swirling had lulled in its intensity, and as Arjun looked closely, he could have sworn that he saw a tall dark figure with fiery eyes and horns on top of its head look down at the tribe. One of the shamans looked up and screamed, 'ENLIL!' And then the shamans began chanting in the same unrecognizable language. The vortex hung over the tribe for long minutes, and the chants of the shamans did not waver. And then, Arjun could have sworn that the entity inside the vortex looked directly at him. But he could have been mistaken, because in the blink of an eye, the vortex descended and covered the chanting shamans. There were screams, and then the vortex, like a tornado, moved away from the tribe, as though being guided by an unseen pilot, and swiftly made its way south over the sands, and was soon lost to sight and sound.

The dust settled, and members of the tribe, slowly, some individually, and some in small groups, began to stand up cautiously. Arjun had lifted Sarah to her feet and smiled encouragingly at her, hoping to soften the terror in her blue eyes. And just as she began a small smile, someone screamed. Arjun whipped around, his Kalashnikov locked and loaded in the blink of an eye, and saw that six of the eight shamans lay dead.

'They willingly gave up their lives, that we might be saved,' said Sarah in her lilting Arabic. It was as though she was singing to him. At any other time, Arjun might have been charmed by the extremely pleasant accent, but the presence of six corpses that had been alive a few minutes back, sort of put a dampener on things. He went to examine their bodies and saw that the bodies had been completely mutilated, as though by some wild animal. Their chests had been torn open, and from what Arjun could make out, their hearts had been removed. Obviously, Enlil was a very demanding God. Arjun had parted with the Shamar once it became clear that the Kurds were no longer in pursuit. Arjun never found out what became of them. It seemed as though they had vanished from the face of the earth.

Now, so many years later, to hear the ancient language of the desert come out of the voice of an old lady in a fisher village a million lifetimes away, was surreal to say the least. But as Arjun got up very carefully, he knew that things were about to change very rapidly, and definitely not for the better. Things were never good when the old gods decided to speak.

With the exception of Shinde, the rest of the group were battle-conditioned and were familiar with danger and blood. Yet the evolving circumstances were unlike anything anyone in the room had ever experienced. With the exception of Arjun. And the rest of the group instinctively gathered behind him in flanking positions. As Baig took up a position on the left of Shinde, he understood with remarkable clarity that this kid was the indisputed leader, and everyone there, including Shinde, would willingly sacrifice their lives for him. Baig wasn't at that point as yet, and he wasn't sure he'd ever be, but he respected the authority, respect, and devotion that Arjun wielded, and if push came to shove, Baig was not unwilling to fight. But how did one do battle with an old lady who was muttering in an unknown language? No doubt something was going to happen, and Baig wasn't sure how he was going to handle it. This was something that hadn't been taught to him at the Police Academy. And while Baig was mulling over the possible eventualities, things went south very fast.

*

Shakuntala's head snapped back. Her eyes were initially glazed and white, as though she had cataracts. Then, as she glared at the occupants of the room and her eyes changed to a mottled gold, her pupils became long and vertical, giving her a very reptilian look. She spoke through split, bloody lips and broken, decaying teeth. The language was indecipherable, the voice guttural.

'Who disturbs the sleep of the dead?'

There was a dead silence from the room, and then Arjun spoke. Baig realised that the kid was speaking Arabic.

'We seek the killer of women. His face is unknown to us. Reveal his identity so that we might put an end to him.'

Shakuntala looked at Arjun long and hard, and then spoke with an undeniable British accent, 'We have met before, warrior. In the sands of Syria.'

*Enlil*, thought Arjun. He bowed and nodded silently. It wasn't healthy to upset an ancient god.

'You are also a taker of lives. What makes you different to this creature that hunts the homemakers?'

So Enlil knew who they were hunting! Sensing that Baig was about to speak, Arjun whirled around, hand raised to still the words that were already out of Baig's mouth.

'You must help us find him. I am sworn to uphold the law and stop this animal that kills senselessly.'

Arjun groaned inwardly. This was not going to end well.

Shakuntala cackled—it was a malevolent sound. 'Is that what you think, Inspector? You are so wrong. He does not kill senselessly at all.'

And then Shakuntala started to shiver and shake, her fists clenching and unclenching, eyes closed. It was evident that she was trying to regain control. Suddenly, her eyes snapped open again. This time, it was her bright brown eyes that took in the group. There was panic in them.

'Do not engage with the entity. It is powerful and evil. It will take back control over me soon, so I don't have too much time.' She looked at Arjun and said, 'The protectors of The Plumber worship Enlil! The Plumber kills in the demon's name. That is why he is protected. Do you understand? Do not believe anything that the evil one says. The Plumber kills for the evil one. He is guided by a secret group. What they all get in exchange, I cannot discern, but you must kill them all. If you only kill The Plumber, they will find another acolyte to take his place.'

'Can you see who he is, mother?' Arjun asked, his voice unnaturally calm. Everyone else in the room, Baig included, was dumbstruck with awe and fear. Arjun's voice kept them from giving in to panic.

'I am trying, and the veil is being parted. I can almost see his face. Oh, Inspector Baig! Oh my God! NO!'

Shakuntala screamed the inspector's name in anguish and gasped in agony as her body was lifted off the ground by an unseen force. She cried out in pain, as her body was slowly stretched out and she hung in mid-air, as though on a rack. And then, her eyes turned once again to mottled gold.

She looked down at the group below her and spoke with the voice of a little girl. The language was still Arabic, but the accent was of the Bedouin from Syria—only Arjun recognized it. To the rest, it was a young girl speaking in an unfamiliar language, and the fact that the sweet voice was coming out of the mouth of an old woman suspended six feet in the air only made things even more terrifying.

'Inspector Baig! Protector of the law!'

The voice changed in the blink of an eye, and it was the guttural rasp of many voices speaking as one again.

'You do not understand the meaning of pain, Inspector. But you will. Oh yes, you will.'

And then Shakuntala looked directly at Arjun.

'I know you, warrior. Your past is drenched in blood, but so is your future. I need not do you any harm. You will cross paths with it several times in your life before you cross over. You will survive, but you will pay a bloody price. You will lose all your loved ones. You are doomed to walk alone, fighting other men's wars, and when you finally die, it will be far away from home. I see your future as plain as the fear on the faces of your men around you.'

Arjun felt a chill run down his back. His parents were practising Christians, but Arjun had seen enough of horror to know that either God enjoyed watching his creations suffer, which meant he had a twisted sense of humour, or that he wasn't all that powerful. Arjun was running with the latter supposition. This old demon knew him well and was predicting a future that Arjun, anyway, had a feeling was definitely in the works. His features tightened with a grim resolve. Shakuntala turned her head once again to Inspector Baig, who seemed as though he were frozen.

'Oh, Inspector! I have a surprise for you.'

Suddenly, without any warning, before the horrified eyes of the onlookers, Shakuntala, suspended in the air, stretched out like a rubber band, began to vibrate. She began to scream in agony. With what seemed to be a superhuman effort, she looked down at Arjun and struggled to make a sentence, her body wracked with violent spasms. 'You have to stop them! Oh, Inspector Baig, you poor, poor man,' she screamed one last time.

And then, before the horrified and shocked eyes of the onlookers below, Shakuntala exploded. It was literally like someone set off a grenade inside her. There was no part of the hut that wasn't covered with the blood, guts, and gore of the sweet old lady.

Lhoncha burst into the hut, gun in hand, panic in his eyes. The visarjan crowded behind him, unable to get through the small door. Losing two kings under his watch would definitely not look good on his resume, and truth be told, he was fiercely affectionate of the young warrior who had boldly walked into his village and killed the reigning king for doing harm to an innocent girl. Lhoncha admired Arjun and had decided in that instant that if something untoward had happened to the teenager, he was going to hang up his spurs. In the fraction of a second during which he burst into the hut, he realized that if he found Arjun dead, it would be a heartbreak from which he would not recover. So, he was pleasantly relieved to find everyone still in one piece, even if they were all a little gelatinous.

Arjun wiped a piece of brain matter from his face. The entire front of his body was soaked in blood, and it was the same for the rest of the group. Arjun was used to things going sideways and fast, but the manner of Shakuntala's passing was something even he wasn't prepared for. He bent down and picked up The Plumber's screwdriver. It was covered with hair and blood. He looked around the group, relieved that everyone was unharmed, physically at least. He looked directly at Baig and voiced the question that was on everyone's mind.

'What was she trying to warn you about?'

***

# Chapter Twenty-Seven

*May 25th, 1985, 2000 Hours, Indian Standard Time, Police Chawl, Colaba*

Nothing about it felt right. In the past, every time a kill had been chosen, it had always felt right. He had been able to see the wickedness of the women and had understood the need to cleanse them. He enjoyed the rituals of stalking them, finding out their timetable, and choosing the right moment to strike. And the final act of cleansing had been a spiritual high which took days to come off.

This time, with this woman, it was different. He couldn't see the evil in her, couldn't feel it like he had in the past with the others. Instead, he was haunted by a sense of doubt, a feeling that perhaps his judgment had been clouded. The certainty that had always guided his hand seemed to waver. The ritualistic thrill he once felt was replaced with an unsettling ambiguity. The timeline was completely off. He should have been ready to kill in two months. But his masters were pushing him, insisting that she was the next one who needed to be cleansed. And it needed to be done now. But he just couldn't see it. And there were these additional orders which didn't make any sense. But he had never questioned his masters before, and he certainly wasn't going to start now.

He had been told that there would be a man and a child who had to be cleansed along with the woman. He had never taken out an entire family, and as he surveilled the residence of the target, against his better judgment, he felt his heartbeat race with excitement. A triple killing by The Plumber would grab headlines across the country. He was already a superstar, but this would definitely seal his place in history. They would talk about him a thousand years after he was gone. He had to exercise all his self-control from getting completely hard.

But at the back of his mind, a small voice kept questioning the choice of his victims. He pushed it away with almost physical effort. He wanted to cement his legacy. This was the way to do it. His masters had guaranteed it. As he watched the woman hang out clothes to dry on the communal balcony, he went cold in his mind as the predator came to the fore. He looked at the building he would have to breach. It was a typical government chawl. A chawl, or *chaali* or *challi*, was a unique type of communal residential structure found predominantly in Bombay. These buildings were an emblem of the city's bustling working-class community, providing shelter to countless families amidst the city's ever-growing urban jungle.

The architecture of a chawl was fairly simple, yet practical, designed to maximize space efficiency. Typically, a chawl consisted of a multi-storied building, with each floor accommodating a series of tiny one-room tenements lined along narrow corridors. Each tenement usually spanned around 12 by 12 feet, barely enough to fit a family, yet it was the heart and soul of many resilient Bombay households. These rooms opened out to a shared balcony or corridor, fostering a sense of community among the residents. The building's façade was often worn with age, displaying the hardships faced by its inhabitants.

Despite the limited space, the life inside a chawl was vibrant and bustling, reflecting the tenacity of its residents. Each room, albeit cramped, was a multifunctional haven, where cooking, cleaning, sleeping, and socializing happened. The interiors were a fusion of necessity and personal touch, with every inch utilized to its fullest potential. The decor often included colourful cloth hangings, family photographs, and religious symbols, blending tradition with the everyday struggle.

Shared amenities were a distinctive feature of chawls. Bathrooms and toilets were communal, usually located at the end of each corridor. These shared spaces could often be a source of inconvenience, but they also reinforced the communal spirit. The residents often formed tight-knit communities, bound by shared experiences and mutual support. The corridors and balconies functioned as social hubs, where neighbours engaged in casual conversations, children played, and festivals were celebrated with collective enthusiasm.

To The Plumber's eyes, this chawl was no different to the ones that dotted Bombay's lower middle-class neighbourhoods, with one exception. The threat level was high due to the fact that a very special type of people inhabited this chawl. Hitting this target in the middle of the day was going to be nothing short of impossible. And then, he smiled as he remembered an ancient adage. *The best place for a tree to hide would be in the forest.*

*

Salma Baig hung out the washing and went in to check on little Parikshat. All of six years old, he was a beautiful boy with the warm brown eyes of his father and an intelligence beyond his years. He was displaying an uncanny love for mathematics that had his teachers perplexed, and his speed at the Oval Maidan when he went for evening football with his friends had his father's chest almost bursting with pride.

She smiled at her son and said, 'Baba, would you like something to eat?'

'Yes, Amma, can I have some cornflakes with milk?'

As Salma smiled and turned to go to the small kitchen to get some cereal for her son, there was a knock on the door. *Probably one of the neighbours wanting something*, she thought as she went and opened the door, wiping her hands on her *saree*. She looked in surprise at the constable standing at the entrance. She didn't recognize him, but that didn't matter. She didn't know everyone from her husband's police station.

'Yes?' she said.

She never saw the blow that knocked her back. The constable was inside in a flash, supporting her falling body, laying her out on the floor. He locked the door behind him, and as she tried to scream, he bent over her and hit her across the jaw with the wrench he had taken out of the bag he had slung over his right shoulder. His movements were practised, smooth, and without a hint of hurry. He had done this many times before. Paresh bent over the prone body to make sure Salma was unconscious and then turned to the small bedroom. Parikshat was sitting on the bed reading an *Amar Chitra Katha*. There was no one else in the small apartment. He had been told that there would be a man. He felt a flutter of annoyance that there would be only two for lunch. Parikshat looked at the strange man, more curious than afraid, as he took out his tool kit. Paresh smiled at the young boy, charming and disarming. 'Don't worry, *beta*. This will all be over very soon.'

*

As Inspector Baig stepped off his police issued Enfield bike and onto the brightly lit street of Paanch Pairi in Colaba, the familiar scent of the sea mingling with the aroma of street food from nearby stalls pleasantly assaulted his olfactory senses. The night was alive with the hum of the city, a gentle breeze carrying the distant laughter of people enjoying the evening. Above him, the sky was a deep indigo, speckled with stars that peeked through the gaps between the towering buildings.

As he approached the entrance to the police chawl, he could hear the faint strumming of a guitar as someone accompanied 'Wish You Were Here' by Pink Floyd, which was being played on someone's two-in-one. The sound echoed through the narrow corridors, and a melancholic tune that seemed to resonate with the very walls of the old building. Baig paused for a moment, allowing the music to wash over him, a brief respite from the day's work. He was against the Western influences that were sweeping across the city, but even he had to admit that Pink Floyd was pretty awesome.

He began his ascent up the rickety wooden steps, each one familiar under his feet. The walls were adorned with fading posters and notices, remnants of community events and announcements. As he climbed, he exchanged nods and smiles with a few neighbours who were returning home or stepping out for a late-night stroll. On the second floor, he encountered Mrs Fernandes, a sprightly woman in her fifties who lived just a few doors down from him. She was standing in the corridor, a basket of freshly laundered clothes balanced on her hip. Her husband was a sub inspector who worked at Gamdevi police station. He was a smart guy and wasn't completely corrupt. Baig liked him and his perky wife. Her face lit up with a warm smile as she saw him.

'Ah, Inspector Baig! Late night again, I see. I didn't see Salma this morning. Or your handsome son. Please give them my regards. I swear, *maa kasam*, Inspector, your son is going to be a lady killer one day. Thank god I have only sons.'

Baig laughed and said, 'I will definitely convey your wishes, and please give my regards to Alfonse. We must go to Kailash Parbat sometime next week and have some *falooda*.'

'Arey, definitely. I will make sure my lazy husband doesn't try to weasel out of this.'

'Good night, Mrs Fernades,' said Baig as he ascended to the second floor.

The hair on the back of his neck stood up. Even though everything seemed to be all right, Baig sensed danger close. His hand went to his side holster, and he unbuttoned the flap. The Pink Floyd song seemed to fade away into the distance as his senses tried to find and fixate on the source of the danger. The feeling got more pronounced as he crept along the corridor towards his apartment.

'What's the matter, Baig?' Jaikeshen Verma, his next-door neighbour, a constable from Cuffe Parade police station, had just stepped onto the corridor for a smoke. He saw Baig creeping along the corridor and followed his colleague, more out of curiosity than concern. This was a police chawl, and nothing bad ever happened at Pace Chawl.

Baig stood outside the door of his little apartment. He had a sinking feeling in his stomach. Something terrible had happened. He opened the door. The lights were off. Jaikishen Verma dropped his cigarette. He could also feel it. The unmistakable sense of death. Baig found himself shaking with terror as he switched on the lights.

Inspector Baig stood frozen at the threshold of his own home, a place that had once been a sanctuary of warmth and love. It had been transformed into a scene of unspeakable horror. The air was thick with the metallic scent of blood, mingling with the familiar aroma of his wife's cooking. The living room, once filled with laughter and the soft hum of daily life, was now a silent witness to the atrocity that had unfolded. The walls seemed to close in around him, the shadows lengthening as if to swallow the light and hope that had once filled this space. Baig's heart pounded in his chest as he took in the horror.

Salma and Parikshat lay on the floor, side by side, their bodies cruelly exposed and vulnerable in death. The killer had been merciless, splitting them open from chest to waist, their insides a grotesque display of violence. Baig's mind struggled to comprehend the scene, his senses overwhelmed by the enormity of the loss.

His wife's face was frozen in an expression of terror, her eyes wide and unseeing. Her hands, which had once caressed his face and held their child, were now stained with blood, as if she had tried to protect their son from the inevitable. Her hair, once vibrant and full of life, lay matted against her pale skin, a stark contrast to the warmth and vitality she had exuded in life. Parikshat lay beside her, his small body a testament to the innocence that had been so brutally extinguished. His face was serene, a cruel parody of sleep, his eyes closed as if he were merely dreaming. A small teddy bear, his constant companion, lay near his outstretched hand, its fur matted with blood, a silent witness to the horror.

Baig's knees buckled, and he sank to the floor. Somewhere in the distance, he could hear Jaikishen yelling for help. But all he could see were the faces of his wife contorted in agony, and Parikshat serene and calm. In the corner, he saw The Plumber's wrench.

*

Khadpa Naresh brought the news of The Plumber's attack to the village. He stood in the main hall of Lingayat House surrounded by visarjan troops and addressed Kalidas, who stood next to Arjun. Khadpa was aware of Shyam Tandel's passing and the ascension of Kalidas to the throne. He knew about the roadmap to the throne and wondered how Kalidas had defeated Shyam Tandel in single combat. Kalidas was tough, but Naresh had no idea that he was tough enough to take out Shyam Tandel. *Never judge a book by its cover*, he thought. Still, he found it odd that the tennis player was allowed into the twin villages, let alone Lingayat house. And that Kalidas didn't actually sit on the throne. And why was that giant Lhoncha standing next to Arjun instead of the king? There were a lot of things that didn't make sense. He decided to get over the narration of the night's events and keep moving on. It was never wise to hang around in an area overrun with the Visarjan.

'The Plumber attacked and killed Inspector Baig's family,' he said matter-of-factly.

A silence descended upon the hall.

'When did this happen?' asked Arjun.

*How odd that the tennis player was asking the question*, thought Khadpa. Definitely, there had been some seismic power shift that he was not aware of. He mentally shrugged and answered the question.

'Not sure, about an hour ago.'

Lhoncha shifted uneasily. 'He attacked Baig's family when he was here with us. Is it connected to us?"

Khadpa was shocked. 'What the hell was Baig doing in the village?' He decided that too much knowledge could end up being extremely unhealthy.

He bowed to everyone in general and said, 'Thank you for your time. I think I will leave now. I just wanted to deliver the news. I'm sure you are all busy.' He turned to leave.

'Khadpa, please stay. You have been a good friend to the village and to all of us associated with it. I am very grateful to you. It is time to bring you into the inner circle.'

Khadpa wasn't sure he wanted to be a part of any inner circle, but something about the tone of the tennis player made him afraid, curious as well. *Who the hell was this kid?*

He acquiesced to the request with a small bow. 'It is my honour to be considered.'

There was a commotion at the entrance of the throne room. Everyone turned to the source. It was Namdeo.

Arjun beckoned to him, and Khadpa was shocked to see the scourge of South Bombay, the one man considered as deadly as Lhoncha, bow his way before the tennis player.

'There is a phone call for you, bhai.'

'Muriel?' asked Arjun, his eyes lighting up.

Namdeo shook his head. 'It's someone talking in Tamil. He won't identify himself, but insists on speaking only with you.'

Arjun froze. Only Muriel knew the number of the phone in the village. She would have never shared it with anyone, and if she had, as obviously was the case, then the person entrusted with the number would be calling with bad news. Something akin to fear lit up his eyes. It was something no one had ever seen. Wordlessly, he left the room following Namdeo. The person on the other side of the phone identified himself as Ramalingam.

'We haven't met, but I know all about you,' he said. Arjun was silent on the phone, paralyzed by the news he knew was about to receive.

***

# Chapter Twenty-Eight

*May 24th, 1985, 1600 Hours, Sri Lankan Time*

The arms handover had taken place in the dense jungles of northern Sri Lanka near Sakkotai Cape. Eight hundred AK-47 Kalashnikovs, rocket-propelled grenades, launchers, and a large amount of ordinance had been appropriated from a warehouse in the Kamchatka peninsula, and transported by land and sea by Chechen mercenaries until it reached Myanmar. From there, Muriel and six hardcore Tamil commandos had taken over control of the merchandise, loaded them onto a grain ship, and sailed down the eastern coast of India, just outside the international water limit. It was a long and arduous journey, and there was always the danger of being intercepted by pirates looking for an easy prey or the Indian Navy. They weren't too concerned about pirates, whom they would make sure received a warm welcome. But the Indian Navy was another kettle of fish. So, they kept their fingers, toes, and everything else crossed as their voyage got underway. As luck would have it, they were blessed with tailwinds and no interceptors and reached their destination hungry, tired, and stressed out, but otherwise none the worse for wear.

Muriel got her first look at Velupillai Prabhakaran. He was in his twenties, looked extremely fit in his battle fatigues and in her opinion, was very handsome. He was also extremely charming.

'Miss Steyns, thank you for delivering the weapons. I know the journey was not easy, and you have the gratitude of the Tamil people. I personally will always be in your debt. Our struggle is just beginning, and these weapons are much needed.'

Muriel stood to attention and said, 'There is no thanks required, sir. I am committed to the Tamil cause and will do everything that I can to help in the foundation of a free Tamil state.'

Prabhakaran snapped to attention and saluted Muriel. Three hundred Tamil warriors all dropped what they were doing and followed suit. It really was, in Muriel's humble opinion, not required, but very impressive.

'Come and eat with us. I'm given to understand that you wish to travel to India immediately. Let us break bread together, and then you will have a contingent of my finest warriors escort you to the coast guard cutter that will rendezvous with you in three hours.'

*

The journey to the rendezvous with the Indian Coast Guard cutter was uneventful. The Sri Lankan army was staying far away from LTTE LTTE-controlled territory. The presence of INS Parikrama, a sleek cutter with state-of-the-art weaponry, further dissuaded any misguided Sri Lankan bravery.

John Moses welcomed Muriel on board, and the coast guard cutter left swiftly. Muriel was surprised to learn that he was a good friend of Arjun and that the machinations of her boyfriend had resulted in the LTTE receiving much-needed protection on the high seas from the Indian Navy. Commander Moses was very discreet and did not question Muriel's presence in Sri Lanka. Instead, he made light conversation about Arjun.

'Do you know that he's a really talented tennis player? We've won a few tournaments together.'

Muriel laughed and said, 'Yes, I'm well aware of his tennis prowess. I had the opportunity to watch one of his tennis matches a while back.'

Their conversation flitted back and forth about sports and movies, avoiding any mention of Arjun. But as she got off the boat at Rameshwaram, John Moses said, 'Tell that idiot friend of mine that he is one lucky dog.'

Muriel laughed and said, 'I will do that, and please accept my gratitude for a safe trip and, more importantly, for the great job that you are doing. I hope we will meet again soon."

'Let's have a few beers at Café Mondegar.'

'It's a date.'

*

She was at Hotel Tamil Nadu in Rameshwaram twenty minutes later. A smart, young, and extremely fit Sri Lankan Tamil met her at the entrance. He smiled brilliantly and said, 'Welcome to Tamil Nadu, Miss Steyns. I am Rajan, and it's my honour to be your driver and companion to Madras. Would you like to rest a bit a freshen up before our journey?'

Muriel returned his smile with a dazzling one of her own. She liked the term 'companion' instead of bodyguard.

'No. I'm ready to start immediately. I need to make the 10 am Indian Airlines flight tomorrow, and it will take us about nine hours to get to Chennai, I think.'

'Oh, please don't worry about the Indian Airlines flight. It will definitely be delayed. But your wish is my command.'

She sank into the comfortable pillows that had been placed by Rajan in the back seat of the ambassador, and as the lights of Rameshwaram faded away, she found that she was exhausted. She quickly fell asleep.

*

*May 25th, 0200 Hours, Indian Standard Time, 30 Kilometres to Trichy*

Muriel snapped awake, fully alert. There was danger. She smelled it in the air.

'We picked up a tail ten minutes back,' Rajan's tone was very even with no evidence of stress.. He leaned back and handed Muriel a .45 Winchester Magnum.

'Don't worry. I have one of my own. Trichy is thirty minutes away. Once we are in the city, I know a safe house with some tough guys loyal to you through cause.'

In spite of Rajan's casual tone, Muriel was worried. How did anyone know of her travel plans? As she mulled over the question in her mind, the lights of Trichy lit up the sky in the distance. She allowed herself to relax a little.

'We've lost our tail,' said Rajan. 'Twenty minutes and we'll be in the city. I'll organize a motorcade for us to Chennai from there.'

'RPG!' screamed Muriel.

The launch was a cough of flame and a whip-crack. The PG-7VL warhead streaked across the road, tail-fin sparks stretching a white hyphen in the dark. Rajan slammed on the brakes, but it was too late. The rocket covered the distance in a heartbeat. It punched the right headlight at 7000 metres per second, vaporizing the chrome bezel and melting the fender into molten lava. It speared the engine block, and half a second later, 700 grams of RDX detonated.

The ambassador did not merely stop. It rose ten feet in the air, the right front corner, now a cauldron of fire acting as a fulcrum. The rear wheels left the ground first, the heavy Hindustan motor's body pivoting on its snout. For one impossible second, the car hung nose down. Then gravity took over. The roof smashed onto the road with a sound like a temple bell dropped from a tower. Flames licked from the engine bay, racing along spilt petrol. The car lay on its back, wheels still spinning lazily, one headlight flickering like a dying firefly.

In the seconds the car rose in the air, Muriel kicked the left door open and sprang out and away from the falling car. She was covered in blood, mostly from the shards of glass that had lacerated her face with innumerable deep cuts.

*Shit! I'm going to need a plastic surgeon*, she thought as she rolled away, the .45 magnum still in her hand. She came into a crouch and scanned for cover, but apart from the scant underbrush, none offered shelter. She was a sitting duck! A long, drawn-out metallic shriek tore through the night as the driver's side door of the overturned ambassador was pushed open from the inside. Miraculously, Rajan had survived! He crawled out and stood shakily, scanning the area for Muriel. He saw her through the flickering lights and smiled.

'Thank God you are safe!' he said with a beautiful smile.

'Get down!' screamed Muriel.

There was wet meat *thwack* like a heavy fist punching through steak, and Rajan's head exploded as a .223 bullet made contact with his skull. His headless torso collapsed like a broken rag doll.

*Sniper!* thought Muriel with fleeting sadness and raised her weapon into the darkness. It was a forlorn hope that she would hit something. Another *thwack* and she screamed in agony as another bullet shattered her gun hand and her magnum became a twisted piece of junk metal. She tried to roll away onto the side of the highway, hoping to find something that she could use as cover while she tried to think. She was out of time!

Suddenly, she was surrounded by six men. The one who was obviously the leader of the hit squad spoke. He was young, in his late twenties. Of medium height and a lean athletic build, he was quite fetching, and his smile only added to his attractiveness.

'Miss Steyns! What a pleasure to finally catch up with you finally. I do apologize for the manner of our meeting, but you have been quite the elusive fox. It took a lot of planning, but it was worth it. I bring you greetings from Colonel Dasanayake.'

Muriel felt an overwhelming sadness. So in the end, Dasanayake had won. He had killed her parents, eluded capture so many times, and now he had her. It was a total defeat.

The young hitman continued, 'I am Lieutenant Malian. I will be your escort back to Sri Lanka, where Colonel Dasanayake is very much looking forward to a long and productive chat with you. Come! We must hurry. We have a jet waiting at Trichy airport for us.'

His light conversational tone only made everything so much more bitter. The tone of the victor. There was nothing left to do.

Muriel looked into the eyes of the young lieutenant and said, 'Not long from now, someone will come for you. He will come for all of you. And you will not escape his wrath.'

She thought of Arjun. She tried to memorize every contour of his face as she bit down on the cyanide capsule embedded in her right molar.

***

# Epilogue

The Indian Airlines Airbus 300 made a smooth touchdown in Bombay at ten thirty in the morning. There were three LTTE instructors on board, and a young tennis player called Arjun. To the casual observer, none of them knew each other. In fact, no one would have guessed that the three very fit, dark-skinned gentlemen were front-line fighters from the jungles of Vavuniya, and had come from northern Lanka on board an Indian Navy coast guard cutter under the command of John Moses. No one would have guessed that young Arjun had welcomed them on the Indian side at Rameshwaram and had accompanied them to Madras, where they had all boarded the IC 426 bound for Bombay. No one guessed anything because no one even knew what to guess. These were ghosts. They didn't exist.

He got off the aircraft ahead of the LTTE fighters and walked swiftly towards the exit. He looked for potential threats. The last thing he wanted was a firefight in the terminal, but if it became inevitable, he wanted to be able to get the drop on the attackers. He had absolutely no doubt that the LLTE fighters would clean up after him. He had heard that there was a big meeting in Antop Hill in a couple of days, and he assumed the LTTE were there for that. As he got out of the arrival hall, he saw some of Wardha Bhai's fighters waiting next to a couple of white ambassadors. He figured they were the welcome party. They looked capable of handling any party crashers, and he walked past them, marginally relieved.

No one gave the young man with the tennis rackets a second look. His relationship with the supply run operations in the south was a closely guarded secret, and no one in Bombay, including the famous Varadarajan Mudaliar, knew of his existence. Much later, after the great Don's untimely death, his relationship with Antop Hill would become the stuff of urban legends. But that would be in the future.

He caught an autorickshaw to Bandra station. He decided against taking a taxi back to Colaba. It was a fairly long journey of about an hour and a half in the maddening Bombay traffic. Taxi drivers liked to strike up conversations and had an uncanny ability to remember faces. Autorickshaw drivers were exactly the opposite.

He could have gone to Santa Cruz station, but there were only slow trains stopping there. There were seventeen stops between Santa Cruz station and Churchgate, and slow trains stopped at every station along the way. Bandra station was a little further by rickshaw, but he would be able to catch a fast train from there, and then there would be only three stops. Definitely a better option.

He decided to walk from Churchgate Station to the Strand. He wanted to feel the crowd, the smog, the surge of the masses jostling against each other as they went about their day. Maybe he would get to see some pretty girls from H.R. and K.C. college as he walked down past Oval Maidan. He needed to dial down the rpm. Needed to start feeling like a young college student instead of an assassin. He found he was looking forward to seeing Brian and Venky again. Maybe get a chance to see Caroline. She was Brian's older sister, absolutely stunning, and completely out of reach. But he didn't really care. He knew he was dead inside. He just wanted to look at something beautiful and forget about the ugliness of war.

He started to feel the battle fatigue wear off as his mind shifted gears, slowly isolating memories of blood and death into the far recesses of his mind. He knew he was in trouble with the dean of his college for poor attendance. Homai Shroff was a stickler for rules. But he had genuine letters from the Indian tennis council that certified his presence at several tournaments in the far north east had been essential.

He took a right on the Colaba Causeway and walked past Electric House. It was a little past twelve in the afternoon when he finally entered Strand. The one-thirty show was going to start soon, and *Sholay* was, as usual, completely sold out for months in advance. He saw Anand, the local black marketeer, walking around in the crowds at Strand Cinema, informing everyone that he had tickets for sale at double the price. A couple stopped him, and they talked a bit, obviously trying to negotiate. Arjun was sure they would be unsuccessful. The demand for a *Sholay* ticket was crazy. They followed Anand into one of the side streets where the transaction would be consummated.

As he walked past Hiroo Kababwala, he saw Richard, the gang boss of Strand, sitting inside the small restaurant with a couple of his henchmen. There was no doubt that the steel tumblers on the table contained some form of alcohol. Arjun was also sure that Hiroo wasn't going to get paid for his *kebabs*. He saw Mandy and Puri, the two Casanovas of Strand, standing near Everest Coffee Shop, smoking and chatting, supremely confident in their status as lady killers. They waved to him, and he waved back. No one even realized that he had not been there for almost three months. He was unimportant, inconsequential. It was good to be back home.

Out of the corner, a figure flashed in his peripheral vision. 'Arey, Vijay Amritraj! How are you? Haven't seen you around for a long time. Everything okay with you?' It was Khadpa Naresh. Arjun bowed and bobbed with a mixture of fear and adulation, and mumbled something incoherently. Khadpa smiled. He was used to that reaction from people. He liked the young tennis player and had christened him after the famous indian legend. 'Don't worry, okay? Anyone gives you any problems, you come see me.'

Arjun nodded and stumbled home. Khadpa smiled at the departing young man and continued on his way. Out of sight of prying eyes, the smile vanished and was replaced with an expression that could only be described as religious awe. Khadpa wondered what the peanut sellers at the gateway would think if they knew the truth. That the young, unassuming tennis player was the 'Ali Baba' the dreaded Afghans talked about.

Arjun passed the Scherezade building on his left, looked up and saw Marisa's unpleasant uncle Frankie, looking down at him. He looked away, not wanting to antagonize the pot-bellied Goan. He looked to his right as he hit the crossroad to his building, and saw the line of taxis that serviced the Fariyas Hotel on his left. Bhagya saw him and raised a casual salute, but no one else noticed him or paid any attention. Bhagya was a part of the inner circle that knew about 'Ali Baba'. He would send the message that the warrior had come home.

As he crossed the Fariyas Hotel, Bhagya caught up with him.

'Arey, Arjun bhai, how are you? Yesterday I saw your father in the market. He was so drunk. I took him back home. He is a real gentleman, but what to do? *Nasha* is nasha bhai. You are too young. One day, you will also know the joy of losing yourself to the nectar of the gods.'

Bhagya lowered his voice considerably as they walked together towards Minoo Desai Marg. His tone was also considerably more respectful. 'You can expect a call at six in the evening, bhai. This is the message I am to give to you. Sorry to talk about your father, but you never know who is watching us.'

Arjun nodded and shook hands with Bhagya. No more words were spoken. He entered Lovedale Apartments. The garage was empty. That meant his mother was out somewhere. There would definitely be no food in the fridge. His father would either be drinking on his own, listening to Shakatak, or would have already lapsed into a drunken stupor. He would have to go to Everest restaurant and get some food for both of them. Arjun sighed. *Welcome back to reality.*

He longed for the touch of love, but he knew it was a gift that was denied to him by fate. He smiled grimly. So be it. Such is life.

*

The cockpit door chime rang, shattering his thoughts and rudely bringing him back to the present. He looked at the monitor. It was the relief crew. He sighed deeply and stretched his limbs. Time to get into the bunks. In spite of all the blood and death, he had the gift of dreamless sleep. The only girl he ever dreamed about was Muriel. Ever so often, she'd visit him as he slept. She was the loss that he had smothered under the alcohol and the business of war. Since that fateful day in Sunder Nagari when the news of her death had shattered his life, he had been told by compatriots and friends that it was only a question of time. Love would find him again. But he knew the truth. After Muriel, he didn't want love and happiness. He wanted blood, he wanted war, and he courted death. But his trip to Valhalla was denied to him again and again. He wanted it to be, but it just wasn't his time as yet.

There had been a girl, some years after Muriel, who had wanted him and wanted to be with him. Easy on the eye, and a class apart, she had shown him love, and she had shown him kindness. But Muriel's death had irrevocably damaged him, rendering him unwilling and, more importantly, incapable of commitment to love. And as he swore an oath to the great leader of the Tamils and got involved in another war, he pushed her away and never saw her again.

Even though the king had fallen, a dream of freedom destroyed by the machinations of a Sicilian and the falling out of brothers, he still heard the words of the doomed Prabhakaran. 'The Tiger will roar again.'

It would not be very long before it would be time to go to war. He knew that with absolute certainty. Whether it was the war in the west that would soon reach a bloody conclusion, or a war in the south that had yet to begin, he knew that he would have to answer the call to arms sooner than later.

Until then, he was a slave to his memories. Sometimes he hated Muriel. She was a stinging reminder that he was fallible, that he had lost, and he hated her for that. That even in his dreams, and even after all these years, she had the ability to take his breath away.

'Everything okay, mate?' asked Captain Juan Bellesconi, the relief captain, staring at Arjun's face. Captain Arjun was extremely popular with the crew and was well known for his wit and his ability to run a relaxed but efficient flight deck. He was always cheerful, and understandably, Juan felt a stab of fear when he saw the look on his captain's face. There was a darkness there that he hadn't seen before.

But it was gone in a flash as Arjun flashed him a boyish smile and said, 'Of course, Juan. You know how it is with these women. It's always some bulshit.'

Juan guffawed, suddenly understanding everything. Women had a way of darkening everyone's thoughts. He himself had more than his fair share of women problems and spent many a night longing for the joys of the single life.

'You think you got problems. Let's have a drink after landing, and I'll tell you my problems. Maybe yours won't seem so bad after you hear the crap I have to go through.'

'You got it, brother.'

'Have a good rest. I'll get the cabin crew to wake you up an hour before touchdown.'

'Sounds good. You have controls,' said Arjun, doing the formal handover of flight controls and communication to Juan and the relief first officer.

'I have controls,' said Juan, formally accepting the handover. 'Have a good rest, sir.'

Arjun lay down in his comfortable bunk and listened to the dull roar of the powerful Airbus engines. It was a comforting sound, and he felt a wave of relaxation wash over him. He liked the night. He revelled in the darkness that the setting sun brought to the world. He remembered a saying: *Daytime is just a dress rehearsal. Everything that is important happens at night.*

Maybe tonight, he would see Muriel again. Sometimes he could smell the sweetness of her breath. He began to drift. 'I'm always there,' he heard Muriel say as his eyes closed and he smiled. In the farthest recesses of his mind, a tiger roared, and as he slipped into oblivion, he thought he smelled blood.

***

# Glossary

- *Arey*: an exclamation of surprise like "Oh!" or "Hey!"
- *Arrack*: a distilled alcoholic beverage made from coconut flower sap, sugarcane, grain or fruit
- *Barfi*: milk-based sweet
- *Bawa*: reference to Parsi men
- *Bedou*: Arab nomad living in the desert, particularly in the Middle East and North Africa
- *Beta*: term of endearment meaning son
- *Bhabhi*: sister in law
- *Bhai*: means brother; used in the underworld to refer to the boss, don or high-ranking gangster
- *Bol*: translates to "tell me"
- *Chaali/Challi*: also known as *chawl*, are multi-family housing typically found in Bombay
- *Chai*: tea
- *Chalo*: translates to "let's go" or "come with me"
- *Chappatis*: unleavened flat bread
- *Chillums*: a pipe used to smoke marijuana
- *Chooth*: an abusive word to describe the private part of a woman
- *Chotey*: meaning "small one" used by gang lords when addressing their subordinates
- *Chutiya*: abusive word meaning "idiot' or "fucker"
- *Dal makhani*: lentil dish
- *Dargah*: mosque

- *Dhansak*: popular Parsi dish made of mutton, lentils and vegetables
- *Dhobi Ghat*: an open-air laundromat where many launderers work
- *Dhurries*: heavy cotton rugs
- *Didi*: sister
- *Dikra*: Parsi term of endearment meaning son
- *Dost*: friend
- *Falooda*: a cold dessert or drink
- *Gaandu*: asshole
- *Gehba*: Arabic abusive word meaning prostitute
- *Gir gaya*: fallen
- *Giraak*: customer
- *Gujju*: Bombay slang for a person of Gujarati origin
- *Gulab jamun*: sweet confectionery or dessert
- *Guruji*: spiritual guide or master
- *Habibi*: Arabic word meaning darling
- *Halwa*: sweet dish consisting of carrots or semolina boiled with sugar, almond milk and cardamom
- *Hamar*: Arabic word for donkey
- *Hashish*: extract of the cannabis plant
- *Havala*: an informal trust-based money transfer system that functions outside the traditional banking system
- *Isshin Ryu*: a style of Okinawan karate founded by Tatsuo Shimabuku
- *Jhinga masala*: prawn dish
- *Kaamwali*: maidservant or domestic hired help

- *Kaeshi-waza*: counter techniques in Japanese martial arts, meaning to reverse or deflect an opponent's attack in order to be able to throw a kick or a hook
- *Kakato geri*: heel kick, bringing down the heel like an axe on the opponent's head
- *Kalaripayattu*: a martial art, using weapons originating from Kerala
- *Kaliya*: dark-skinned person
- *Kanji*: rice porridge
- *Katana*: long single-bladed Japanese sword
- *Kebabs*: grilled or roasted meat or vegetable dish
- *Keema*: minced meat dish
- *Khabaris*: informer or confidential informant
- *Kiriotoshi*: striking down, referring to a powerful cut or technique
- *Kumite*: free-style fighting
- *Laijutsu*: a Japanese martial art focused on the quick and fluid drawing, cutting, and sheathing of a sword from its scabbard in one fluid motion
- *Lassi*: a sweet or savoury Indian drink made from yoghurt or buttermilk
- *Maa kasam*: translates to "I swear by my mother"
- *Maa ki chooth*: an abusive word referring to a mother's private part
- *Maal*: derogatory word on the streets of Bombay referring to an attractive girl
- *Madarchod*: translates to "motherfucker"
- *Makiuchi*: a type of sword cut used in Japanese martial arts

- *Namaste*: means "hello" or "goodbye"
- *Nasha*: high intoxication from drugs or alcohol
- *Nephilim*: fictional bodyguard units attached to Saddam Hussein
- *Niko-dachi*: literally means "cut stance". Used in Japanese fighting techniques
- *Nimbu paani*: lime water
- *Om*: a mystic syllable or chant appearing in Hinduism, appearing in most Sanskrit recitations and prayers
- *Pakoras*: Indian savoury dish
- *Panchnama*: a legal document recording the evidence and findings at a crime scene in the presence of two or three witnesses
- *Pav*: a type of Indian bread originally from Goa
- *Phirangi*: translates to "foreigner"
- *Puja*: worship ritual
- *Raand*: Hindi term for prostitute
- *Raees*: wealthy
- *Rooh*: Arabic term for spirit
- *Rotis*: Indian bread
- *Saab*: sir
- *Sai*: traditional Okinawan martial arts weapon
- *Salaam*: greeting
- *Saree*: traditional Indian woman's dress
- *Shaitan*: translates to devil
- *Sharmutha*: translates to "whore"
- *Shiana*: Bombay term for the tough guy of the neighbourhood

- ***Shurikens***: a weapon in the form of a star with projecting blades or points
- ***Sicario***: contract killer or hitman
- ***Supari***: contract killing or hit job
- ***Tsubame gaeshi***: a fabled sword technique
- ***Urumi***: a flexible whip-like Indian sword
- ***Wallah azim***: translates to "I swear by Allah the Magnificent"
- ***Yaar***: friend, beloved or companion
- ***Zukin***: a hood

I would like to thank Kevin and his amazing team at Nu Voice Press for their patience and dedication in bringing this story to life. Without you guys, this would not be possible.

# About the Author

Rohan Kailasam was born in Chennai and grew up in Mumbai. After finishing college and finding his MBA course uninspiring, he went to Texas. He became a commercial pilot before returning to India and joining Air India, initially based out of Mumbai. He has since worked for several foreign airlines.

An avid fitness enthusiast, he plays tennis and holds a black belt in *Ishin-Ryu* karate. He is currently a student of Brazilian *Jiu-Jitsu*. His other passion, apart from writing, is music; he plays the piano and is the frontman for the Chennai-based rock band, Helmsdeep.

*The Mercenary's Shadow* is his second book, and like *Wastra*—his first book—it is written above the clouds at 40,000 feet where turbulence shakes loose the truth, and the view reminds us how small we really are.